The Killing
of Mummy's Boy

Joan Ellis

First published in 2014
by Joan Ellis Publications
Isle of Wight
England

www.joan-ellis.com

ISBN 978-0-9930091-1-2

Cover design : Chee Lau

Printed in Great Britain by imprintDigital.com

For Doug

With thanks to the man on the train for showing me the workings of the criminal mind.

Chapter one

[Waterloo to Portsmouth 2013]

'I slit someone's throat,' the man told the woman on the 4.20 from Waterloo to Portsmouth.

It was Sandra's first journey back to London since she had moved to the Isle of Wight a few years before. Having a stretch of water between her and the mainland made her feel safe. The Solent could be expensive to cross; some people thought twice before making the journey. She liked that.

Once on board, she had found an empty table and taken off her coat before absentmindedly plucking a stray blonde hair from her cardigan. A man was watching her from the aisle. She followed his gaze. To her embarrassment, her fingers were resting against her left breast. Flummoxed, she struggled with her case, making several unsuccessful attempts to lift it onto the luggage rack.

'Let me,' he said.

Now it was her turn to watch as he swung the case up over his head and positioned it on the shelf. His white T-shirt rode up revealing the lower half of his torso. Her eyes tracked the thin line of black hair that ran from his navel and disappeared under the waistband of his jeans. He flopped down in the seat opposite and honed in on the box of doughnuts she had put on the table. The glossy icing and the multi-coloured hundreds and thousands glinted through the cellophane window. They were her treat. She couldn't get them on the island and always made a point of buying half a dozen from the kiosk at Waterloo station.

'Did you make those?' he asked.

They were obviously manufactured; the brand name was emblazoned across the side of the box. She shook her head.

'My sister bakes cakes for the café on Ryde beach. Do you know it?' he asked.

She glanced at him, momentarily trying to picture where he meant before shaking her head and checking her phone. No messages. She sighed and slid the phone into the pocket of her handbag where she kept her Oyster card. The travel card wasn't there. Panicking, she rechecked her bag and looked underneath the seat. Nothing. She must have dropped it after topping it up at the station. Luckily, the card was registered so at least she wouldn't lose any money. Quickly, she took out her mobile again, scrolled down the address book and clicked.

'Hello, I'd like to report a lost Oyster... sorry...can you hear me now?' she shouted. 'My name? Sandra, Sandra Williams...Dove Cottage, Isle of Wight. PO30 5AB.'

She bit her lip impatiently.

'5A 'P'? 'P' for 'papa'? No, it's 'B', 'B' for ...'

The man smiled at her and her mind went blank.

'Bravo,' he whispered over the top of his newspaper.

She gave him the thumbs up by way of thanks.

''B' for 'bravo',' she said. 'Yes, the card is registered...hello...can you still hear me?'

The line went dead. Irritated to have lost the signal, she sighed and locked her phone. The man threw down his newspaper, making her jump and reached into the pocket of his jeans. Fanning out three Oyster cards on the table, he pushed one towards her.

'Here,' he said.

His nails were bitten, his cuticles ragged and bloody.

'No, thanks, it's yours,' she replied.

'Have it,' he insisted.

'No, I don't need it. I'll get a replacement. Why have you got so many?' she asked lightly.

He shrugged, gathered up the cards and put them back in his pocket.

2

'I always lose something when I go to London,' he told her.

'Where in London?' she asked, leaning forward, seizing the opportunity to talk about her home town.

'Leyton. Me girls live there.'

East London, of course, his accent was a giveaway. But a Dad? She would never have guessed he had kids. He seemed free, uninhibited by responsibility. Only someone with children knew the particular pain they could bring. As her friend had warned her when she had told him she was pregnant, 'Congratulations! You'll never be so happy or unhappy in your life.' At the time, it had struck her as nothing more than a jaded comment probably the result of one too many sleepless nights. She had no idea what he meant. Now, sadly, she knew only too well.

'How old are they?' she asked, genuinely interested.

'Eight and nine. Haven't seen 'em for years,' he said dismissively as if 'years' was just another word for 'hours'.

She raised her eyebrows at him.

'Been away,' he told her by way of explanation.

Based on his muscular appearance, she imagined him on an oil-rig, braving all weathers.

'I'm Ben, by the way. Drink in The Lud, down the road from me in Ryde. Know it?'

She nodded.

'Never seen you,' Ben said.

'I know it but I don't drink there.'

'Why not?' he asked, offended.

She shrugged hoping her indifference would draw the conversation to a close but he was not easily deterred.

'What's wrong with it?' he demanded.

3

'Nothing,' she lied.

Sandra had nipped in there once to use the toilet. She could still smell the inside of the cubicle and picture the misspelt filth scrawled on the walls. There was no paper left on the roll and she had resorted to using the inner cardboard tube.

Ben leant towards her, his elbows on the table and stared into her eyes. Alarmed, she recoiled and looked around for somewhere else to sit but the carriage was full. Four young race-goers on the opposite table were imbibing ready-mixed gin and tonics from cans. One of the two women lay slumped against her partner's shoulder, her weight pinning him against the window. The other man was boasting loudly about his winnings.

Sandra's ex-husband had been a gambler and would have lost the family home from under them, had she not divorced him when she did.

She picked up a copy of The Metro from the floor and flicked it open creating a barrier between her and her unwanted travelling companion.

'Can I see that?' he asked pushing his copy of The Times towards her. 'I can't read this.'

If her newspaper distracted him, she was happy to let him have it. She folded it and placed it on the table. Without so much as a glance at the front page, Ben jettisoned it onto the seat next to him.

'You've kept yourself nice, for your age,' he said addressing his remark to her chest.

She was wearing her low-cut, cream top. Her hand moved towards her throat and her fingertips felt for her rose locket. She rubbed it gently against her thumb, anxious to cover her chest with her arm as she did so.

His face was set in a permanent smile, like a dolphin's. His biceps bulged under the thin fabric of his T-shirt. Despite herself, she smirked.

'What you doing later?' he asked.

'My husband's meeting me at Ryde,' she lied without missing a beat.

4

He looked at her left hand and grinned knowingly. No wedding ring. He let out a little snort, disguised as a cough. Sandra inwardly admonished herself. She was getting careless, having removed the ring earlier and forgotten to put it back on. A cheap metal band, it made her fingers itch but she chose to wear it as part of her disguise of normality and respectability. Usually, it kept any unwanted attention at bay too.

'Off to see my girl now,' he told her gleefully.

Relieved she would soon be free of him, she smiled.

'She's a prostitute.'

Sandra gasped. It was clear from Ben's ever widening grin he enjoyed her reaction.

'She'll do anything for me. Dresses up … got all the gear. Last time, she wore her Grand-dad's sailor suit.'

From the tawdry description, Sandra pictured a scrawny blonde, dead behind the eyes, sporting an ill-fitting white shirt and blue trousers, a nautical cap at a jaunty angle, splayed across a crumpled bed waiting for Big Ben to strike.

'Just doing what me Dad told me, 'Never hurt a woman, Ben. If you want sex, pay her, don't rape her.'

Sandra gasped but tried to mask how unnerved she was. She had to get away from him, stand in the corridor, if necessary. Before she could move, he jumped up.

'Just nipping to the loo, watch my stuff,' he ordered.

This was her chance. Once he had disappeared, she could lock herself in another toilet and stay there until she reached Portsmouth Harbour.

Just as she was about to move, one of the men opposite stood up, blocking her exit, and made several frustratingly abortive attempts to extricate more drink from his rucksack on the luggage rack. He swayed back and forth battling with zips and buckles. Sandra was so desperate to get out she was about to offer to do it for him when he succeeded in liberating two cans and sank gratefully back into his seat.

'Miss me?' Ben asked sitting back down.

Not wanting to antagonise him, she forced a smile. To put some distance between them, she checked her mobile again.

'Has it gone six?' he asked in an agitated tone.

Again, desperate to appease him, she checked the display and shook her head.

'Can't miss the Hover,' he said.

She relaxed, almost laughed with relief. He was catching the Hovercraft that meant he would get off the stop before her at Portsmouth and Southsea.

'You're in great shape. Bet you've never had kids,' he said, leaning over table.

He was so close, she could see the lumps of mercury filling his back teeth.

'I've got a son,' she told him then immediately regretted it.

Fortunately, he wasn't listening. His eyes were all over her.

'Why haven't you seen your children for so long?' she asked in an attempt to distract him.

'Been inside,' he replied lifting his eyes from her cleavage and looking her in the eye, keen to gauge her reaction.

Sandra looked over at the men opposite for help but their fixed grins were evidence of too many G&T's. Useless.

'What for?' she asked, faking nonchalance, her heart beating in double time.

Sandra wondered if he could hear it thudding. By the look on his face, he enjoyed having her undivided attention and made the most of it, taking his time to reply. Any hope he had been sentenced for a minor crime began to fade.

'This and that...my third time,' he boasted, the fear he induced forcing her to hold his gaze.

'What did you do?' she demanded, her voice rapid but strained.

'I slit someone's throat.'

'Teas, coffees, sandwiches?' the steward asked halting the refreshment trolley alongside their table.

Sandra's relief at his arrival turned to disappointment when she turned to look at him. The steward would be no help. His frail body failed to fill what appeared to be the smallest sized uniform. She must weigh more than he did.

'Stick some ice in there for us, mate,' Ben smiled, holding up a small plastic cup.

Young and keen, the lad obliged, scooping in ice-cubes.

'Cheers,' said Ben, calmly filling his cup from a bottle he had concealed inside a plastic bag.

She watched, disgusted as he knocked back the drink.

'Cider?' he asked proffering the cup.

She shook her head, discreetly wiping her sweaty palms on the seat. Desperate to convince herself he wasn't a murderer, she tried to convince herself he was just another petty criminal who had to big himself up in order to gain kudos with the lowlifes who hung out in the Lud. To her horror, he seemed to read her mind.

'Here's my ID card,' he said flashing a small plastic card just long enough for her to recognise the official government insignia. 'I have to keep it with me in case I get stopped by the police.'

Sandra took it as confirmation of his crime and contemplated moving again. Supposing he came after her? She didn't want to provoke him. If he were to attack her, who would come to her aid? Have-a-go heroes rarely travelled by train these days.

'You wouldn't do it again, would you?' she asked trying to keep her voice slow and steady. She hoped her tone conveyed more of a statement and less of a question.

'What?' Ben asked, casually refilling his cup. 'I wouldn't do what again?'

The cider bubbled over the top of the beaker and ran down his hand. He sucked it lasciviously off his fingers, one by one, his smirking eyes never leaving hers.

'Slit someone's throat,' she said loudly hoping another passenger would overhear and rescue her.

'Nah. That was year's ago,' he replied casually as if murder was nothing more than harmless boyish behaviour he had long grown out of.

Sandra froze. He might have a knife. Not wanting to goad him, she struggled to fix her features into a neutral expression.

When she had boarded the train, she was unaware of his existence. Now she was privy to his worst crime. At least she hoped it was his worst.

Perhaps she could get off at the next stop? Slowly, she reached into her bag and took out her phone. Her hand was shaking.

'On train with murderer. Help,' she texted her friend, Rob.

Logically, she knew there was nothing he could do but she had to let someone know, just in case. Why had she allowed this to happen? What was she doing still sitting here, let alone talking to him?

'Is that work?' he asked watching her wait anxiously for her phone to respond.

She nodded rapidly. Best not say anything, she was a hopeless liar. He would see right through her. Then again, it was partly true; she did work with Rob.

'Tell 'em you're busy,' he laughed. 'Tell 'em you're with me.'

Rob's reply flashed up on her screen.

8

'Murderer?!!! What you like?!! x'

Oh no. He thought she was joking. Trust Rob. There was no point replying.

The train stopped. Her body flooded with adrenalin, ready to run. If she timed it right, she could get off just before the doors closed ensuring he couldn't follow her. As she was about to make a dash for it, the aisle filled with the people who had just got on. They milled about with their bulky bags, wandering through the train looking for somewhere to sit, blocking her exit. Her heart sank as the whistle blew and the train pulled away.

Fear turned to anger as she watched him wedge the bottle under the crook of his arm and refill his cup.

'Haven't you had enough?' she shouted.

What was she playing at? He had probably cut someone for less. But it was unnerving enough sitting opposite a self-confessed murderer, let alone a drunk one.

'Last little drop,' he said surprisingly good-naturedly as he screwed the cap firmly back on the bottle and lifted the drink to his lips.

'Perhaps if you drank less, you'd see more of your kids.'

She shocked herself. Why wind him up? If the past few years had taught her anything, it was not to say a word out of place. But, she couldn't stop, delivering the words like gun-fire.

'You drink too much,' she told him, picturing her ex-husband downing another Scotch. Turned out it wasn't the only thing on the rocks, their marriage was floundering too.

'You sound like my Mum,' Ben laughed.

She flinched. Just hearing the word 'mum' unnerved her. Did it still define her? She knew it did but believed her son may have other ideas.

'You're right. Too much drink ain't good,' he said staring intently at her throat. 'Nice pendant. Can I 'ave it, 'ave it for my girl?'

'No,' she said her fist tightening around her precious rose necklace.

9

Her cheeks flushed. He saw and laughed.

'I'm going to call you 'Rose' like the one round your neck.'

How dare he? She opened her mouth to say something but stopped.

'Not upsetting you am I, Rose?'

He reached across the table and placed his hand gently on her forearm. She pulled away as if scorched.

'Sorry, shouldn't have done that, should I, Rose?'

His slow, apologetic tone was almost convincing.

'Don't mind me touching you, do you, Rose?'

'My name's Sandra,' she asserted before she could stop herself.

'I know. Sandra. Sandra Williams.'

He laughed. She froze. Of course, he must have been listening when she reported her lost Oyster card. How could she have been so careless, giving out her details in public?

'It's going be nice tomorrow,' Ben said. 'I'll fire up the barbie and have a party. Wanna come? You can get the number 9 bus from Newport. You live there, don't you?'

'No,' she said quickly.

'Yes, you do. You've got a Newport postcode,' he said. 'Dove Cottage, Isle of Wight. PO30 5AB.'

Her insides liquefied. Her cottage was in Shorwell, a remote village five miles south of Newport but close enough to share the same postcode. Her neighbour only ever used his house at weekends. The set-up had always suited her but now a murderer knew where she lived she would relish a regular presence on the other side of the party wall.

If he was aware of the terror he had induced in her, he did not show it. Her mind somersaulted as she tried to recall what other information she had let slip.

'Sandra,' he repeated slowly, rolling the letters around his mouth as if tasting them. 'S-a-n-d-r-a? Nah, that's not you. No, you're my Rose.'

She shifted uneasily in her seat, hoping the group opposite had overheard. It was too much to hope for. The older man was still jammed against the window. Much to his delight, every time the girl inhaled, her breasts threatened to escape her bra. The other girl, her stilettoes discarded, rubbed her foot slowly against the other man's ankle.

'Come to my flat. 150 East Hill, Ryde. I'm always there. I don't do nothing.'

Of course, he didn't. The leach.

'How do you pay your girl then?' she asked recklessly, calling his bluff.

Perhaps, his sordid tale: the murder, the prostitute and the neglected children, was nothing more than his attempt at a sick chat-up line.

'I give her this,' he said brandishing the half-empty bottle of cider.

'You'd better stop drinking it all then,' she chided as if admonishing a child.

Her misguided boldness was akin to madness and just as uncontrollable.

'You're right, Rose. Last little drop.'

He unscrewed the lid and poured himself another cupful, downing it in one.

'How did you cope, locked up for years?' she asked still trying to trip him up.

'Inside you're fed, warm and got no bills to pay. And I could get anything I wanted,' he gave her a sly look, teasing her, tempting her to find out more.

'How?' she asked.

'Let's just say you ladies are designed to carry more luggage than men,' he said with a wink, his eyes on her crotch.

She picked up the newspaper and put it across her lap. This time Sandra knew better than to show she was shocked.

'Let's say a woman smuggles you in a mobile phone, how do you charge it?' she asked desperate to catch him out.

'Wire off a kettle flex and screws out the bedstead. Easy.'

Sandra wasn't convinced. He could have seen it in a film or on television. Unfortunately, his next admission erased any doubt.

'I was inside with Bewley before his trial.'

Sandra swallowed hard and looked away. Bewley had been found guilty of murdering a young boy years ago. He had always protested his innocence but the weight of evidence against him was overwhelming. His victim had been the same age as Sandra's son and shared the same name, Carl. Consequently, the case always had an uneasy resonance for her. She listened intently to Ben.

'After the trial, Bewley confessed to his cellmate. When me and the boys on the wing heard, we wanted to put him over the railings.'

He looked at her to ensure she understood he had meant to kill him. She blinked.

'The screws wouldn't let us do the bastard but they looked the other way when we kicked his head in.'

Sandra recalled seeing Bewley's picture on the front page of every paper shortly after he was sentenced, his face so badly beaten he was unrecognisable from his earlier mug-shots. Only the headlines shouting his name confirmed his identity.

'Not upsetting you, am I, Rose?'

She shook her head. Again, he reached across and touched her arm. This time, she did not dare pull away.

'Come with me, Rose. I get my passport in a few days. We can go anywhere we want.'

Out of nowhere, the idea took hold. Like a wild fire in her mind, igniting long-forgotten sensations. For a moment, she fantasised about what being with a brute like him would be like. She imagined him being very different from her po-faced ex-husband.

'Rose?' he said squeezing her arm gently.

Her eyes flickered towards him but she said nothing. Suddenly, he got up. Sandra held her breath but he simply lifted her case down as the train approached his stop, Portsmouth and Southsea.

'Can I have one?' he asked nodding at the doughnuts.

'No.'

'No?'

The dolphin smile disappeared. In its place, a look so powerful it compelled Sandra to open the box. Calmly, as if being offered them at a party, he selected the chocolate one before walking towards the door.

'See ya around, Rose.'

Chapter two

[Isle of Wight 2013]

Sandra reminded herself to keep her big mouth shut in future.

She couldn't wait to leave the carriage and stood the short journey to Portsmouth Harbour, desperate for the train to stop and the door to open. She half ran, half walked along the platform and down the slope towards the Catamaran. Knowing she had plenty of time before the next boat, she headed for the toilet dragging her case into the cubicle behind her. After locking the door, she collapsed against the wall, her hands clammy, her mouth dry. The acrid stench of industrial cleaner caught in the back of her throat making her feel sick. What a fool. Given she prided herself on her newfound anonymity, she had done a great job of etching herself in Technicolor on a psychopath's brain.

Using her thumbnail, she prized opened her rose locket, turning it to study the picture of her son's face. If just looking at an image could wear it out, Carl's photo would have faded long ago.

Here was proof of the happy, carefree life they had once shared. Carl was smiling, his eyes screwed up, squinting into the sun, overjoyed with his new scooter, her gift to him on his seventh birthday. It was taken in their garden at Muswell Hill. That glorious, perfumed space that had been the backdrop to so many golden and indolent days with her little boy. She could still smell the chamomile lawn and hear his laughter as he rode down the long manicured sweep of grass towards the back of the house.

'Watch me, Mum! Watch me!' he yelled, swerving to a halt beside the yew hedge. 'Wow! Did you see that?'

She grabbed her camera from the bench.

'Smile, Carl.'

Immediately, he grinned obligingly into the lens. As she pressed the shutter, he laughed and sped away.

Then, the scream.

14

Instinctively, she dropped the camera and ran towards the front garden. The scooter was on its side, the back wheel spinning. Carl was a little way off, face down on the path, a trickle of blood meandering like a worm across the paving stones. Frantically, she squatted beside him.

'Carl! Carl! Talk to Mummy.'

She knelt down on the ground beside him, muddying the knees of her white trousers.

'Carl?'

'My…head…hurts.'

'Mummy kiss it better,' she said, brushing her lips against his grazed cheek.

'Get off,' he said pushing her away and getting to his feet.

Staggering backwards before getting up, she was relieved to see it was just a flesh wound. Nothing a dab of antiseptic and a plaster wouldn't put right.

She was his mother but had been unable to protect him then and she certainly could not shield him from danger now.

That job fell to strangers, trained police officers heading up the Witness Protection Programme.

It would soon be Carl's birthday but unlike all those years ago, she could not take his photo this year. The most she could hope for was a call, made from an untraceable location, as always. At least she could hear his voice and speak to him. Texts and emails were too risky. Carl wrote letters but each one took six weeks to reach her after going through the rigorous security process demanded by the Programme. She looked forward to holding the pages he had held and reading the words he had written. Recently, the paper had reeked of cigarette smoke. Who could blame him? He needed something to relieve the stress.

Sometimes it seemed like he was the one being punished, banished as he had been to the furthest corner of the country, alienated from his family and friends. Even his new job left him feeling frustrated and unfulfilled.

Sandra suffered too. Every day, she feared he would be killed in a reprisal attack, his life taken in return for the life sentence his evidence had secured.

She shivered and checked the time on her phone. The Catamaran was leaving in four minutes. She unlocked the door and ran through the departure hall to join the queue, relieved to be just another face in the crowd.

'You cut that fine!' the ticket collector said with a smile.

Ignoring his comment, she hurried down the tunnel and onto the boat, choosing to sit alone by the window. Looking out across the Solent, she replayed her encounter with the stranger on the train and felt inwardly embarrassed at how flirtatious she must have appeared. Fancy even talking to the man, let alone leading him on just to make herself feel a little less invisible. Pathetic. As for telling him she had a son, that was an unforgivable breech of trust. But her words could not be unsaid.

Blending into the background had never been her forte. Less of a wallflower and more of a burgeoning rose, people remembered her. What had been a blessing in her previous role as Director of a London PR agency had become a curse, ensuring she was often remembered for things best forgotten.

Her innate sense of right and wrong left her compelled to speak out if she witnessed an injustice and she had always encouraged Carl to do the same. Now look where it had got him, living in fear with an invented past and an uncertain future. Even his name had been changed, supposedly to protect the innocent. It rankled with her that he had been forced to live a lie for telling the truth.

'If you go back to London, you will be murdered,' the police officer had told Carl. 'There's always someone happy to step up, a family member out for revenge or someone from the gang who wants to be seen as some sort of hero. Unfortunately, you weren't to know it but you couldn't have picked a more notorious family, the Elliotts will not let this go. You're the enemy, they want you dead.'

The words had cemented themselves into the very fabric of her being, the bricks on which her new life would be built. Sandra wasn't eligible to join the Witness Protection Programme but instinct told her to leave London. If the Elliotts couldn't find Carl, they would come after her.

Suddenly, her phone vibrated in her pocket making her jump. Automatically, she clicked on the email. Much to her annoyance it was just an online bookseller suggesting new titles. Recently, she had bought several paperbacks from them and since then they had bombarded her with new titles she might like to read. Smart.

Such technology in the wrong hands meant Carl's whereabouts were just a click away. These days, social media made it all too easy to track someone down. Carl couldn't afford to leave a digital footprint. The police had made that very clear. Even a photo of him could give away his whereabouts. All it would take to flush him out would be an iconic landmark or a stretch of familiar scenery. It would be tantamount to giving the enemy his co-ordinates.

As the Catamaran slowed, a voice announced their arrival at Ryde. Sandra joined the throng of people threading their way off the boat and up the ramp. Some headed towards the station to catch the old London Underground train that ran along the pier. Others enjoyed reunions with loved ones in the car park where they embraced before loading their luggage and driving away to what Sandra imagined were idyllic lives.

She set off resolutely on the long walk down the pier, enjoying the feeling of being suspended over the water and getting glimpses of the waves below. At that moment, the island struck her a uniquely beautiful place. Something about the view of the town from half a mile out to sea reminded her of Venice with its elaborate, arched palazzos hugging the waterfront. It may have been a leap of imagination not shared by others but it didn't bother her; she only had herself to please.

Her phone vibrated again. A text.

'Hope you didn't chat up any more murderers on the boat!!!! x'

It was her friend, Rob, carrying on what he thought was a harmless joke.

Annoyed, she threw the phone into her bag.

The sound of the Hover skimming the waves alarmed her, reminding her of the man on the train. He would have caught the earlier one and arrived here about an hour ago. She could just make out The Lud across the road from the pier and hoped Ben wasn't waiting outside to greet her.

She told herself she was being silly. Although their encounter had unnerved her, doubtless it had been nothing more than a game to him. He would have forgotten her already. Nonetheless, her legs shook, her right foot like a puppet's, pawing uselessly at the pavement, momentarily unable to take her weight. She held onto the railings to steady herself, suddenly aware she was shivering.

Eventually, she reached the end of the pier and rounded the corner into the bus depot where she was relieved to see the No 9 to Newport.

'Shorwell, please,' she told the driver breathlessly, handing him the fare.

She went upstairs and sat in the front seat where she tried not to glimpse inside other people's homes. But with their curtains open, their cosy lives were laid bare. She looked away, not wanting to be reminded of the normality she would never again experience.

The bus terminated at Newport where Sandra changed onto the No 12.

'Hello, there,' said the driver. 'Been anywhere nice?'

She smiled briefly and showed him her ticket before finding a seat near the door.

To most people, familiar faces and friendly greetings were a charming aspect of island life but recently Sandra had found it an unwelcome intrusion.

As they neared Bowcombe, the houses gave way to fields and farms. The sheep and cows were a welcome sight.

The driver stopped at The Crown in Shorwell without her even having to ring the bell. It unnerved Sandra; he must have remembered where she lived from a previous journey.

'Have a good evening,' he said closing the doors behind her.

Sandra walked along the narrow lane and up the stone path to her cottage. It was in darkness. She wasn't the sort to leave lights and lamps on timers, never convinced anyone would be fooled into thinking she was at home when she wasn't.

Turning the key in the lock, she pushed open the door and automatically clicked on the light. The smell of curry greeted her. She had made a large pan of madras the night before she left so she wouldn't have to cook when she got back. She was looking forward to the bottle of Chablis waiting for her in the fridge. Three glasses was usually all it took to blot out the past and have the required soporific effect.

She carelessly wheeled her case over the mail, having noted it was mainly brown envelopes and nothing from Carl.

She bent down and collected up the letters. The impersonal marketing shots could go straight in the bin and the bills would have to wait. A flier with the headline, 'No wind farms in West Wight' took her interest. She picked it up, revealing a small, rectangular plastic card. It was obviously some clever piece of advertising, a mock credit card perhaps to convince people to want one. For a moment, she was back at work, pitching smart ideas to clients. For a moment, she felt good, like her old self. Then, she examined it closely.

It was an Oyster card.

Chapter three

[London 2011]

Chopping shallots always made Sandra cry. Smaller than onions but more potent, they got her every time. She dabbed at the corners of her eyes with a piece of kitchen towel before referring back to the recipe book propped open on its stand on the vast marble work surface. Dessert, dark chocolate mousse, was prepared and chilling in the fridge. The fillet steak in brandy sauce would be cooked when her three colleagues arrived. She had invited them to dinner by way of thanks for the hours they had put in on a successful pitch. It was a big win for the agency, securing her yet another pay rise. She glanced at the clock, seven thirty. They were due at eight.

The cast-iron pan was heating on the hob. As she poured in a thin stream of olive oil, she heard Carl's key in the door and smiled to herself.

'Hi love. You're late. Good day?' she asked, her back to him, slicing vegetables with her Sabatier knife.

Chop, chop.

'How was college?' she persisted.

Chop, chop.

'Carl?' she called, wondering whether she needed to cut up another shallot. No, stick to the recipe, four should be enough.

Chop, chop.

'Just need to sit down,' he replied.

'How did the exam go? Coffee in the pot but if you fancy something stronger, I've just opened a nice bottle of ...'

'Just need to sit down, Mum.'

Chop, chop.

'Go through to the lounge, love. Relax. I'll be with you in a sec.'

Chop, chop.

'Just need to sit down. Just …'

Chop.

She turned to see her son, clutching the work surface with both hands, his face ashen. He looked like his insides had been sucked out. She dropped the knife and ran to him.

'Carl!'

Her arm around his waist, she helped him to a seat.

'What's wrong? Are you in pain?' she asked kneeling beside him.

'Just need to sit down,' he repeated, his voice thick, his body distorted and awkward like he was made out of Meccano.

She stroked his cheek gently like she did when he was a child. He turned away. Her fingers were wet.

'I just left him, Mum.'

'Who?'

He looked at her, his eyes full of tears. She barely recognised him. Flakes of rusty blood clung to his straw blond hair.

'I left him dying in the dirt like a rat. His throat cut. Blood.'

'Who?'

'Dunno. Some bloke.'

'Where?'

He looked up and glared at her. She reached out to touch his arm. The sleeve of his denim jacket was spotted with red.

'The park.'

'What? D'you mean the one at the back of us?'

Carl nodded, his eyes closed.

'Are you okay?' she asked.

'His throat was cut, Mum.'

'Oh my God,' said Sandra gently brushing his fringe out of his eyes. Specs of dry blood attached themselves to her fingertips. Horrified, she wiped her hands down her skirt. 'Are you hurt, darling?'

He shook his head.

'What happened?' she said gently.

'I was walking along the path, opposite the skate park when I heard shouting. A bloke had just let his dog off its lead and the thing had gone racing off into the bushes so when I heard screaming, I thought it was attacking someone. I ran in and saw some guy slumped against the wall.'

'And?' she prompted.

'Blood. The slit was like a smile.'

'Did you see anyone else?' she asked anxiously.

Carl looked straight ahead as if he was reliving the moment. He sniffed loudly and wiped his nose with the back of his hand.

Turning to pull a square of kitchen paper from the dispenser, she noticed the pan was smoking. Grabbing the handle, she threw the skillet into the sink and turned on the cold tap creating a cloud of smoke. Her eyes stung.

'Did you see anyone else?' she repeated turning off the tap.

'Yes,' said Carl, chewing his lip. 'He was grinning. Smirking, proud of what he'd done.'

Sandra spun round, shaking

'How do you know it was him?'

22

'He had a knife. He was covered in blood. So much blood. I didn't know that ...'

'Oh my God,' she interrupted, her voice thin and raspy. 'Why didn't he run when he heard you coming?'

'I don't fucking know. Don't ask stupid fucking questions.'

Sandra rocked backwards, shaken by the velocity of his response. She had never heard him swear. Then again he had never witnessed a murder before. Who could say how he should react? Carl lifted his hands to his face, his long slender fingers covering both eyes, pressing hard against the sockets. She could hear him sobbing.

'Carl, I'm so sorry, come on,' she said putting her hand around his shoulders.

Immediately, he pulled away. His face was one big open mouth making him look like a macabre clown. As he spoke, a line of drool, like albumen, swung from his lips.

'I ran away. Your precious fucking son left a dying man. Happy now?' he roared, raising his clenched fists above his head. 'I left him for a fucking jogger to find. There you go, Mum. Bet you're proud now, eh? Still think we're so fucking superior because we live in a big house and I went to a private school? Well do you?'

This wasn't Carl talking. He had witnessed evil, seen one man kill another. It suddenly occurred to her it could have been far worse. A few moments earlier and it could have been Carl lying there, bleeding to death.

'Carl, don't torture yourself, don't dwell on it.'

'You didn't see it. Christ.'

He was right. A terrible image had been indelibly inked on his memory, one of the many things in her son's life she could do nothing about.

As a single parent, she had often felt inadequate. She knew she lacked certain qualities that Carl's father had in spades. He was, when the mood took him, very funny and could make Carl laugh, tricking him out of a tantrum. He could be surprisingly patient too. It crossed her

23

mind to ring him. She had his number somewhere. But what was the point? Somehow, he would make it all her fault. Best keep him out of it.

What Carl had seen had been horrific and unprecedented. She could do nothing to erase the graphic images left behind, let alone salve his torment. At some level, she understood his ordeal had only just begun.

She took out a bottle of Remy Martin and poured him a large glass.

'Here,' she said gently pushing the glass into his hand.

He took a mouthful, his face hidden behind his long blonde hair.

'You phoned the police?' she asked.

Carl looked up, his eyes wired, his tone hard.

'Oh yeah, I stood there, took out my phone and dialled 999, while the bloke cut me too. Of course, I didn't call the fucking police.'

'Sorry, don't worry, I'll ring them,' she said, putting her arm around him again. 'He can't have got far and I daresay the jogger has reported it by now.'

Carl fell against her, gripping her arm. He was hurting her, his fingers pressing into her flesh until they found the bone. She eased away and took his hand in hers.

'Carl, this is very important,' she said slowly and steadily to ensure she held his attention. 'Did the killer see you?'

He nodded and vomited just as the doorbell rang.

That night, two mothers lost their sons.

Chapter four

[Isle of Wight 2013]

The man on the train knew where Sandra lived. She would have to be on her guard, ensure the doors and windows were kept locked maybe even get a spy-hole fitted. Her neighbour lived on the mainland and only came down at the weekends otherwise she would have asked him to keep an eye out.

At least, she hadn't mentioned where she worked. Her office at St Mary's Hospital had suddenly become something of a haven, with the soupy mix of body odour and cheap perfume reassuring her she was not alone. Even the low level cacophony of computer fugues and tapping keyboards felt comforting. All of a sudden, the sound of sound made her feel safe.

She picked up a wad of papers but the words on the page swam together. The only thing she could see clearly was the Oyster card lying on the mat and the leering face of the murderer who had put it there.

The last time she had felt this edgy was during the trial when she had heard things she wished she hadn't. The prosecution's case had rested on Carl's eye-witness account supported by DNA evidence. Sandra had never understood how her son and the jogger were the only people to notice a youth covered in blood running through a park in broad daylight.

The press had a field day, particularly the red tops, regularly filling their pages with lurid details of the defendant and his family. From what Sandra could glean, murder was in Lee Elliott's genes, his family a motley bunch of low-lives. His father was serving life for manslaughter. His brothers were in and out of prison and his mother provided a series of alibis for her feckless brood.

Lee Elliott was a street rat. He went for the throat, killing for money. One of his jobs was to ensure drug debts were paid in full. Non-payers swiftly became non- people.

Watching from the gallery, Sandra had found it surreal experiencing the rituals of English law first hand. The judge and silks apart, most people seemed well-versed in the legal system. Sandra assumed this was because they had either made countless appearances in the dock or, as in Sandra's case, they had watched too many courtroom dramas.

The prosecuting counsel, a slick, articulate young man tied the tawdry facts into a neat parcel that he presented as a fate accompli to the jury. When they retired to consider their verdict and unpacked the evidence, the gory details would have splattered into their laps like entrails, leaving them with only one verdict: guilty.

Elliott's long-suffering counsel struggled to defend his client. He did his best, claiming Carl's ability to identify the killer had been impaired. Citing the Weapon Focus Effect research by Loftus et al, he argued Carl was less likely to recall the assailant accurately because of the anxiety he would have experienced when confronted by the horrific incident. At that point, Sandra had looked over at the victim's mother. She was a forlorn-looking woman who became visibly agitated at the prospect the accused might get away with murder, her son's murder.

Fortunately, the jury paid no heed to what was generally perceived to be schoolboy psychology on the part of the defending barrister. Lee Elliott was found guilty and sentenced to thirty years in prison.

A life for a life.

Little did the jury know, they had just handed down the same sentence to the star witness, Carl.

Sandra shuddered.

None of her colleagues knew much about her personal life, let alone that she had a son. It was safer that way. They could think what they liked just so long as they never knew the truth, the whole truth.

She sat down and put her password into her computer.

'Morning Sandra,' said a middle-aged man waving his hand in front of her face. 'Fancy a brew? I've got a lovely Lady Grey.'

He indicated the box of tea-bags in his hands.

'Sorry, Rob. I was miles away. Yes, lovely, thanks,' she said gratefully.

He was the one person who made her job bearable. His relentless quest to find himself a man was as fervent as Sandra's current desire to stay single.

'You escaped then?' he asked.

'From what?'

'Your murderer? I nearly fainted when I got your text yesterday.'

He perched on the edge of her desk, expectantly. Sandra sighed; Rob, with his love of gossip, was the last person she should have involved.

'Sorry, Rob. Don't know why I sent it; not like there was anything you could do. I'm fine.'

Sandra clicked on a file on her desktop.

'Don't apologise. It was well exciting.'

'You should get out more,' she replied drily hoping to finish the conversation before it began.

'So, he didn't chop you up and bury you under the floorboards, then?'

She glared at him. For a nice guy, sometimes he could be very crass.

'No, but he did come to my house last night,' she told him.

'Oh and people say I'm a fast-worker. What you like?'

'I didn't invite him, Rob,' she admonished. 'He just turned up.'

Usually, she was a very appreciative audience for Rob's camp humour, laughing obligingly at his double entendres. Most days, it was the only thing that kept her going. The trouble was he had no 'off' switch.

'He had overheard me telling someone my address. Then he must've caught the Hover and somehow got to the cottage before me. Luckily, he'd gone by the time I got home.'

'How did you know it was him? Dust for prints?' he asked still in character.

27

'He put something through my letter-box.'

'Is that a euphemism?' Rob asked, still smiling.

'Shut-up, Rob. You never know when to stop do you?' she said, her voice shaking.

When she saw Rob's hurt reaction, she immediately regretted what she had said.

'Sorry, Rob but the man terrifies me.'

'Sounds just my type.'

'Rob, for God's sake. Drop the act. What bit of 'he terrifies me' don't you understand?'

He looked genuinely chastened, 'Let me get you that tea.'

'Hang on, please,' she said catching hold of his arm. 'What do I do if he comes back?'

'Don't worry. How about I come home with you tonight?'

Sandra smiled. Rob was kind if somewhat delusional.

'Thanks, but he's three times your size.'

'Are you saying I'm a wimp?' he joked. 'Seriously, you can stay at mine. But, no hanky-panky, I know what you heterosexuals are like,' he said with an exaggerated wink.

At last he had achieved his aim. He made Sandra smile.

'What are we heterosexuals like, Rob?' asked Kim, their line-manager suddenly appearing beside him. 'I would love to hear your views but unfortunately I am far too busy. Unlike you two. Now, if one of you can spare a moment to take these notes to A&E, I won't sack you.'

With that Kim handed Sandra a sheaf of papers and walked out of the room.

'Sarky cow,' said Rob when she was out of ear-shot.

'She's got a point. I'll run these down now.'

'Allow me,' he said taking the papers from her. 'Today, errand boy; tomorrow, captain of industry. Besides, the lift's broken and there's a couple of hunky mechanics working on it. Going down!'

He mimed something obscene and checked Sandra's reaction. She was smirking. If he achieved nothing else all day, she knew he had done what he had set out to do - made her happy.

Unfortunately, her grin disappeared the minute he left the room. It was going to take more than his double-entendres to cheer her up.

Her screen had gone blank. She jabbed randomly at the keys before switching her computer off and on again. Nothing.

'Can you help me, please,' she asked the work experience girl sitting at the next desk.

'Is it plugged in?' she sighed without even looking at Sandra.

It was a reaction Sandra was all too familiar with. Carl used to pull the same face whenever she asked him to retrieve a document she had spent all weekend working on, only to have pressed the wrong button and lost the lot.

'Did you save it, Mum?' he would ask sharply, knowing full well she hadn't.

Shoving her out of the way to get to the keyboard, he would enter a magic formula, miraculously retrieving the missing file from the ether. She had never understood how to do it herself because he would never take the time to show her.

'There you go,' said the girl crawling out from underneath Sandra's desk as the screen came back to life.

'Thanks, thanks very much,' gushed Sandra gratefully.

'No problem. Is this yours?' asked the girl waving a piece of paper. 'It was on the floor.'

Blood test results. They must have fallen out of the patient's file when Rob snatched it. She took them and headed out of the office along the endless corridors towards A&E.

She had hoped work might take her mind off the murderer but unfortunately that wasn't the case. She worried he would be waiting for her when she got home, lurking in the lane, ready to grab her when she passed. Why did she speak to him? What the hell had she been thinking? Perhaps, she should stay at a hotel, just for the night? Her budget would not run to it being a long-term solution. Maybe, she should move on again? Leave the island? Get out while she still could?

Perhaps she would take Rob up on his offer. Then again, staying at his place was not ideal. According to him, he spent his evenings, 'Kissing one guy 'good-bye' at the back door as another came through the front.' Sandra suspected it was another of his euphemisms, either that, or wishful thinking.

She was getting worked up over nothing. The murderer lived in Ryde, twelve miles away. He was hardly going to keep schlepping to Shorwell just to harass her. From what he had told her, he wouldn't even be able to afford the bus fare.

These days, the A&E department was the one place that made her feel lucky. Unlike most of the people here, she was in good shape, physically at least. Admittedly, some looked in suspiciously good health but others defined the word 'emergency'.

A woman was frantically stripping her baby's limp body of its clothes as the infant cried incessantly.

'She's burning up,' the child's mother was yelling.

Sandra remembered the time when Carl was having difficulty breathing. He could only have been about eighteen months old. Petrified, she had dashed outside with him in her arms, desperate to get him some fresh air. When the paramedics arrived they had put an oxygen mask over his face. It was so big it covered his tiny features. As they tended to Carl, working quickly and methodically, they asked questions, endless questions.

'How long has he been like this?'

'Is he allergic to anything?'

'Is he asthmatic?'

'What? You put your baby to sleep in the same room where you had just sanded and varnished the floor?'

How could she have been so stupid? The ambulance-man had shot her a look of disgust and shaken his head, all the while working on Carl, doing a job that would not have been necessary had she done hers.

'Have you got the blood results there?' the receptionist snapped.

'Yes,' said Sandra handing her the papers

Her maternal instinct got the better of her, 'Any chance that little baby could be seen next?' she asked pointing at the squalling infant, wearing only a nappy.

The receptionist raised her eyes from the screen.

'Excuse me?' she replied tartly. 'I am doing my job. I suggest you do yours. He's next.'

Dismissed, Sandra turned to leave. Then she saw a couple at the entrance. It was the woman who caught her eye, dressed in just a pair of shorts and a top, her body illustrated with tattoos. A skull breathed fire along one arm and a flock of blue butterflies fluttered up one arm. She was laughing, lifting up the man's tee-shirt and tracing a line with her finger down from his belly button to the waistband of his jeans. Sandra couldn't be sure. She only caught a glimpse. The girl was blocking her view of the man with the muscular build who looked like he might work on an oil-rig. Or kill.

Chapter five

[London 2011]

The officer in charge of the Witness Protection Programme, was an old-timer who knew everything there was to know about the game that ended in life or death. The low lives had taught him all the tricks.

His thin lips barely moved when he spoke, like he was conserving his energy for something more important. He even ran his words together as if he was paying per minute to talk. Sandra had to strain to hear what he was saying. His face gave nothing away, his eyes were dulled by having seen too much.

'If you could live anywhere in this country, where would it be Carl?' he asked when deciding where best to relocate him.

'Manchester,' Carl replied. 'I went to the uni there.'

'Well, that's one place we won't be sending you.'

Sandra shot the man a look. He nodded back, a cross between a grimace and a grin.

'Sorry, but if he's told me, he's told his mates. Manchester is the first place people will look for him.'

Carl rolled his eyes and flopped on the sofa, exasperated, flinging his long arms into the air and bringing them down over his face.

'Shit, man!'

His despair was palpable.

'Carl!' she said.

'Well, my evidence gets the police the conviction they want but my life is fucked. That bastard Elliott is laughing. He'll be released one day. I'll live like a fucking fugitive forever.'

'Carl! Don't. The officer is trying to help you.'

'I did the right thing, Mum, just like you always wanted. So why does it feel like I'm in the wrong?'

She couldn't answer him. For once, Sandra took little satisfaction from knowing her son had done the right thing. As the prosecution's star witness, he was a wanted man.

The officer looked out of the window, observing a woman unload her shopping from her car. When he eventually turned to speak it was in a soft, almost fatherly tone.

'Know one thing, Carl. You're in real danger,' he said turning away again.

He had just spoken the words no mother wants to hear. She needed him to look after her son, just like she had always done. But how could they protect him against men with knives and guns? Men with no respect for their own lives, let alone anyone else's?

Why Carl? If only he'd gone for a drink that night with his mates like he usually did instead of walking home through the park. If only he hadn't run out of money and given the pub a miss.

'Most people in the Witness Protection Programme see it as an opportunity for a fresh start,' said the officer.

'A fresh start? What are you talking about?' she asked defensively. 'My son was not embroiled in some sort of corrosive gang culture. He did nothing wrong. He simply did his civic duty.'

'And what if I won't do it?' Carl asked the officer, resentment seeping from him, like pus from an open wound.

The officer paced across the room, taking his time to reach the piano at the far end of the room.

'Your choice,' he said calmly. 'The programme is entirely voluntary. It's there to protect you. We can't be held responsible for your safety if you don't sign-up.

He lent over the keys to examine a framed photo of Carl.

'First day at school, huh?' he asked.

'How d'you know?' replied Carl.

'Your uniform is too big and your shoes too clean for it to be any later in the term. You went to the private school in Highgate, right?'

Carl nodded.

'My friend's son went there, the fees crippled him.'

The officer looked at the sheet music propped open on the stand and smiled knowingly.

'I never did learn to read music. It's like a whole language that I just don't speak,' he said, carefully turning the page. 'You're a bright kid. You understand what I said – if you don't sign-up to the Programme, your life is at great risk.'

He flipped the page back and allowed his words to hang in the air like a rotting carcass.

'I'll risk it,' Carl snapped back.

Again, the officer was in no hurry to respond, walking slowly back over to the window and adjusting the curtain to get a better view of the woman taking the last of her shopping indoors.

'What are you looking at?' Carl demanded.

'Here, take a look. What d'you see?' the officer asked pulling back the curtain. 'A woman unloading her shopping. Or a woman unloading more shopping than she needs? If it's the latter, perhaps she's concealing someone in her house?'

'And perhaps she's bloody bulimic,' said Carl.

'Carl!' shouted Sandra alarmed he could be so rude, the officer was only trying to help.

'Carl, if you don't stick with this, you won't see Christmas,' said the officer.

It was a harsh approach but one that Sandra thought might just work on her son. She wondered if the officer had children. If he did, they must be grown-up. Judging by his grey hair and red thread veins snaking across the bridge of his nose, he had to be late fifties or early sixties. Her guess was he lived alone; when he had removed his jacket earlier, she had noticed only the front of his shirt had been ironed. No advert for the police force, his exhumed appearance suggested too many late nights and insufficient daylight.

Sandra took heart from the fact he was an old hand and as such would have met Carl's type before, a smart, well-educated kid who thought he knew it all. Sandra knew her son would come round eventually; she would make sure of it.

'Fuck this,' said Carl leaping up.

'Sit down,' the officer growled.

'Don't tell me what to do,' said Carl.

Even as he spoke, his words sounded like the dying embers of defiance.

He flopped back onto the sofa, hitting the sofa hard with the flat of his hand. The officer stood with palms pressed together, the tips of his index fingers resting against his nostrils before striding over to the marble mantelpiece and picking up a posed shot taken at Carl's graduation. He examined the underside of the silver frame.

'What did you get your degree in?' he asked.

'You're the detective, you tell me,' said Carl.

'Well, I'd say English.'

'How did you know?' Carl asked like a child watching a magician produce a coin from behind his ear.

The officer smiled and gestured towards the walls, lined with books.

'Just an educated guess.'

Sandra could see Carl was beginning to take notice. He sat forward when the officer spoke and did not interrupt.

'I knew two witnesses who refused protection. One had a petrol soaked rag and a lit match put through his letterbox. The fumes killed him before anyone could get to him. The other, a young woman with a kid who insisted she didn't need our help, was dead within the week.'

Something in the officer's tone told Sandra he had been the one to break the tragic news to both families. The sudden realisation that she could be the next one getting the knock on the door propelled her to her son's side.

'God forbid, Carl. Just do as he says,' she begged taking him by the arm.

He pulled away from her.

'You've got no choice, Carl, your Mum can see that.'

The officer glanced from mother to son. Sandra knew he had just played his trump card.

It was obvious she had indulged her son from the day he was born. He had enjoyed a privileged upbringing: private school, piano lessons, a four-bedroom house for two. There was even a new car on the drive next to her Porsche. No prizes for guessing who that belonged to.

The officer would have spotted he was an only child; the photographs covering every surface said as much. There they were, just the two of them, getting soaked on the log flume at Thorpe Park, enjoying ice-cream on Brighton Pier, and more recently, dining at a selection of expensive-looking restaurants.

'Okay, I think we're done,' the officer smiled at Sandra, picked up his jacket and made his way to the front door. 'I'll be in touch.'

Sandra knew the officer had seen enough to draw his own conclusions. If he had deduced Carl was a mummy's boy who had long since lost contact with his father and was now willing to comply with anything in order to stay safe, he was right.

She followed him into the hall and opened the door for him.

'Thank you, officer, I think you've just saved my son's life.'

Chapter six

[Isle of Wight 2013]

'Happy birthday to you. Happy birthday to you. Happy birthday dear Carl, happy birthday to you,' Sandra sang, grasping the receiver with both hands and holding as close as she could to her ear.

If she could have climbed into the telephone to get closer to him, she would have done.

'Yeah whatever, thanks, Mum,' he said wearily.

He didn't sound thrilled to hear from her but she was grateful for the clear line.

'Happy birthday, Carl,' she said over brightly to compensate for his unenthusiastic tone.

She repositioned herself on the sofa, a glass of wine positioned next to the newly-opened bottle on the floor. 'Doing anything special later?'

'Nah, work tomorrow,' he laughed ruefully.

Typical Carl, she thought. Always doing the right thing.

'Did you get my card?' she asked picturing the huge twenty-one picked out in silver glitter against a blue background, with the words, 'To my wonderful son' emblazoned across the top in gold. 'You know what the island post can be like ...'

'Yeah,' he cut in.

'When did it arrive?' she asked trying to think of something to say, anything to keep the conversation going.

'Dunno.'

She heard him strike a match and inhale.

'Oh, Carl. You're not still smoking, are you?'

'You're not here. Don't nag. It doesn't affect you,' he told her, exhaling loudly.

Events seemed to have made him more aggressive, less patient. Hardly surprising after everything he had been through.

Resolving to keep the tone light, she reached down for her wine and took a mouthful, before stretching out and repositioning the cushion into the small of her back.

'You okay?' she asked.

'Fine.'

'Job going well?'

He sighed.

She swung her legs round and sat up straight, holding the glass away from the sofa, careful not to spill it.

'It's my twenty-first and you're talking about work?' he asked incredulously.

'Just asking, love' she said gently.

'Why?'

His voice had a sharply-honed edge causing her to soften her tone.

'So it's your big day, any plans?'

'Nothing, I told you,' he snapped.

Silence.

'Carl?'

'What?'

She changed tack.

'I popped up to see Nan the other day. She sends her love and says to wish you a happy birthday. She says sorry she forgot to post your card but gave me a cheque for twenty-one pounds. Said to put it in your Post Office account so you don't spend it.'

Her speech was rapid, desperately trying to hold his attention. To her surprise, he laughed.

'Ah, Nan. She's always done that, sent me a pound for every year. She's a legend but she shouldn't give away her money. She should spend it on herself.'

Good old, Nan, always able to work her magic on Carl. Relieved, Sandra raised her glass to her mother and took another gulp.

'She doesn't understand why you haven't been to see her. I just told her you've been busy, was that okay?'

'Yeah, fine. Thank her for the money, yeah?'

He made the statement sound like a question by inflecting at the end of the sentence. It was a recent habit, no doubt purloined from American sitcoms. It irritated her but she reminded herself this was his twenty-first birthday, and this conversation was her only opportunity to share in his special day.

'Carl…'

'Mum, gotta go, someone's at the door. Talk soon, yeah?'

'But…'

She stopped. It was pointless. Besides what was she going to say?

'Happy Birthday, Carl and by the way I met a murderer on the train, he knows where I live and he's stalking me.'

'Mum, call you next week, yeah?'

'Okay,' she said reluctantly. 'Happy Birthday, Carl. I love you.'

'Straight back at you,' he said.

'What's that supposed to mean?' she demanded taking another mouthful of wine.

39

'Means 'love you too'.'

He may as well have added 'Doh!' to demonstrate how out of touch she was with the latest lingo. Exasperated, she refilled her glass.

'Mum,' he said suddenly. 'Don't worry but ...'

'What?' she asked jumping in quickly, her voice thin and reedy, the panic rising.

More silence. More nothing. She took a big mouthful of wine and immediately followed it with a second gulp.

'Talk to me, Carl.'

She reached down and topped up her glass. She could just picture Carl with the phone wedged between his chin and his thin, hunched shoulder, stubbing out the butt as he simultaneously reached for another cigarette. She heard him strike another match, light up and inhale.

'I'm going back to London.'

'Not to live?' she asked gulping back her wine.

'Yeah.'

'NO!' she cried jumping up, her foot catching the stem of the glass, spilling red wine on the landlord's rug. 'Shit, Carl!'

'Calm down, Mum.'

'I've got wine all over the bloody carpet. Carl, you can't go back. They'll kill you.'

'Chill out! I'll be fine.'

'Fine?' Fine' is how you describe the weather.'

She was stunned he could be so cavalier, after everything that had happened.

'Lee Elliot is banged up. He can't get to me.'

40

'But his family can.'

'I can disappear in London. It's a big place. I'll be the needle in the haystack. I can have a life. Anyway, I'm fed up lying. I've got a shit memory and I'm always screwing up.'

'Carl, please don't do this,' she begged.

'I can't stay where I am. It's too small. Too claustrophobic. As soon as I open my mouth the locals know I'm different and it makes them suspicious. You know what these villages are like. Everyone knows each other's business. Or thinks they do.'

She couldn't argue with that. Even the bloody bus driver knew where she lived. She needed a refill and went into the kitchen where she took a half-full bottle of wine out of the fridge pulling the cork with her teeth.

'What's that? You drinking? It's not even lunch-time. For God's sake. And what about work? You can't go into a hospital stinking of booze.'

'Just raising a glass to my son on his birthday,' she told him defensively lifting the drink to her lips. 'I've got the morning off. I'll be fine by this afternoon. Anyway. Never mind me; it's you I'm worried about.'

The wine tasted good. As the cool elixir seeped through her body, it assuaged the panic at the thought of what could happen to Carl if the Elliotts got their hands on him. He had grassed up one of their family for God's sake.

Thankfully, the alcohol had begun to blur the edges and the world seemed a less hostile place. She had discovered the benefits of drinking many years ago. As a director of a PR agency, it had gone with the territory, the glue that sealed the deal. Now, she regularly relied on its restorative properties, often by-passing food in favour of a liquid lunch.

She put the phone on speaker and propped it against the knife block.

'You can't go back to London,' she shouted.

'It's my life,' he replied.

41

This was her worst nightmare. What the hell was he playing at? She walked unsteadily to the sink, squatted down and hunted in the cupboard for another bottle of wine. Her search threw up a can of air freshener and a desiccated bluebottle. She recoiled and tumbled backwards. Then, using the back of a chair as ballast, she pulled herself to her feet.

'Mum? Are you still there?'

She grabbed the phone and after several attempts succeeded in clicking off speaker mode.

'Why? Why London?' she asked.

'Debs is there.'

'Debs? Who is Debs?' she asked. 'For the love of God, Carl. You'd risk your life for some girl?'

'Mum, I've moved on.'

'Moved on?' she shouted into the receiver, incensed. 'Move back and you'll be dead within a week.'

'Don't exaggerate. Anyway, Debs works in the City. End of.'

'So, how, how, how on earth did you, did you meet her?' she asked failing in her attempt to sound sober.

'In the pub. She's got a holiday home near the beach at Polperro.'

She had to find the right words to make him see sense but the wrong ones got in the way.

'You, don't know, I, er, I, Carl, am yous mother and yous, you must...'

Another drink would sharpen her thoughts. She picked up her glass. It was empty.

'You're drunk,' he declared sounding disgusted. 'Anyway, it's happening. Get over it. I can't stay buried in the countryside.'

She sobered up in an instant.

'But you're happy for me to bury you in London because that's what will happen if you go back.'

'Okay, I am hanging up. I can't talk to you when you're like this.'

She had to keep him on the line and try and talk some sense into him.

'Don't, Carl. Please don't, don't go.'

When he spoke again, his voice was measured, his temper only just under control.

'Be happy for me. Oh, Mum, don't start crying for God's sake..'

'But Carl,' she wept.

'I've got to go to London, Debs is pregnant.'

And with that he hung up.

Chapter seven

[Isle of Wight 2013]

He knew where she lived. The man on the train knew where she lived. The murderer knew where she lived.

It made coming home a terrifying experience. Each time she was forced to walk in his footsteps. Each time, she was fearful, not knowing what or who she might find.

The terror had not lessened over time, it had got worse. As soon as she stepped off the bus and the doors closed behind her, she was alone but for the fear that had become a constant and unwelcome companion.

This time she quickly stole past trees and bushes avoiding the whispering shadows that could be disguising potential danger.

When she reached the cottage, her heart hammering, she wondered if the man had looked through the window to get a glimpse of how she lived. She hated the idea of him intruding in that way.

Her hands shaking, she managed to unlock the door on her third attempt. She went in and closed it quickly behind her. The room, with its functional, unfashionable furniture was not to her taste. The only precious object was the photograph of Totland Bay that hung in pride of place, above the fireplace. She had taken it on Carl's birthday two years ago. Since he had been on the Programme, she had been unable to celebrate with him in person and had had to find other ways of marking the occasion. That year, the weather had been particularly good and she had decided on a drink at The Waterside. She had sat outside the pub, surrounded by people but alone with her thoughts watching the sun go down. As it set over the sea, she had captured the moment.

Locking the door and flicking on the radio, she relaxed as the DJ's silky smooth voice seemed to single her out from his millions of listeners and speak to her alone. It was an old broadcasting trick but she didn't care. The mindless chatter was soothing and suited her just fine.

'Do you ever get that?' asked the DJ. 'You're walking along the street and someone says 'Hi ya, mate. How's it going?' And you're thinking 'Do I know you? Or are you just some weirdo?' Ha, ha. If that's happened to you, tell us. Text the word, 'stranger' to ...'

She quickly turned it off, her mind jolting back to the man on the train. What if he came back? What if he was here, hiding inside the cottage?

Sandra froze, her heart pounding against her ribs.

'Dove Cottage, Shorwell, PO30 5AB,' she could hear herself saying on the train. "B' for bravo. 'B' for bravo.'

"More like 'S' for 'stupid',' she thought bitterly.

Cautiously, she crept upstairs and flung open her bedroom door causing the handle to bang against the wall. From the doorway, she could see the whole of the room, even under the bed. Nothing. Her wardrobe was on the landing. She pulled the door and it swung open. Her scant collection of clothes hung like husks on the rail.

As she approached the bathroom a wild face greeted her. She leapt back terrified before realising she was looking at her own reflection. Breathing heavily, she headed back downstairs and into the kitchen.

She sat at the table and told herself to calm down, there was nothing to worry about, the man had played his sick little joke, game over. Gradually, her heartbeat slowed.

She decided a cup of tea would soothe her nerves and she reached into the fridge for the milk. Spotting half a loaf of bread, she put two slices into the toaster before opening the cupboard where she kept her special plate.

Carl had spotted it in a junk shop in Brighton on one of their many excursions and had asked to have his pocket money early so he could buy it. It was one of the few gifts he had given her over the years and she treasured it.

It was not in its usual place but it was always in the cupboard above the sink, behind the casserole dish. She glanced across at the shelves and work surfaces. No sign of it. Frantically, she tried to recall when she had last used it. It had been just before she had left for London.

Her cheese sandwich had tasted all the better for being eaten off such precious crockery. She remembered using the last of the washing-up liquid to wash it up. She checked the bin. Sure enough, there was the empty bottle.

As she turned back she saw it in the sink. She went over and picked it up. It was covered in crumbs and smeared with a dark, sticky substance. She sniffed it suspiciously. Marmite. She had bought a new jar recently but not used it. She opened the cupboard, found the pot and unscrewed the lid. Sure enough, the seal had been broken.

She clung to the edge of the sink. He had been back to her house and this time he had been inside. He must have wanted her to know; just like before he made no attempt to cover his tracks.

How the hell had he got in? She was always so careful to lock up. She felt the vomit rise in her throat. She bolted upstairs and into the bathroom where she flung herself over the toilet. Looking down into the porcelain bowl, she was repulsed and shocked to see it was full of dark, foamy urine.

She knew it couldn't possibly be hers. She had not used the lavatory that morning; she had peed in the shower.

Chapter eight

[Isle of Wight 2013]

After a brandy to steady her nerves, Sandra phoned the police. She was relieved to be dealing with a woman officer who she assumed would be more understanding. Sandra was anxious to dispense with the formalities as quickly as possible, giving her details before she was even asked. The officer was clearly not used to working at Sandra's speed preferring to take her time and input the information onto her system in a slow, thorough manner. Sandra paced the room, silently berating the woman's tardiness.

'Okay, so you've got all that? Right, someone's been in my house, an intruder,' Sandra explained.

'Any signs of a break-in, madam?'

'Not that I can see but I know he used the toilet ...'

The stench of urine clung to her nostrils. She topped up her drink and took another mouthful.

'... and he ate my food. He ...'

'How do you know it was a 'he'?' interrupted the policewoman.

'Because I recently met a man on a train and he knows where I live.'

'Sorry, madam, I need to be clear. Do you know the intruder?'

The officer sounded as if she was losing patience. Sandra tried to focus but she felt disconnected, like she was swimming underwater.

'Ben, his name is Ben. You'll have him on file. He's a murderer, he cut someone's throat.'

At last, she was getting somewhere. She sat forward on the sofa, desperate to remember anything else that might identify him.

'I see, madam. And what makes you think it was the same man?'

The officer's voice was flat and pragmatic.

'I told you, he knows where I live.'

Now it was Sandra's turn to sound irritated. Surely, the silly woman had enough to go on?

'Did you give him your address? Invite him to your home?' the officer persisted.

More questions. Why? Just go and find him.

'No,' Sandra shouted impatiently. 'I live alone. Why would I ask a murderer to my house?'

The police officer seemed very slow on the uptake.

'Are you writing this down?' Sandra asked slamming down her glass. 'You don't seem to understand. Let me start again. The man overheard me telling someone my address. Then he came round and put an Oyster Card through my door. Now he's actually been inside my house.'

'An Oyster card?' asked the officer incredulously.

'Yes, yes, it's a London travel card, like a credit card. But ...'

'Yes, I know what an Oyster Card is, madam. I am simply trying to ascertain if the law has been broken. So did anyone actually see this man in your house?'

'No, but it had to be him. Who else would it be?'

'So, you have no way of knowing whether or not it was the person you met on the train?'

'Who else would it be? What's got to happen before you take notice? Has he got to cut my throat too?'

'Has he threatened or assaulted you in any way?'

'No, I...'

'And definitely no sign of a break-in?'

'No, you've asked me that once. '

'Just clarifying the facts, madam.'

What a waste of time. Sandra sighed audibly.

'So, all we know for certain is that someone put an Oyster card through your door?'

The woman started every sentence with 'so'. It grated on Sandra.

'What about him getting into my home and using my plate and my toilet?'

Sandra was aware she was beginning to sound faintly ridiculous.

'Could you have left the house in a rush and forgot you'd used the plate and the toilet?'

'If I'd done that why would I be ringing you?'

Sandra drained the glass, swishing the brandy around her mouth before swallowing it.

'So, from what you're telling me, it seems no crime has been committed.'

'No crime? Someone has been in my house. There must be something … oh forget it,' said Sandra wearily.

'Would you like our Crime Prevention Officer to come round and advise on how to make your property more secure? I can arrange an appointment now if you like?'

'Crime Prevention? Isn't that like shutting the door after the bastard has bolted?' she said clicking the phone off and throwing the handset onto the sofa.

Light-headed but lucid, she knew exactly what to do. She would call back another time and talk to someone more experienced.

The acrid stench of burning alerted her to the bread still in the toaster. She flicked it out with the end of a wooden spoon.

She scraped the worst of the charred bread over the sink and watched as the white porcelain became flecked with sooty black. She tried a piece of the crust then threw what was left of the slice in the bin.

Staggering into the living room, she made it onto the sofa where she lay down and gratefully rested her head on a cushion.

A sharp rap on the door woke her. She sat up. Not daring to move, she wondered if she could reach the phone and call the police. Her fingers crept slowly along the settee. Just a couple more inches.

The knock came again. The letterbox lifted and a pair of bespectacled eyes peered directly at her. She let out a little gasp and her nerves stood to attention. She held her breath.

'Hi Sandra. Sandra, it's me Stephen from next door? Are you there?'

She leapt up.

'Stephen? Hang on, just a sec, I'm coming.'

She ran to the door and opened it.

Stephen stood there. Blinking at her with his hands behind his back, he looked just like an owl.

'Sorry to disturb you, Sandra but I've been away. I had to pop back to oversee some work I've had done on the cottage. Anyway, it's all finished, thank goodness but sadly I've got to go back to the smoke. Just got a very lucrative contract. No rest for the wicked, eh? So, I won't be here for a while. Shame, especially with this lovely weather we're having.'

Sandra stared at him. What the hell was he talking about?

'Oh sorry, I almost forgot,' he said producing a slim white envelope and handing it to her. 'This appears to have been wrongly delivered to me. The postman must have muddled up Dove House with Dove Cottage. Easy mistake to make.'

She took it from him. The name and address was typed clearly enough but the postmark had been obscured.

'I don't know when it came. Like I said, I haven't been around for a while. Nothing urgent I hope?' he asked looking past her into her living room.

The letter was likely to be from one of two people, Carl or Ben. One would make her day; the other would make her terrified.

'Are you okay? You're shaking. I didn't mean to frighten you.'

He sounded genuinely concerned.

'I'm fine, really,' she said just wanting him to go. 'Thanks for bringing it round. Goodbye.'

Forcing a smile, she shut the door.

As Sandra tore open the envelope a small square photograph, fell into her lap. She didn't recognise the young woman with the long blonde hair. Sandra turned over the letter to check the signature. It was from Carl. But her joy was short-lived. She looked at the date. Tuesday 11th June, that was only yesterday. Through the Witness Protection Programme, Carl's letters had taken about six weeks to reach her. This one had taken a day. The address confirmed her worst fear. Carl had lied to her; he wasn't going to move back to London, he already had.

16 Blenheim Crescent, Primrose Hill, London, NW3 1TF

Tuesday 11th June

Hi Mum,

I am living in London with Debs. That's her in the pic, stunning, isn't she? Our baby will be beautiful. We're having a girl, by the way.

This house is like something out of 'Hello' magazine. Debs inherited it when her parents died.

Haven't mentioned the Witness Protection shit to her - didn't want to stress her while she's pregnant. So don't say anything.

By the way, she thinks you've had a bit of a breakdown. Told her about your old job and our house and she asked why you'd left it all behind.

I made up some crap about burn-out and depression. If she asks, just play along.

Luckily, she earns a fortune so I don't have to work. I quite fancy acting. I've had enough practice; I've been playing at being someone else for years.

Carl

PS. My landline: 0207 721 4566. Speak soon.

Chapter nine

[Isle of Wight 2013]

Sandra punched Carl's new number into her phone. How could he be so stupid? What was he thinking? That was the trouble, he wasn't. He had acted on impulse and to hell with the consequences.

As she was about to enter the final digit, she stopped. She knew from The Programme that a landline number could be easily traced. She couldn't risk it.

After several mouthfuls of brandy, she went up to bed and lay on the duvet listening to a branch tap dance against the window. Unable to sleep, her thoughts, a kaleidoscope of pain, fizzed like white noise behind her eyes.

Carl had got a woman he had just met, pregnant. The poor girl had no idea who he really was or what he was involved in. If he hadn't told her he had been on a Witness Protection Programme, chances were she didn't even know his real name.

Then again, it can't have been easy for Carl, cut off and isolated, living a fictional existence. God! What a bloody mess but what could she do? Carl had taken the reins.

She understood him wanting a relationship. But wanting out of the Programme? Total madness. And why go back to London where the Elliotts would be straight onto him?

She could still picture Lee Elliott's mother watching her son in the dock. The only time she took her eyes off him was when Carl gave his evidence. Then she stared defiantly ahead. Sandra had felt intimidated by this woman with a bulbous nose and huge jowls, who seemed to be made entirely from suet. When Carl had finished, she got to her feet and yelled in her North London accent, 'Fucking liar. You can't hide from us.'

A motley band of youths, unmistakably her sons, jeered and nodded like a hydra with an ASBO from the gallery.

'Silence!' the judge had told them. 'Or I shall have you removed.'

Too late. The matriarch had issued her warning.

Sandra's heart raced just thinking about it. She had warned Carl enough times. Unlike her, the Elliotts were not governed by integrity and morals. They followed their own corrupt code. Spruced-up, drugged-up and tooled-up, they policed their patch. To them a Stanley knife was not an implement to cut carpet but a weapon to cut flesh.

When she opened her eyes the next morning, the first thing she saw was crack in the ceiling. It had been there ever since she had moved in but recently it had got bigger. It was in the shape of a 'Y' and looked like it had been drawn in pencil with a shaky hand. The tail was longer than ever and meandered over a third of the way across the room. She made a mental note to tell the landlord.

Digging the sleep from her eyes, she sat up and swung her legs over the side of the bed. The floorboards felt warm against the soles of her feet. Unsteadily, she made her way across the landing and down the stairs.

She thought about phoning Carl but decided against it. Even if her son had thrown caution to the wind, she knew to be careful.

The brandy bottle was an increasingly welcome sight. Her friend always there for her. She went to pour herself a glass but there was none left. Funny, she didn't remember finishing it last night.

Even if Carl wanted to be reckless she was going to follow the advice of Witness Protection. They advised letters and phone calls from untraceable locations were preferable to emails and texts. Spontaneity was a thing of the past but it was a small price to pay for his safety.

Sandra found a pen and paper and a small bottle of whiskey. She poured herself a shot, just a drop to kick start the day and enable her to write a letter to her son.

Dear Carl,

I am horrified you have moved back to London. Not only are you endangering your life but your girlfriend's and your unborn child's too.

I can't believe you haven't told Debs about your past. I am sure she would never agree to any of this if you had been honest with her.

Opting out of Witness Protection is madness. I understand your frustration but you need to be cautious.

Contact the police. They will help you.

Carl, be careful. Who is this girl? What will happen when she finds out you lied to her? And what sort of a life can you hope to give your baby?

Think about it.

I love you.

Mum x

She took another mouthful of whiskey before adding a final thought.

PS. Thanks for telling your girlfriend I am completely gaga. I will endeavour not to disappoint if I meet her.

She read the letter out loud. It struck exactly the right note. She celebrated with another nip of whiskey.

Amongst the detritus that had accumulated in the kitchen drawer, safety pins, unsharpened pencils and paperclips, she found a book of first class stamps and an envelope. She hammered the stamp on the envelope with her fist before sliding the letter inside and licking the seal too quickly causing her to cut her tongue on the sharp edge.

She copied the address from Carls' letter before writing his name at the top then thought better of it and changed the 'C' to a 'D' and put it to 'Debs' instead. If he wouldn't take notice of his mother, perhaps he would listen to his girlfriend.

Glancing at her phone, she saw she had just five minutes to catch the morning post. If she hurried she would just make it. She flung on her coat and put on an old pair of shoes she kept by the door. Realising she had them on the wrong feet, she kicked them off and started again. 'Come on, come on,' she told herself. Stuffing the letter into her pocket, she ran out of the house. It had been raining; the cobbled path was slippery. She skittered along the lane, sliding across the wet leaves. When she got to the main road, she could see the mail van parked outside the village shop where the postman was already emptying the box. She ran the last few yards before darting across the road.

'Wait, please,' she cried. 'Please, please wait.'

The postman smiled at her as she caught her breath and dropped the envelope into his bag.

'Thanks very, very much. It's very, very urgent.' she slurred congratulating herself on how sober she sounded. 'Thank God I caught you.'

'It must be your lucky day,' he told her.

'Yes,' she said as she slipped off the kerb and fell head first into the road.

Chapter ten

[Isle of Wight 2013]

Lying flat in the tunnel, a white light illuminated Sandra's thoughts. After an intense examination by unseen eyes, her fate would be obvious. Heaven or Hell. Ascend into the arms of angels or descend into the Devil's lap. As a lapsed Catholic, she knew how it worked.

She must be in purgatory, the waiting-room for unclean souls, waiting to be cleansed. She was full of sin; this bit could take some time.

'Keep still, please,' the disembodied voice said. It came from outside the room issuing orders from behind a computer screen.

The dimensions of the tunnel were no greater than those of a cylindrical coffin. Some sort of conveyor belt had delivered her into this tomb. She just hoped she could get out the same way.

A clanking noise filled the space followed by an urgent buzzing. Then silence.

'How many years has it been since you last saw Carl?' asked her inner critic. 'Two, three? At least he did the right thing, just like you wanted. But now he lives in fear. One wrong word and Bang! Bang! He's dead.'

The clanking started again. Sandra breathed in deeply. Encased in white light, like a celestial mummy.

'Happy Mother's Day. Happy Father's Day, Sandra,' said her tormentor, drilling down into her brain. 'You got to play at being both parents. Did you listen to your son? Really listen? Like you are having to listen to me now?'

Self-doubt pricked and perforated her confidence.

'Just one more, very still, please,' order the voice.

She tried to shut out another stream of taunts.

'You taught your son to do the right thing. He is a beacon, shining a light on the scum, scum like the Elliotts: the dealers, the users, the pimps and the whores, the murderers.

Think about what I am saying. You have plenty of time, day after day, stretching ahead of you, all alone. Can there be a worse hell?'

If there was, Sandra couldn't think of one; time with no end, full of regret and remorse.

Her inner critic was always ready to berate her. Usually, she shut it up with a stiff drink.

'Easy money makes for an easy life. The less fortunate, have it harder. Perhaps the scum are people who have simply picked the wrong path. Went left instead of right. Easily done. Everyone has free will. But perhaps the rich are freer than others.'

She wanted it to stop.

'Imagine Carl. Now, imagine him born into a family who only knew one way, the wrong way? How bent out of shape would he have been?

The voice pushed on, mining her mind for the truth.

'Let's look to the future. A future you will have no say in. Carl has a girlfriend now. And soon they will have a baby of their own, a child to teach the difference between right and wrong but that's not going to be easy when one of the hands rocking the cradle belongs to an accomplished liar'.

Sandra blinked and the voice stopped. In its place, the relentless banging.

Soon she would know her fate. Lee Elliott's face swam into view, leering at her, his idiotic sneer mocking her. She had spent every day of the trial scrutinising him, mesmerised by his Adam's apple like a piece of flint pushing out from under his flesh.

She was suffocating, buried beneath stark white light. Now nothing. Only silence. Silence she could hear.

Chapter eleven

'There's no sign of anything sinister on your scan. Don't look so scared, that's good news. An MRI is never pleasant but very thorough.'

The consultant, a squat, well-fed man attempted to disguise his bulk with a voluminous blue check shirt.

Sandra looked around at the blue curtains drawn around her bed and felt the stiff, coarse hospital sheets rubbing against the backs of her legs.

'How long have I been in here?' she asked.

The doctor referred to his notes.

'24 hours. You were admitted to the ward yesterday morning.'

She had lost a day. How did that happen?

He pinched the bridge of his nose between his thumb and forefinger in an attempt to stifle a sneeze. Suddenly, he snapped forward, opened his mouth and ejected a cloud of droplets over the bedclothes. Sandra recoiled.

'Your observations are fine and your bloods are clear. But...' he paused, his finger running along the words as he read the notes. '... you might want to think about how much you drink.'

Sandra studied his big fat pious face. He may be a doctor but knew nothing about her pain. It poisoned her soul and could not be numbed with tablets.

'How much d'you drink a week?' he asked.

Sandra shrugged.

'A rough guess?' he persisted.

He furrowed his brow and stared at her, his pen poised to commit her sins to paper. She did not answer. How could she? She drank to forget not to keep count of the bottles.

'I don't know,' she said truthfully.

'Shall we say, three or four glasses a day?' he asked.

The numbers jangled inside her head.

'Sounds about right,' she lied.

'And spirits?'

'Occasionally.'

He scribbled something on his pad. She was transfixed by his huge girth. Each check on his shirt was about an inch wide and she began to count the blue and white squares in an attempt to calculate the circumference of his waist.

Twenty-eight, twenty-nine, thirty and that was just the ones she could see. Double it and that would be closer to the truth. The man was obese. 'Physician heal thyself,' she thought, contemplating the amount of food and drink he must have to consume to maintain his size. Gluttony. Like her, he too was not without sin.

'I can get the nurse to come and talk to you about cutting down. Excessive drinking can be dangerous, as you've discovered to your peril. You gave yourself a very nasty blow to the head when you fell.'

'I was hit by a car,' she told him fearing he had muddled her up with another patient.

'There is no mention of a car. The notes just say you fell into the road.'

Her head was spinning. A car hit her. She was sure of that.

'But, I remember. I gave the post-man my letter, stepped into the road and was hit by a car. Look at my arm, it's all bruised,' she said showing him.

He gave it a cursory glance.

'That would've happened when you fell. You had a very nasty blow to the head but don't worry, we've given you a thorough check-over. I gather you were lucky and someone was on hand to call an ambulance.'

'But it was a hit and run. Surely someone called the police?'

He shook his head.

'We've got no record of that. Anyway, the good news is you can go home. I'll arrange for some painkillers for you. But it's very important you don't drink with them or you'll be back in A&E again,' he said with a brief twitch of his facial muscles, a smile, of sorts.

'Hippocratic oath? More like hypocritical,' she mused to herself.

As soon as the doctor left, Rob appeared carrying a plastic bag of black grapes. They looked perfect, as if plucked from a still life painting.

'Morning, Sandra. How are you? Hung-over?' he asked sitting down on the bed.

She flinched.

'Sorry,' he said getting up immediately and repositioning himself in the chair beside her. 'I was waiting outside and couldn't help overhearing what the doc said.'

'Fat bastard telling me how to live,' Sandra said bitterly.

'Apparently you were a bit pissed when they brought you in,' he said. 'I got the inside track off one of the paramedics. Apparently, they were well surprised when they turned up at the scene to find our very own admin assistant, Sandra, sparko in the road.'

Rob helped himself to a grape, popping it into his mouth and rolling it from side to side before squishing it with his back teeth and swallowing it. She hoped he wasn't planning on eating them all the same way.

'Want one?' he asked, spitting the pips into the bag. 'I can peel one for you, if you like, Tulluluh.'

'No, thanks. Did they say anything about what had happened to me?'

'No, only that you'd had a fall and hit your head. Why?'

'Just something the doctor said, not to worry.'

She feigned nonchalance but she was perplexed. There was a car. She was sure of it.

'Don't get comfy,' she told Rob. 'Just waiting for the nurse and then I can go home.'

He peered at her.

'That looks painful! Your poor old face. What you like?' he asked. 'How many Pinot Noirs was it? Ohmygod just imagine, if you'd pegged it, I'd have had to have done your spread sheets!'

She knew he was testing her to see where the line was and gave him a smile. He was only trying to cheer her up; she knew that. He grinned.

'I could kill a cuppa,' he told the tea lady when she appeared.

The woman looked nonplussed.

'It's okay. I'm a brain surgeon,' he told her. 'Just here, examining my patient.'

He pointed at Sandra before putting his index finger to his temple and making little circling motions.

The tea lady tut-tutted and moved towards the next bed.

'I suppose a Jammy Dodger's out of the question, then?' he called after her. 'Didn't know you could get a sense of humour bypass on the National Health.'

Sandra sniggered but the sickening pain in her ribs ensured her good humour was short-lived. God-forbid, she should cough or hic-cup.

'Drink? And I don't mean wine,' Rob asked his hand on the water jug.

Without waiting for a reply he quickly poured her a glass of water and held it to her lips. She took a few sips before sinking back into her pillow.

'You mustn't get dehydrated. Ohmygod. That happened to me last year and I...'

Sandra had stopped listening and watched the shrivelled woman in the opposite bed, her long, leathery tongue snaking incessantly in and out of her loose-lipped mouth.

'I hate grapes,' Rob said, enjoying another handful. 'Look, they've come all the way from South Africa. They're got more Air Miles than me. I've never been off the island. No wonder I'm single. Where's that nurse? We need to get you out of here; this place isn't exactly party central. '

Sandra lifted her hand, hoping to stall his incessant chatter. But Rob was on a mission to make her smile.

'Don't try to talk,' he grinned. 'Just nod once for 'yes' and twice for 'no'.

'Get my coat?' she asked.

'Why? Have you pulled?' he laughed.

Sandra ignored him and watched as he opened the locker and pulled out her jacket. Brown and shapeless, he looked at it disapprovingly.

'Once you're better, I'm taking you clothes shopping.'

'Is there a letter in the pocket?' she asked impatiently.

He felt inside and shook his head.

'Thank God,' she whispered.

She had posted it before the accident. Debbie could well have read it by now. All this pain and discomfort had been worth it. She was happy. She had done the right thing.

'Who are you writing love letters to?' Rob asked.

'My ...' Sandra began but stopped short of saying 'son'.

Since the trial, she had had to deny his existence too many times. She hated doing it because she felt it was tempting fate. But she had no choice.

'Well, I'm sorry to be a party-pooper but I told she-who-must-be-obeyed I was only nipping out for a skinny latte. If she knows I've been down here with you, you won't be the only one eating hospital food. Ohmygod! I had my appraisal this morning. What a joke. She asked me what I 'brought to the party?' I said 'glamour and grooming'. She wasn't impressed.'

Sandra didn't reply. The elderly lady opposite now had a visitor. A middle-aged man was sitting beside her bed. Sandra jerked forward to get a better look.

'Mark my words,' said Rob following Sandra's gaze. 'That one will be up by tea-time, partying and showing off her fandango. Oh, hello, granny's got a toy boy. Nothing says 'brute' quite like a shaved head.'

Fingers of pain, tightened around Sandra's rib cage and she let out a little cry.

'Steady,' he said, easing her back against the pillow. 'I know you're experiencing a bit of a drought but there's no need to throw yourself at anything with a pulse. At least wait for that swelling to go down before trying to pull. Ohmygod! The Brute's coming over.'

Rob sucked in his gut and beamed at the man approaching the bed who looked like he might work on an oil-rig.

'Rose?' said Ben easing himself onto the edge of her bed.

'What are you doing here?' said Sandra shrinking back into the bed.

'Calm down,' he laughed standing up and lifting his hands above his head in a gesture of mock surrender.

Just like before, his tee-shirt rode up, revealing his bare midriff and the thin line of dark hair that snaked down from his navel. Sandra shifted uncomfortably. He leant over her, allowing his smoky fingertips to brush against her nostrils before gently touching her swollen cheek.

64

'Looks nasty,' he murmured. 'Tell me who did that to you, Rose. I think I need to pay them a visit, don't you?'

'She had an argument with the tarmac,' said Rob.

'Leave me alone,' Sandra said jerking her head away to avoid his touch.

Her leg was shaking. She tried to catch Rob's eye but he was too much in awe of The Brute to notice.

'Sorry, it must hurt like hell,' he said letting his hand rest on the bedcovers.

'Why are you here?' she asked.

'Visiting Mum. She's over there,' he replied waving at the elderly, vacant-looking woman. 'Dodgy ticker, bless her. Been overdoing it. Still, I can come and see you both now.'

'No,' said Sandra, pulling the sheet up above her shoulders. 'How did you know I was here?'

'You'll have to excuse her, she's had a blow to the head,' smiled Rob. 'You can come up and see me anytime.'

'You're not my type, mate,' he said before bending his face towards Sandra's. 'Get well soon, Rose. If you need me, just shout.'

He grabbed a handful of grapes and squashed them into his mouth with the flat of his palm.

'Look after her. Rose is a special lady,' he shouted at Rob as he swaggered out of the ward.

'Still my beating heart,' said Rob waving his hands in front of his face. 'Who was that? Did you see the size of his gluteus maximus?'

Sandra thought she might be sick. Rob took her hand and stroked it.

'You okay? Who was he? Why did he keep calling you Rose?'

'He was the one I texted you about,' she said. 'You remember, the man on the train. The murderer on the train.'

Chapter twelve

[Isle of Wight 2013]

Ten straight stems, ten tight buds like pouting pink mouths, wrapped in cellophane lay on the doorstep to greet Sandra when she arrived home from hospital. Roses, the cheap kind, a fiver a bunch, she thought, the sort she used to buy for her mother whenever she was stuck in traffic on the North Circular Road in London. Trapped in her car, drumming her long, painted nails impatiently on the steering wheel, a sallow-skinned woman in a headscarf, jumper and long skirt would approach, grinning and showing her bad teeth, a bucket of blooms under one arm, five for three quid or ten for a fiver. It was a small price to pay to put a smile on her Mother's face albeit not for long; the flowers never lasted and were invariably dead by the next day.

The only person who knew about the accident and cared enough to leave her flowers was Rob but he was at work.

The blooms stared defiantly up at her, challenging her to take a closer look. Her head and shoulder hurt as she bent down and pulled out the small, white card. On one side, written in blue ball-point, just four words, 'Roses for my Rose'. On the other was a mobile number.

Shaking with fear and anger, she turned to see if anyone was about. Only the birds calling to one another from their vantage points in the foliage broke the silence.

'How dare he? The bastard,' Sandra thought as she walked around the side of the cottage to the dustbin.

Lifting the lid, she jettisoned the flowers in, headfirst. She paused before reaching down to retrieve the card, before slipping it into her pocket. It was evidence. It proved he had done it. It proved she wasn't imagining it.

A sudden noise startled her. She turned to see a pheasant fly out of the bushes. Such ungainly creatures, she thought, like bumble-bees, not designed to fly.

She walked back to the front door and quickly opened it. Once she was safely inside, she locked it, her heart racing.

Her headache, an intense throbbing behind her eyes, was getting worse. She reached inside her handbag. Where were her painkillers? She tipped out the contents onto the table and a small white plastic bottle rolled obligingly towards her. Twisting the lid frantically clockwise and anticlockwise, she eventually lined up the plastic arrows correctly and flipped open the lid. Two smooth white tablets tumbled into her palm. She opened her mouth and dropped them in. They tasted bitter. Walking into the kitchen and ignoring the doctor's advice, she opened the bottle of whiskey and took a swig.

Back in the living room, she crossed over to the table and picked up one of the two leaflets given to her at the hospital: *'Head injuries – a patient's guide.'*

'If you experience headaches, blackouts or vomiting, go straight to your nearest accident and emergency department.'

If she did that, she'd never leave the place, she thought ruefully. Opening the other pamphlet, she was annoyed to see someone, probably that interfering doctor, had underlined the Alcoholics Anonymous helpline number.

'Bloody cheek,' she thought casting it aside.

Gradually, the pain began to ease. Relieved the medication was kicking-in, she wandered back into the kitchen. The big box of doughnuts she had bought at Waterloo Station almost a week ago was on the table where she had left it. There were only a couple left but in the middle was a big, round grease stain, all that remained of the doughnut the man on the train had taken.

Her hand hovered over a ring doughnut with garish pink icing. It looked fine but would taste stale. Then again, she couldn't remember the last time she had eaten. As she leant forward to pick it up, her head felt like it was filling with bubbles of blood. Feeling unsteady on her feet, she sat down.

Within a few moments the sensation passed and she reached into her pocket and took out the card, turning it over in her palm. It was the proof she needed. She phoned the police. This time she had no intention of being fobbed off and, after giving her details and a brief outline of what had happened, she demanded to speak to a senior officer. Eventually, a curt, business-like voice came on the line.

'How can I help? I understand someone has delivered an Oyster card and a bunch of flowers to your home?' he asked.

'I'm being stalked by a murderer,' Sandra slurred thanks to the cocktail of drugs and alcohol. 'He's everywhere I am. The train, my house, even the bloody hospital.'

She took another mouthful of whiskey and swallowed it in one gulp.

'Have you been threatened?' the officer asked.

Sandra didn't care for his tone.

'No, but ...'

'No threat, verbal or physical?' he persisted.

'Not exactly, no.'

'What do you mean by 'not exactly'?' he asked suddenly more attentive.

'He knows where I live and has come to my house at least three times now, uninvited.'

'When you say 'uninvited'...'

'I mean I didn't bloody invite him,' she snapped. 'I didn't ask him to come.'

The booze was talking for her, making her bold.

'He tried to kill me. He had me run over.'

'What makes you think it was the same person?'

'Who else would it be?' said Sandra struggling to keep hold of the conversation.

'Did you report the incident?'

'No, I was unconscious at the time,' she said enjoying her own sarcasm.

'You're making a very serious accusation, madam. Do you have any evidence?'

Questions, bloody questions. All this red tape was tightening round her brain.

'Any proof?' he repeated.

'He leaves me things. Things I don't want. Oyster card, roses.'

'Could it be someone you know? Someone you have perhaps had a relationship with?'

Frustration boiled inside her.

'The man is a murderer for God's sake. What part of that don't you understand?'

'Do you know who he is?' the officer asked suddenly alert.

'His name is Ben.'

'Ben what?' he asked suddenly sounding more alert.

'I don't know but his mobile number is.... hang on.'

She read the number off the card and heard him tapping the digits into his computer before repeating them back to her.

'Thank you. That's very helpful. And what does he look like?'

'Early forties, shaved head, muscular, very muscular, tall, about six foot and ...' she paused, picturing him in her mind's eye. She liked what she saw.

'And?' he prompted.

Sandra came to.

'A London accent. He has a very strong London accent. Very common.'

She spoke the words like gunfire. The sooner he had a description, the sooner he could find him.

'Anything else? Anything at all?'

His tone was more sympathetic, as if he had switched off the public servant and activated his inner human.

'Can I get a restraining order against him?'

'Madam, like I said, no crime has been committed. If and when he actually does something, tell us and we can act.'

'So he's got to kill me first? In the name of God, this is madness.'

'I am sorry you feel that way, madam.'

'I am sorry you feel that way,' Sandra parroted back to him. How she hated that phrase. It was just a smart way of saying, 'The way you feel has nothing to do with me.'

She felt sick. Mixed with the whiskey, the pain-killers had become pain-inducers. Like an ill-fitting shoe, her skull felt two sizes too small for her brain.

'You say he's a murderer. Do you know when or where this alleged crime might have been committed?'

Sandra lost her tenuous grip on the conversation. The officer burbled on, 'Oyster card…roses… hospital visit'. He made the bastard sound more like a good Samaritan than a vicious assailant.

She imagined the policeman, having grown bored of their conversation, clicking off his screen to surf the net for a mini-break or a set of second-hand golf clubs.

'I need someone to protect me. Now. You let these criminals out of prison, tell us they've been rehabilitated and then something like this happens.'

'Do you have a friend or relative you can stay with?' he asked unaware Sandra was opening a bottle of wine, one from the case she had brought from London when she moved, the good stuff, once reserved for special dinner parties.

70

'Anyone at all?' prompted the officer.

Rob. She could stay with Rob. No, she couldn't involve him in all this. It wouldn't be fair. He was lovely but would be no use if things turned nasty. Perhaps she could go to London and stay with Carl. After all he had invited her. She wouldn't have to tell him the real reason; there was no need to worry him.

'Madam, can you hear me? Would you ...'

Cutting the officer off in mid-sentence, she clicked off the phone and went to bed.

The following morning, Sandra woke with a headache. Hangover or the after effects of the accident, she had no way of knowing. All she knew was it hurt like hell. She went downstairs for some water. The pink envelope lying on the mat immediately caught her attention. She didn't need to know the handwriting to know who it was from. She ripped it open.

16 Blenheim Crescent,
Primrose Hill,
London, NW3 1TF

Dear Sandra,

Thank you for your letter.

I hope you don't mind me writing to you but Sam is worried about you. He explained the tremendous stress you were under at your previous job. It can't have been easy for you. We are both relieved you are now getting the help you need.

It's clear you are concerned about Sam moving to London and his relationship with me. I love him very much and will look after him and our new baby. We hope you will play a big part in her life. Sam will make a wonderful father.

Perhaps, we can visit you before the baby is born? I holidayed on the island as a child and have happy memories of long summer days on the beach at Seaview.

I know this must be quite a lot to take in but try not to worry. Call any time and you are welcome to visit whenever you like. I am sure we will be great friends. I hope so.

With love

Debs and Sam xxx

Sandra screwed up the letter and threw it against the wall. How patronizing, being written to like she was a mad woman. The silly girl had obviously fallen for Carl and his ridiculous story about her having a breakdown. There was no way she could stay with them; they would have the men in white coats waiting for her the minute she stepped off the train at Waterloo.

She struggled for breath. It felt like she was inhaling carbon dioxide. She put her hand to her mouth, too late as the vomit splattered over her shoes.

Chapter thirteen

[Isle of Wight 2013]

Sandra was not the sort to play the sick card. It had been a while since the accident. Apart from the odd headache and one side of her body feeling like it didn't belong to her, she convinced herself she was fine. It was nothing a drink couldn't cure. She pushed the duvet back and sat up.

The very thought she would be working at the hospital at the same time as the man on the train was visiting his mother made her want to stay cocooned in bed. He might have a legitimate reason to be on the ward but Sandra knew there was nothing legal about him.

She leant back against the headboard and picked up her phone. She checked the time, it had just gone seven-thirty, and then called Rob's mobile.

'Sandra! Ohmygod! Please say you're coming back? I'm so bored I even considered doing some work yesterday.'

He was like a puppy, brimming with boundless love. Thank God for Rob.

'Meet me outside the hospital, in about an hour?' she asked.

'Are you sure? Isn't it a bit soon to be coming back to work?'

'I'm fine, a bit sore but ...'

'Okay, I'll be waiting for you, paramedics on standby, just in case you keel over again. Health and Safety and all that,' he laughed.

She clicked her mobile off and threw it in her bag. The bruising and swelling made having her usual shower, impossible. She washed as best she could with a flannel over the sink. Even getting dressed was frustratingly slow. Putting on her knickers was the most challenging. She sat on the edge of the bed and made several attempts to bend down and push her feet through the leg-holes before giving up and allowing her pants to drop to the floor. They would just have to stay there; it was too much effort to retrieve them. The rigmarole of putting on a bra was out of the question. She shuffled onto the landing and selected a long skirt from her wardrobe. Despite, the fabric being too thick for the muggy weather, it was easy to put on and the perfect cover up. She teamed it with a loose fitting blouse and pushed her feet into a pair of flip-flops before walking tentatively downstairs. Dressed for both summer and winter, she felt ridiculous. Then again, who cared? She couldn't remember exactly when she had become invisible but the older she got the more used she became to being ignored.

She hobbled about the cottage and eventually managed to secure all the windows and to double-lock the back door. She glanced at her phone again to check the time. Damn. Her bus was due in less than half an hour; she had better get a move on.

Breakfast was two painkillers washed down with wine. She picked up her bag, left the house and locked the door behind her.

As she walked through the gate and onto the lane, her awkward gait meant her feet seemed to find every raised cobble and loose stone throwing her off kilter and slowing her down. Consequently, she arrived at the stop with just seconds to spare and thrust out her good arm when the bus appeared.

'Morning,' the driver said with his usual avuncular grin as the doors hissed open. 'Back to work already? No rest for the wicked, eh?'

She paid her fare and made her way to the nearest seat by the window. Sometimes, she wished people would keep themselves to themselves. Perhaps, Carl was right, there was a lot to be said for the anonymity of London.

She sat down and looked out at Shorwell Shute, forever in the shade, proudly displayed its green, glossy banks resplendent with lush ferns. By contrast, the fields approaching Bowcombe were parched. Sympathizing with the sheep in their warm coats, hiding from the sun under the trees, her long skirt trapped the heat uncomfortably around her thighs.

Those painkillers seemed to be working over-time; she was imagining farmers dolling out parasols to their livestock and offering them grass smoothies. She felt light-headed, almost happy.

'Nice to see you smile, Rose. Turn that frown upside down, eh?'

Sandra turned. Only one person called her 'Rose'.

The man on the train was now on the bus, staring straight at her.

'Sorry, I was upstairs texting when I spotted you getting on,' he said. 'So I came down to see you.'

'Get away from me,' she told him.

'You don't mean that, Rose,' he said as cocky as ever.

They were the only two passengers on the lower deck. She considered getting off at the next stop but worried he would follow her. She could tell the driver. But what would she say? Ben hadn't done anything. She decided to sit tight and pray he got off before her.

'How's it going then, Rose? Kissed any more tarmac lately?' he joked swinging himself down onto the seat next to her.

She squeezed up close to the window. Why was he on her bus when he lived in Ryde? What possible reason could he have for being in the West Wight? She stared out of the window, determined not let him get to her. He parted his legs, closing the gap between them. The heat from his thigh increased the amount of perspiration pooling between her legs.

'Relax, Rose.'

She was horrified to be both repulsed and excited by him. She told herself to get a grip and stop being so bloody stupid.

Sensing her discomfort, he laughed and made a point of resting his arm along the top of the seat behind her head. She leant forward to try and avoid contact and noticed two thin estuaries of sweat form a river of desire between her breasts. The itchy fabric irritated her bare flesh and she shifted her weight from one buttock to another. All the while, his breath was on her neck, warm and pungent. Just knowing she wasn't wearing any pants intensified her sudden and unexpected feeling of illicit pleasure. She wriggled. His proximity perplexed her. One moment, she felt like hoisting up her shirt and forcing herself against him, the next she wanted to punch in the window and climb out.

'This yer first day back at work?' he asked.

She nodded.

'Bit soon innit?' he said turning his head to gauge her reaction. 'No sense in killing yourself over a job. Should've got your doctor to sign you off for a bit and milked it.'

Horrified at such a suggestion, she turned to look at him. His mouth twisted up at the edges, like the crust on a Cornish pasty.

'You hot?' he asked parting his legs even wider and pressing his thigh firmly against hers.

It was the most intimate physical contact she had had with anyone since hugging Carl 'goodbye' the night he had left for his new life. She had clung on to her son but his embrace had been all too brief and perfunctory. He had been the first to break away. His heart may have been hardened to their parting but hers was broken.

Her headache had all but disappeared, all she could think of was the man. Her body pulsated to an exciting new rhythm. This killer made her feel alive.

She knew it was wrong but the sensation was delicious, dangerous and dirty. The last time she had felt like this she was sixteen and about to lose her virginity to Ross Wheelen on the back seat of his Vauxhall Viva.

Through the window, she could see Carisbrooke Castle, high on the hill. Newport, her destination, was just minutes away. She should have been glad to escape his attentions but wanted to stay with him, go all the way. When the bus turned right at The Waverley pub, she fell against him and made no attempt to sit upright.

'Rosie!' he mocked, placing his hand on her arm.

It broke the spell and her body stiffened as her lust turned to dust.

'Come on, Rosie. I've given you a travel card and a bunch of roses. Not a crime, is it?' he asked.

'You should know.'

'I thought you'd like the flowers. Thought it was a nice thing to do.'

'It's pathetic.'

'Did you just call me 'pathetic'?' he asked his eyes widening in anger.

'No,' she said. 'Of course not.'

'Just being nice,' he said sounding nasty.

'Nice? You broke into my house, didn't you? You've been stalking me ever since we met.'

'What? Don't be daft.'

'You used my loo and stole my food,' she shouted loud enough for the driver to hear.

She pressed her knees together, ashamed at having played a dangerous game with a dangerous man. She felt vulnerable without knickers but it was too late for modesty. She tugged her skirt down over her knees all the same.

'You think I was in your house? Believe me, Rose, you'd know if I'd been inside,' he laughed, mocking her.

'It was you. I know it was,' she said.

But even as she said the words, she doubted herself. The thought it could have been someone other than him had never even occurred to her.

'Not guilty, Rose. Cross my heart and hope to die,' he said, crisscrossing the left-hand side of his chest with the forefinger of his right hand.

Something in his child-like gesture made her think he just might be telling the truth.

'Then who the hell was it?' she demanded, her voice cracking.

'Dunno. I came to your cottage twice: once with the Oyster card and the other to leave the roses. 'A rose for a rose',' he quoted from the card.

She tried to read him. He looked plausible enough.

77

'Why would I break in, Rose? If I wanted to see you, all I'd have to do is knock.'

His eyes travelled away from her face, down her throat, across her breasts and settled disconcertingly in her lap. And just for a moment, he made her feel something she hadn't felt in years.

Wanted.

What was she thinking, letting him manipulate her?

'Excuse me,' she said standing up.

'Why? What you done?' he laughed but did not move.

She tried to push past him.

'Steady on, Rose. No rush. We're both getting off here. It's the last stop,' he told her as the bus turned into the depot.

He made no attempt to get up even after the driver had applied the hand brake and opened the doors. Cornered against the window, she jabbed at him.

'Move! I'm late for work.'

Slowly, he got up and swaggered towards the door. He waited and watched as she made her way towards him. Aware she wasn't wearing any knickers, she wondered if he was aware she was naked beneath her skirt.

'Wanna share a cab to the hospital? Mum might be coming out today,' he said ushering her off the bus.

'No.'

'Thought you were late for work, Rosie?'

'I lied,' she told him walking away.

'Naughty girl, never had you down as a fibber, Rose,' he shouted after her.

She ignored him and watched as he walked away. The bus to the hospital wasn't in yet and she didn't want to risk waiting just in case Ben came after her. She hurried off towards Church Litten. The painkillers were wearing off. Her head ached and walking was slow and difficult. What was usually a fifteen-minute stroll to the hospital, took her well over half an hour.

Not surprisingly, when she finally arrived at the hospital, there was no sign of Rob outside. She went up to her office and wanted to leave as soon as she arrived. The air felt thick and oppressive and all she could hear was the tapping of keys. It was early, but people were already getting out their home-made sandwiches, peeling back the top layer of bread to inspect the fillings. They all looked so disappointed. God knows why, thought Sandra, presumably they were the ones who had chosen to make the same dull thing day after day.

She dropped her bag on the floor and pulled out her chair as Rob approached.

'Sandra. Where have you been? I've been trying to call you.'

'Sorry, my phone must be on silent,' she said wiping her sweaty palms down her skirt.

'No wonder you're hot and bothered, The Brute is in the building. I came over all faint when I spotted him.'

'You saw him?' she asked her voice urgent.

'Yes, a cab dropped him off at the door while I was waiting for you. He is the sweetest …with his mum all day yesterday and the day before that.'

'All day? Are you sure?'

'Yeah, the nurses told me he never leaves her side. I'm close to my Mum too. That mother-son bond is so special. Oh, sorry, Sandra,' he said wrongly assuming, like everyone, she was childless.

If only he knew. The reason she was full of regret was not because she didn't have a son but because she did.

'Don't worry, he seems like a lovely guy,' said Rob.

'Just because he's got big muscles doesn't mean he's got a big heart.'

'The heart is a muscle. Anyway, I think he made up all that stuff about being a murderer to impress you. Some women like all that stuff, don't they? Look at those girls who write to men on Death Row.'

'Rob, for God's sake, he's not to be trusted. He broke into my house.'

'Have you told the police?' he asked sounding excited.

'Yes, for all the good it did. They want evidence not a middle-aged woman's fantasies.'

He rested his hand on her forearm.

'Wait there.'

He bustled off and returned a few minutes later.

'There you go,' he said handing her a drink.

'Thanks,' she said, her smile as weak as the tea.

She put the mug down on her desk, slopping liquid over the edge to form what looked like a map of Asia on a pile of papers.

'Shit!' she said, her hand shaking as she slid the sodden top sheet into the bin. 'I can't stay, knowing he's downstairs.'

'That should have been recycled. She-who-must-be-obeyed said ...'

Before he could finish, she grabbed the stack of paper and threw it all in the green recycling bin.

'There. Happy now?' she screamed.

Rob's eye-brows flew up into his hairline.

'Sandra, have your tea and calm down,' said Rob gently. 'He's not here to upset you, he's just visiting his mum. But if it makes you feel better, I'll keep an eye on him. It'll be my pleasure,' he winked.

True to his word, he spent the rest of the day popping up and down to the ward, tapping the nurses for information. According to them, Ben only ever left his mother's side to visit the toilet or hospital shop for more chocolate, crisps and fizzy drinks.

For the first time that day, Sandra smiled. She enjoyed the irony. The stalker was being stalked.

Chapter fourteen

[Isle of Wight 2013]

Sandra's first day back at work left her exhausted and in more pain than she had anticipated. Knowing the man on the train was just yards from her, unnerved her. On her way out, she asked Rob to go down to the ward with her and check on his whereabouts. Only too happy to enjoy another glimpse of The Brute's raw masculinity, Rob stood with her as they spied on him as he fed his mother a bowl of custard, carefully wiping her mouth after every spoonful, all the while talking and laughing with her.

'Ah, that's cute,' said Rob.

Sandra smiled in agreement before reminding herself the hand that held the spoon had also held the knife that killed a man.

After saying 'good-bye' to Rob, she caught the bus into town where she stopped to buy some eggs and a couple of bottles of Chardonnay. An omelette and a glass or two of wine would make an easy supper.

The bus was punctual leaving the depot and the driver wasted no time in getting her home. It was such a beautiful evening, she even considered stopping for a drink in the garden at The Crown, the perfect place to escape her worries and unwind with a drink in its magical garden with doves and a stream. Unfortunately, her head began to ache again and she decided to head home.

The smell of stale cigarette smoke hit her as soon as she walked through the front door. The aroma was so strong she expected to see someone standing there, cigarette in hand.

Her mouth felt dry like it was full of dead butterflies, their powdery wings having absorbed all the moisture. If she was breathing, she was not aware of it. Tentatively, she walked across the room taking small steps. When she reached the kitchen the smell of nicotine was less noticeable but turning back into the living room, the aroma hit her again.

She wanted to cry with fear but knew better than to make a sound. Her hand on the banister, she waited at the foot of the stairs, straining to hear if anyone was still in the house. Nothing. Her foot shaking on the bottom step, she slowly made her way onto the landing. The door to her bedroom was half open and she could clearly see her unmade bed, just as she had left it. The bathroom and spare bedroom were both empty. The only noise was the dripping tap. Leaning over the bath, she turned it off and shuddered. She never used the bath or shower that morning; she had washed at the sink.

Her heart thumping, she went back down the stairs. She scanned the living room and spotted a spent match in the fireplace. Where the hell had that come from? She didn't smoke and never lit a fire for fear a stray spark would catch the thatch alight. She picked up the match and jerked back out of the inglenook. Straightening up, she found herself eye-level with the picture of Totland Bay, the one she had taken at sunset on Carl's birthday.

She gasped, her right hand flew to her mouth.

The sun was burnt, nothing more than a black hole. Someone had stubbed out a cigarette on the sunset.

She lifted the photograph down. Only a few weeks ago, she had accidently knocked it off its hook when she was cleaning and smashed the glass. If only she had replaced it, this could never have happened. Holding the edge of the frame, she worried at the burn mark, circling the hole with her forefinger.

And in that moment she knew the truth.

The person she had blamed for the unnerving goings-on, was not responsible for this. Ben did not deface the picture. How could he have done? He had been at the hospital all day. She had seen him. So had Rob.

Perhaps he had been telling the truth and it wasn't him who had used her toilet or ate her food either. Nonetheless, she found it hard to believe he was entirely innocent.

She got up and walked towards the front door to ensure it was locked. Her right knee gave way and she had to grip it with both hands to stop it shaking.

She grabbed a bottle of wine from the carrier bag, unscrewed the top and put the rim to her lips. Warm white wine, something she would never have touched in her past life, tasted good. She rolled the liquid around her mouth before gulping it down. These days, it took longer to have the desired effect but after the fourth mouthful, she felt calmer and the pains in her limbs subsided to a dull ache. She thanked God for Dr. Chardonnay.

For reasons she could not explain, she found herself wishing it had been Ben in her house. Then, she reminded herself, the man was a murderer, a nasty piece of work. No woman in her right mind would want him anywhere near them. Perhaps, Carl was right. She was crazy. She must be. Why else couldn't she stop thinking about Ben and the way he had made her feel on the bus? But, it wasn't just the musky longing he had stirred in her. It was something far more potent.

Love. The love she had seen Ben show his mother was real. It was the love her son had never shown her.

She picked up the picture and remembering how she had felt the moment she took it. She had been lonely, missing her son on his birthday, wishing things were different and she could be with him. Would he have been feeling the same way? She doubted it very much. Placing the picture on the table, the wine had helped to dampen down some of her initial terror. At last, she had concrete evidence a crime had been committed. There may even be fingerprints. The police would have to take her seriously now.

She picked up the phone and demanded to speak to the same officer as before. She wanted continuity and to prove her case. After a few moments, the familiar sardonic voice came on the line and insisted Sandra repeat her details even though she knew he had them. Pedant.

'I told you all this before,' she snapped. 'For God's sake. Do your job and get round here now. He could still be in the house or hiding in the garden...'

'Have you been drinking, madam?' he asked and Sandra thought she heard him stifle a yawn.

'What are you the bloody Wine Police? Of course I've been drinking. It's a shock to discover someone's been in your house and defaced your property.'

'Madam, I...'

'Having a glass of wine is not a bloody crime.'

Stupid man. She was entitled to a drink. It was none of his business. Whatever next, an alcohol-meter under the stairs, totting up every tot of whiskey?

'Any idea who it might be?' he asked as if talking to a small child.

'No but it's not the person I told you about. It's not Ben.'

'Do you smoke?' he asked.

Sandra could hear him, clicking his mouse.

'Are you saying I did this?' she asked incredulously.

'No, madam, I ...'

'And for the record, I don't smoke.'

'Any sign of a break-in?'

His tone slipped into automatic as he trotted out the same old questions.

'No but they could've set the place on fire. It's a timbered thatch, Grade two listed, for God's sake.'

'Okay, madam. I've got everything I need for now. I'll send over our Crime Prevention Officer. He'll advise you on securing the property.'

'This isn't some tin-pot break-in; this is bloody arson!' she exclaimed.

'He'll be with you first thing, if that's convenient? And, we can investigate this further once ...'

Yada, yada, yada. She clicked the phone off and considered ringing her neighbour, Stephen to ask if he had seen anything suspicious. Then she remembered he had told her he was going away. She hadn't seen a light on in his place for days; he had probably already left.

The smell of smoke lingered but was not as strong. She felt violated, her home infiltrated by a stranger. She went into the kitchen, grabbed the damp dishcloth and used it to wipe down all the surfaces. Just as she was about to clean the picture frame, she stopped herself. What was she doing, getting rid of valuable evidence?

She had had enough. She grabbed the wine and went up to bed. The more she drank, the safer she felt and the better she slept.

When she eventually woke the following morning, she rang work, explained about the break-in and said she would be in later.

A knock on the door cut the conversation short. Shaking, she made her way downstairs.

'Who is it?' she demanded.

'The Crime Prevention Officer.'

'Show me your ID.'

The letterbox clattered opened and a small plastic card on a chain was pushed through.

'Okay,' she said as the card was retrieved.

She opened the door to a tall, lanky man who looked shocked to be greeted by a woman wearing just a long baggy T-shirt. Nervously, he twirled his ID card through his fingers.

'Crime Prevention Officer,' he said awkwardly.

She nodded and let him in. He was so tall he had to duck to get through the door and had to remain stooped to avoid hitting his head on the beams. After a cursory glance at his notes, he examined the front door.

'That lock is pretty basic,' he told her disapprovingly. 'Not fit for purpose.'

'Yes, it's a rented place. The landlord doesn't like spending money.'

'He should want to protect his property. These locks are very easy to work free. If someone wanted to break-in all they'd have to do is swipe something like a credit card between the door and the frame,' he said demonstrating with his ID card. 'Then they just push back the lock and open the door.'

He looked at her to check she understood before jotting down some notes on his pad.

Sandra showed him the burnt picture.

'How odd,' he muttered before returning to his comfort zone: locks.

'First thing to do is get a five lever Mortice lock fitted on your front entrance.'

Sandra's front entrance hadn't been used in so long she would welcome an intruder. The man, unaware of his double entendre, continued.

'Has anyone else got a key to the property? Landlord, friend, relative?'

She shook her head, wondering if she would ever throw open the doors to her portal again. The encounter with Ben on the bus had rekindled urgent longings, long forgotten.

'No signs of a forced entry,' he declared, examining the bolts on the back door.

Sandra should have been paying attention. Instead, she fantasised about forcing herself on Ben. She felt like she was smiling inside her knickers.

'Fit new locks on all of them,' he told after he had inspected the downstairs windows. 'Is it okay if I check upstairs?'

She nodded and waited in the living room. She couldn't stop thinking about Ben. Pushing her hair back from her face with one hand, she made no attempt to pull down her thin T-shirt as it rode up over her knees.

'Use the loft much?' he shouted as her hand travelled down over her breasts.

'No,' she called, imagining her palm was Ben's as it cupped her left breast.

'Okay if I have look?'

'Fine,' she said, her hand working its way under her T-shirt, over her belly and inside her pants.

'Do you mind passing me my torch?' he shouted.

'Sorry?' she gasped, enjoying the waves of pleasure flooding her body.

'My torch. I left it by the door. As soon as you can please.'

'Shit!' she thought. 'Shit.'

'Hang on,' she told him flustered.

'It's okay, I'll come down.'

'No! No! I'll get it!' she shouted, pulling down her T-shirt and grabbing the torch before he could see her, all flushed.

He had ruined the moment. Frustrated, she went upstairs where all she could see was his long legs and feet as he stood with his head and shoulders inside the entrance to the attic.

'Thanks,' he said as she placed the torch in his outstretched palm.

She waited as he worked the beam around the rafters.

'Can you see anything?' she asked anxiously.

'No,' he told her, clicking off the torch.

'There's a retractable ladder just inside the hatch if you want to go up and look around.'

'No, it's fine.'

He emerged, blinking rapidly, his thick-lens glasses magnifying his pupils and his sandy hair flecked with pieces of thatch.

'Right, I think that's everything. So, locks on all the windows and doors, and an alarm system. A small one should be fine for a property this size.'

'I can't see the landlord paying for this,' she sighed.

'It's in his interest to keep his property secure. But the most important priority is your own safety, obviously.'

He looked at her and she stared back. Her well-being had long since ceased to be important. Keeping Carl out of harm's way was all that mattered.

'In the meantime, you can consider putting lights on timers and perhaps join the Neighbourhood Watch scheme?' he asked as if suggesting she enrol with the WI.

'It'll take more than a sticker on the front door to keep out whoever is getting in,' she told him, aggression and fear mingling in her voice.

'I'll put all this in my report. Anything else I can help you with?'

'Will someone come and check the place for fingerprints?'

He looked disconcerted at the suggestion.

'You'll need to discuss that with the duty officer at the station. There's a good locksmith on Gunville Road in Newport. We're not allowed to recommend places but if you look in the Yellow Pages, you'll find him.'

He smiled at her.

'Thanks for your time,' she said remembering her manners.

She couldn't help noticing his shocked expression as he clocked the proliferation of bottles spilling out of her recycling bin. She knew what he was thinking, 'Wow! You drink a lot.'

Alone again, the fear ebbed back into her veins. Her hands were shaking. She reminded herself the officer had checked the cottage. There was no-one here.

A pain gnawed at her stomach. She couldn't remember when she last had a proper meal and went into the kitchen. The fridge was empty except for the eggs she had bought. But she couldn't face cooking them. Instead, she opened the cupboard and thrust her hand into a box of cereal. She forced a fistful of wheat flakes into her mouth, where mixed with her saliva, they formed a hard ball which she spat into the bin.

A half-drunk bottle of apricot liqueur left over from Christmas and shoved under the sink, caught her eye. It had been her present to herself. The only one she had received. Before the court case, Sandra thought drinking in the morning was only ever socially acceptable on Christmas Day when she liked to invite the neighbours over for Bloody Marys. She thought it an apt way to celebrate and thought the Virgin Mary would approve.

Pouring what was left of the syrupy liquid into a tumbler, she downed it in one and noted ruefully she had become a glass half-empty kind of girl.

Drinking early this early in the day made her drowsy and she went upstairs to lie down. It felt wrong to go back to bed. Had she had a man with her, it would have been exciting and illicit. The frisson of afternoon delight had stayed with her since she had bunked off school to spend the afternoon with Dave Brown, an upper sixth former renowned for his prowess with fifth form girls. He didn't disappoint and had been well worth missing double art for.

Lying stretched out on top of the duvet, she stared up at the ceiling where the once-white paint had turned an unattractive shade of taupe. The crack in the ceiling looked worse than ever. The 'Y' shaped twig had become a bough, its branches spreading overhead.

Work could wait, she closed her eyes and thought of Ben. With any luck the ceiling would collapse as she slept. At least she would die happy.

Chapter fifteen

[Isle of Wight 2013]

The sound of a door banging woke Sandra. She realised it was her front door as it made a particular noise.

'Carl?' she shouted, disorientated having just woken from the dream she frequently had about her son. The one where they were back home in London, living together like nothing had ever happened. 'Carl, is that you?'

Even as the words travelled down the stairs, she knew it couldn't possibly be him. She was in her cottage with its pink painted walls and familiar crack in the ceiling.

Her heart was beating so fast she thought she might collapse. She stayed as still as she could. Straining to hear if anyone was in the house, the only noise she could hear were cars in the distance. Breathing was difficult; air came in rapid gasps.

After a few minutes, she forced herself to get up and walk to the window. There was no sign of anyone on the lane. Please God this didn't mean they were in the house?

She inched her way across the floor and out onto the landing, every step fraught with fear. The door to the bathroom was open. She could see there was no one in there.

Slowly, she went over to her wardrobe and listened. When she was certain no-one was inside the cupboard, she opened the door. It was empty but for her clothes hanging like chrysalis. She went downstairs, treading softly as if the steps were made of glass.

The living room was empty. She checked the cupboard. Again, she listened at the door. Silence. Cautiously, she hooked it open with her foot. Nothing. With just the kitchen to search, she became increasingly fearful, her heart beating against the insides of her chest like an animal trying to escape. To her relief, the kitchen was empty and the windows were secure.

She had never felt more terrified. It was a waste of time calling the police and she couldn't worry Carl. Not now. He had enough to cope with. There was always Rob but she didn't think it was fair to involve him.

However, there was one man, one man whose criminal mind would think like her intruder's.

Ben.

With the sort of utter conviction that was usually the preserve of the clinically insane, she took out the card he had given her and rang the number.

Her hands shook and it took several attempts before she got the digits in the correct sequence. She heard it ringing then clicked the phone off as soon as she heard Ben's voice. What was she thinking, inviting a murderer into her life? She hesitated before quickly punching in the number again.

'Hello Ben? It's Sand…Rose. This is Rose.'

'Rosie,' he laughed. 'I knew you wouldn't be able to resist me.'

His arrogance was staggering. But this was just the attitude she needed.

'Fancy a drink?' she asked before she changed her mind.

'Rosie,' he mocked. 'You naughty girl.'

'Can you meet me or not?' she snapped.

'Sure,' he replied his tone softening. 'Where?'

'The Crown, down the road from me?'

'When?'

'As soon as you can.'

'I'll be about an hour if you promise to make it worth my while.'

He was enjoying playing with her. But this wasn't his game. She was calling the shots.

'Okay,' she assured him.

'Dirty girl. Bell you when I'm in the pub.'

'But, you haven't got my number.'

He laughed.

'You phoned me, remember? I'm putting you on Speed-dial.'

Cursing herself for being so careless as to not block her number, she hung up and went back upstairs to get ready.

She pulled her T-shirt over her head and walked over to the floor-length mirror concealed behind her wardrobe door. Her long legs were still slender but the once taut flesh had softened. She turned sideways. Her belly was soft and smooth without any stretch marks. The only tell-tell signs of her ever having been pregnant was a silvery white line that ran horizontally just above her pubic bone, her battle scar, the only remaining evidence of her emergency Caesarean.

An unwelcome memory of Gaz Elliott flashed into her mind. During the trial just as Carl was giving his evidence, the youth had stuck his tongue out at her and made rapid licking motions.

Sandra felt dirty, defiled and instead of her usual shower, she decided on a hot bath. She put the plug in and turned on both taps before locking the door. It made her feel safer, even though she knew she was alone in the house. As the room filled with steam, she rubbed away the condensation from the mirror over the sink to reveal her reflection. Fortunately, there was still some evidence of the attractive young woman she had once been. Her complexion was golden from weekends spent on the beach. And her eyes were big and blue, like Carl's.

As she sat in the bath, the warm, silky water wrapped itself around her like a sheet. She lay back and looked up. There was a crack in the ceiling she had never noticed before, no doubt a continuation of the one in her bedroom. The place was falling apart. She must tell the landlord.

Slowly, she got out and towelled herself dry. In the back of the cabinet, she found some body lotion. Carl had given it to her as a birthday present and she had used it sparingly to make it last. Thick and unctuous, it smelt of bergamot oil. She smoothed it over her body, thinking of Ben with every touch. It worked better than any pills as the aches and pains that had plagued her since the accident seemed to melt away.

Unlocking the bathroom door, she padded softly into her bedroom where she picked out a pair of black lace knickers from her drawer. The last time she wore them was years ago, after her husband had left and she had thrown herself into an ill-fated affair with a man half her age. Much to her surprise, the matching bra still fitted. She decided stockings were too obvious and tights too much of a chastity belt. It had to be bare legs. Selecting a black dress from her wardrobe, she pulled it on over her head. The jersey fabric was forgiving and the bias cut concealed any lumps. It had cost her a small fortune when she bought it but it made her feel like a million dollars.

She brushed her hair before piling it on top of her head and securing it with a single Diamante pin. A slick of lipstick, some perfume and she was ready. She was dressed for a date but meeting a murderer. What was she playing at? Then again, playing by the book hadn't got her very far; it was time to break some rules.

Her mobile rang, making her start.

'I'm here,' said Ben and hung up.

She wasn't expecting him so soon.

After checking all the windows were secured, she downed a large whiskey for Dutch courage, slipped on her heels, slung her bag over her shoulder and left the house, locking the door behind her.

Her body tingled with anticipation as she walked into the pub. She scanned the bar. A young couple studied the menu chalked on the blackboard and an elderly man supped a pint alone at the bar.

Her heart sank. Ben wasn't there. Why did she even think someone like him would do the right thing?

'Rose!'

Ben swaggered towards her.

Half repelled, half ridiculously pleased to see him, she fluttered inside.

'Half of cider, love and whatever the lady wants,' he told the barmaid.

'White wine,' Sandra said trying to sound sober as she opened her purse before dropping it on the floor.

'Oops. You started early. Looks like I've got quite a bit of catching up to do. Make that a pint,' he told the barmaid.

Sandra scrabbled around, picking up the coins. Ben offered her his hand.

'There you go, Rose,' he said helping her up. 'You don't have to kiss my feet, y'know.'

He paid for the drinks and after pocketing the change, steered Sandra towards a corner table.

'Cheers,' he said sitting down opposite her. 'So this is where you hang out when you're not chatting up strange men on trains.'

They both glanced around the pub, with its flagstone floors and open fireplace.

'I don't usually drink here,' Sandra said. 'It's very nice but I prefer ...'

Suddenly, she felt Ben working the ball of his foot between her thighs underneath the table. She glanced down and noticed his discarded shoe under his chair.

'What can I do you for, Rosie?'

She felt his toes against her silk-wrapped crotch and surrendered to the sensation. It was delicious, like on the bus, only better because this time she was ready for him. He held her gaze as he massaged her underneath her dress.

'Rose?' he prompted. 'Tell me what you want.'

He reached down under the narrow table and grabbed her hand, pulling it towards him. He placed her palm between his legs. She

95

gasped. The couple turned to look at her. Embarrassed, she pulled away but not before she had felt him pressing against her palm. She shifted her chair backwards forcing him to remove his foot.

Neither of them spoke for a while.

'I want you,' she told him flatly.

'I know,' he replied.

'I want you to help me.'

'Oh?'

She couldn't tell if he was mocking her.

'Someone has been in my house. They leave clues. At first they did silly things like eat toast and use the loo but recently it's got nasty. They burnt a picture of mine and this morning I was in bed and heard the front door slam so they must have been in the house.'

She shuddered at the thought.

'Sounds like someone's having a little game with you, Rose. I need to sort 'em out.'

'I don't want any trouble. I just want it to stop,' she told him firmly.

He finished his drink and wiped his mouth with the back of his hand.

'Another one?' he asked indicating her glass.

She nodded and watched him. She liked the way he kept one hand in the back pocket of his jeans when he walked.

'The police aren't interested,' she said when he came back with the drinks. 'Insufficient evidence, apparently. According to them, an un-flushed loo, a plate of crumbs and a burnt picture, don't cut it.'

Ben laughed.

'What's so funny?'

'You. You trust the police. And you're posh. 'An un-flushed loo',' he mimicked.

'Can you help or not?' she asked impatiently.

'Cos I can. How about we go back to your place and I suss it out?'

'No,' she said suddenly alarmed.

'Well, how can I help if you won't let me in? Don't you trust me?'

'I don't know you. Forget it. I shouldn't have come.'

She made a move to leave.

'Sit down, please, Rose,' he said gently. 'You're not afraid of me, are you?'

She didn't reply because she didn't know the answer.

'You don't have to be. I would never hurt a woman. I've told you that. If some bastard's been frightening you...'

'I've told you; I don't want any trouble.'

He smirked and took another mouthful of cider.

'How's your Mum?' she asked suddenly wondering if the elderly woman in the hospital bed was his mother or just a convenient ruse, the perfect excuse to be in the hospital where she worked.

'Much better, thanks,' he replied a smile of genuine relief lighting up his face. 'They're letting her out tomorrow.'

He made it sound as if the hospital had given her time off for good behaviour.

'She had us worried but mum's a fighter.'

'How old is she?'

'Eighty-five. Got a shock when I come along. Didn't think she could have no more kids.'

'What was wrong with your mum, nothing serious I hope?'

'Cancer.'

He looked down and picked up his beer mat, standing it on its end.

'I'm so sorry,' said Sandra wishing she hadn't asked.

'Thanks. Funny innit how they can fly a monkey to Mars but they can't cure the big 'C'?'

Ben was turning the mat faster and faster. Gently, she placed her hand over his and let it rest there. He stared out of the window, lost in his own memories.

'You okay?' she asked.

'Fine. You've just got to get on with it, haven't you? Ain't nothing no-one can do.'

She sighed, feeling sorry for him.

'So, then, Rosie, still want me to check the house over?' he asked changing the subject.

'Yes, please. Just nip to the loo,' she told him, getting up.

'Loo,' he repeated, mimicking her voice.

She laughed. The more she got to know Ben, the more she liked him. She went into the toilet and texted Rob.

'Not well, please let them know I won't be in today. I'm with Ben. He's coming back to my place but not for what you're thinking. S x'

It was a precaution, just in case. But something told her she was in safe hands.

Chapter sixteen

[Isle of Wight 2013]

'This is well old,' said Ben admiringly as he stood in the doorway to Sandra's cottage.

'Seventeenth century. Mind your head on the beams.'

He ducked and made his way over to the sofa where he sat down and looked instantly at home.

'White wine okay?' she asked disappearing into the kitchen.

'I'd prefer beer.'

'Sorry. Whiskey?'

'Only if it's a large one.'

When she returned with the drinks Ben was looking at her photo of Totland Bay.

'Nasty,' he said pointing at the burn mark.

'Yes,' she said taking it from him and replacing it on the wall.

'Nice picture, did you take it?' he asked.

She nodded.

'Clever girl.'

She had never met anyone like him. Good and bad bound together with muscle and bone. He was like an animal, proud and confident, king of his kingdom.

He leant back and crossed his arms behind his head. Once again his T-shirt rode up like it had on the train when they first met. As always, her eyes travelled along the line of black hair that snaked down from his navel. She wanted to trace it with her finger.

'What you looking at?' he asked.

'You,' she replied.

He got up, opened his arms and she walked towards him. She grabbed his shirt and pushed her hands up underneath. She held him like she never wanted to let him go.

'Hey, Rose,' he whispered as he heard her sobbing into his shoulder. 'That's okay, let it out.'

'Sorry,' she sniffed as her mascara stained his shirt. 'I'm just so scared all the time.'

'Ssch. I'm here now. I'll sort it.'

He held her face in his hands. When his lips met hers, his kiss was deep and slow with none of the aggression and urgency she had imagined.

Eventually they parted and she rested her cheek on his chest. Without a word, he took her hand and led her upstairs. She hadn't been with a man for a long time. She felt nervous and began to doubt Ben. She hardly knew him and until recently, had every reason to think he was the one stalking her.

'I can't do this,' she said bursting into tears again.

'I'm the one who should be crying. No-one's ever said 'no' to me before,' he said with a smirk.

He had taken her rejection well making her angry with herself for leading him on. Standing there knowing she had dressed for sex in skimpy underwear and high heels, she felt a fraud.

'Perhaps you should go,' she said.

'If that's what you want, Rose but I came to help you.'

'You don't have to…'

'I know I don't but I want to,' he insisted. 'I'd like to.'

'Really?'

'Well, I'm here. And we're not doin' nothing else,' he winked. 'Only joking with yer, Rose. Come on let's make a start.'

He checked the bedroom windows first.

'He'd have to be a midget to get through them.'

'Yes, they are very small. That's why the place is so dark.'

'The windows ain't been tampered with,' he announced after having checked them all.

'I know. The police couldn't find any signs of a break-in. Just told me to get some locks and an alarm fitted.'

He let out a throaty laugh.

'Ain't a lock could keep me out,' he told her, reminding her again of the sort of man she was dealing with.

'Really, you can go, I'll be fine.'

'Rose, you need me. You wouldn't have asked me here otherwise. Let me help.'

Ben was no good but he wasn't all bad either.

'Most alarms are a joke. But if it makes you happy, I'll fit one for yer.'

'Thanks. I'll pay you.'

'Forget it. My mate works in security. I'll make a call and have it done in a day.'

'That's brilliant,' she said understanding that Ben having a mate who worked 'in security' probably meant the locks would be free of charge.

They headed downstairs to the kitchen and finished their drinks.

'Thanks for that. I best be off now and I'll be back to do those locks soon.'

'Please stay,' she said refilling their glasses and handing one to him.

'You've just missed the last bus.'

'You're having a laugh, aren't you?'

'No, this is Shorwell, not Ryde. Buses only run late Fridays and Saturdays. Please stay, Ben. I'm frightened.'

She shifted uncomfortably from foot to foot, sipping her drink, waiting for him to reply.

'I'm going to do me back in sleeping on that thing,' he said with a grin as he indicated the sofa.

'Tough,' she said with a grateful smile. 'I'd offer you the spare-bedroom but the ceiling leaked and it's still damp in there.'

'Oh Rosie. Shame to waste your sexy undies.'

'How d'you know?' she asked, embarrassed but excited.

'Ah! So I was right!' he said his grin broadening.

'How can you tell what knickers I'm wearing?'

'X-ray vision. That and when you came back from the loo earlier, your dress was tucked into your pants. Black lacy ones, yeah?'

Sandra covered her face with her hands.

'No, oh God.'

She wasn't bothered he saw her pants. She was mortified he saw she was gagging for it.

'I'll go and get you a duvet for later,' she said going back upstairs.

As she was getting the bedding, all she could think of was bedding Ben. Dumping the duvet on the floor, she ran downstairs, excited.

'Ben, I've ...'

Then she saw something that made her stop breathing.

Ben, naked on the sofa, her kitchen knife in his hand.

Chapter seventeen

[Isle of Wight 2013]

'Come here, Rose,' Ben whispered patting the space on the sofa beside him.

Sandra didn't move. The body she had longed to enjoy only minutes earlier, terrified her.

'Don't be scared, Rose.'

She was aware her breathing had become loud and obvious.

'Trust me, Rose,' he said his dolphin smile belying the menace laced through his voice like strychnine.

Trust him? He was naked with a knife. A more threatening sight she could not imagine. Her body shook as she stood, transfixed by the six-inch blade. In the hands of a murderer, her Sabatier carving knife was transformed from a kitchen implement into a lethal weapon.

Unlike her, he had been in this situation before. Slowly, she lowered her eyes away from his face to the blade.

'Put the knife down, Ben,' she said trying to keep her voice steady.

'Sorry, Rose, I can't do that. Sit down, next to me, there's a good girl.'

She did not move. Her eyes were fixed on him as he sat, his legs splayed apart. The sight of his flaccid cock did nothing to allay her fear that he was about to rape her. He looked the sort who could be primed and ready for action in no time.

Her mobile was on the mantelpiece but she couldn't reach it without going past him. He followed her gaze and shook his head.

'Wouldn't do that if I were you, Rose.'

Pointing the knife at her, he leapt up, grabbed her phone and sat down again.

'Ben, please, you're frightening me,' she pleaded, her voice thin and reedy.

She should never have trusted him. What a fool she had been to let someone like him turn her head. All it took was a flirtatious comment and a salacious look.

He beckoned her over.

'Come on, Rose sit down and I'll give you the knife.'

Her eyes widened.

'Ben, I'll …'

'Scream? No you won't. No-one will hear you. The bloke next door isn't in. I checked.'

She felt hollow, a husk of a woman.

She inched forward. Her heart thumped and her tongue felt too big for her mouth. Lowering herself onto the end of the sofa, as far away from his splayed thigh as she could get, her eyes darted sideways. To her surprise, his penis had retreated and was barely visible. Instinctively, she locked her knees together.

'Relax, Rosie,' Ben said.

Then he grabbed her, put his arm around her neck, and the blade at her throat.

She waited. Not daring to breathe. Suddenly, Ben released his grip and threw down the knife.

'Trust me now, Rose?'

She stood and jumped away from him.

'Of course, I don't, you bastard, you mad bastard,' she shouted. 'What the hell?'

'I could've killed you but didn't,' he said firmly. 'It proves you can trust me.'

'I can't trust you. You're mad. I'm calling the police,' she yelled her hand snapping out to retrieve her phone from him.

Gripping the mobile, he raised his arm above his head.

'Behave! Or you'll spoil everything.'

Too terrified to move, she stood still.

'You left yourself open to attack. I could have had you.'

She was not interested in his sick explanations. She grabbed the knife, pointing it at him like a dagger.

'Give me the phone. Now!' she shouted in a voice she didn't recognise.

She stepped towards him, the blade raised above her shoulder. Dropping the phone, he grabbed her wrist, her fingers sprung open and the weapon fell from her hand.

'It's okay, Rose,' he said softly as he let go of her. 'You're in danger. I wanna help but you gotta believe I'm on your side.'

She rubbed her wrist. It was true; he could easily have killed her. And probably have got away with it too.

'You're a psycho,' she yelled at him, tears of anger and relief, racing down her cheeks.

'Cheer up, Rosie,' he said as he picking up the knife and holding it alongside his thigh. 'What d'you reckon is bigger. The knife or my pork sword?'

'You are disgusting. Put some bloody clothes on.'

Sandra watched as he placed the knife on the floor in front of her.

'Sorry for frightening you but learn to protect yourself. If your visitor is some crazy smack head, there'll be no reasoning with him.'

The shaking had stopped but she wanted him out of the room, just for a minute.

'I need a drink,' she told him. 'There's whiskey in the kitchen. Get me one.'

'Nice try,' said Ben grinning. 'But you can't bullshit a bullshitter. You were going to do a runner, weren't you?'

'No, I just want a drink,' she repeated, getting up and going into the kitchen.

She poured herself a whiskey and downed it in one. She could hear Ben moving about. The alcohol mixed with adrenaline hit her at ninety miles an hour. Instantly befuddled, she didn't know what to think. Was he her friend as he claimed or her foe as she feared?

Returning to the living room, she was relieved to see he was dressed.

As she approached he grabbed the knife, rushed forwards and grabbed her. She screamed. He clamped his hand over her mouth, pressing the blade against her flesh.

'Rose, do what I say and you won't get hurt,' he instructed.

His palm muffled her screams. Trying to bite his flesh was as ineffectual as a new-born puppy trying to maul a tiger. Ben tightened his grip.

'Right, Rose, get your hand and push your fingers up hard between my arm and your neck. Go on. Do it. Harder! Good, now turn your head. Quick!'

With her head jammed under his arm and the point of the blade in her neck, she did as he had said. With one jerk, she was free. It was easy, too easy. Perhaps it was another one of his tricks, one only an ex-con like him would know. She spun round.

'Clever girl. You escaped.'

She laughed, an insane guffaw that quickly turned to tears.

'You really hurt me,' she said rubbing her neck. 'This isn't a game. This is my life. If you're planning on killing me, get on with it. Do it, just do it. Go on.'

She was shaking, her whole body goading him. As he stepped

forward, she stood her ground, full of inane, inappropriate self-confidence.

'I could've killed you,' said Ben. 'I want to show you how to defend yourself.'

'No, you get a kick out of terrifying me and parading about naked, you mad bastard.'

He shook his head.

'Wise up, Rose. Don't invite strange men back to your house, especially not a 'mad bastard' like me. And don't be a victim. I can't be with you 24/7.'

'I don't want you anywhere near me,' she scoffed, wiping the snot from her nose with the back of her hand.

'It's not me you've gotta worry about, is it?' he asked bringing his face close to hers.

'Get out,' she told him looking at the door.

'You need protecting but you need to tell me who from.'

Sandra deflated and collapsed down on to the sofa. Ben's methods were unorthodox but there was no denying they worked. She could hardly believe it but to her surprise, she trusted him.

'Who are they, Rose? They say the victim often knows the killer.'

The whiskey messed with her mind, she couldn't think straight. One minute Ben was her protector, the next her attacker.

'You're just trying to frighten me so I have to rely on you,' she said. 'Yes, that's it, you've put one of your mates up to this. You're in it together.'

'Rose,' he said forcing her to look at him. 'I can walk away from this shit anytime. You can't.'

She inhaled deeply. He was right there.

'Ah!' he said pointing at her. 'I knew it. Someone's after you, aren't they?' he asked, urgent and excited.

'I... don't... know,' she faltered remembering Gaz Elliott's face leering at her in the courtroom.

'Liar,' Ben shouted, his voice expanding to fill the space between them.

Sandra stayed silent to compensate. She had been careful to cover her tracks before constructing her anonymous life on the island. If the Elliotts were behind this, how did they find her? The only person from her old life who knew where she lived was Carl.

With sickening clarity and speed, she pieced things together. Carl had written to her and put his new address on the letter. Drunk and anxious, she had replied, carelessly printing her address across the top of the page.

Two pieces of paper. Two envelopes. Two lives in the balance. Four if she included Debs and her unborn baby.

And Carl had lied to Debs. The girl would have no idea certain information had to be kept secret in order to keep Carl alive. The consequences were unthinkable.

'Rose?'

'How do I know you're not in on this?' she asked. 'I could have you arrested; I've got the knife with your prints all over it.'

He stood with his arms folded.

'You're not going to call the police. You need me. If you had someone else they'd be here instead of me, a stranger you met on a train,' he laughed. 'Get us another drink, Rose. It's going be a long night.'

'What?'

'You heard,' he winked, handing her the knife. 'Oh and stick this back in the block. We don't want any accidents.'

She looked at the blade, turning it back and forth.

'No-one ever tell you not to play with knives, Rose?'

She went into the kitchen and tiptoed over to the cupboard where she carefully concealed the knife behind a stack of plates. She returned a few minutes later with two fresh tumblers of whiskey and gave him one.

'Cheers,' he said raising his glass.

Sandra watched, as he took a mouthful then swilled the spirit around, puffing out his cheeks and squishing the liquid between his teeth as if it was nothing more than cheap mouthwash. Eventually, he swallowed causing his Adam's Apple to shoot up and down.

'You're hiding something, Rose. What's a good-looking girl doing stuck out 'ere all on her own?'

'None of your business,' she replied trying to keep her voice steady.

'How can I help if I don't know nuffin'?'

He gave her a moment and when she did not reply, he got up and went to the door.

'Ben. Don't go,' she said.

His hand flicked the lock open.

'You want me mixed up in your shit but I'm not allowed to know what's goin' on.'

She ran to the door and grabbed his arm.

'Stay, just for tonight.'

'One minute you're threatening to have me arrested, the next you're begging me to stay. I don't get you.'

Ben had never harmed her. Not once. Nonetheless, he was a killer, just like the Elliotts. Perhaps, it was time they met their match.

'I'll tell you everything in the morning,' she promised.

'Why not now?'

'I'm tired.'

'I'm not sure about you, Rose. Maybe you're the one who can't be trusted,' he said turning the tables.

She felt uncomfortable, being the suspect, not the victim.

'Ben, please I ...'

'Calm down. I'll stay on one condition.'

'Okay,' she nodded. 'What is it?'

'I keep the blade with me.'

Her heart thumped, her eyes flickering towards the kitchen.

'It's in the second cupboard on the left, bottom shelf. I'm right, aren't I?' he said with a smirk.

She nodded in disbelief.

'How do you know?'

'Told you, you can't bullshit a bullshitter. I listened, counted the number of footsteps you took. Then I heard you open the cupboard door. The bottom shelf was a good guess.'

Ben was as sharp as any blade, always one step ahead of her.

'Don't panic, Rose. I won't murder you in your bed. But if that bastard turns up, God help him. Slitting throats is my speciality.'

Chapter eighteen

[Isle of Wight 2013]

Sandra lay in bed looking at the small chest of drawers she had half-heartedly pushed against her bedroom door. God knows why she had bothered. If Ben had a mind he could shift it easily. And if she was honest, she didn't want to keep him out. She liked the idea of him creeping up the stairs and overpowering her.

His behaviour unnerved her but she couldn't expect normality from a psychopath. The definitions did not put her off him. On the contrary, she liked the way he terrified and excited her in equal measures, making her feel alive. Unlike her ex-husband who when he could be bothered, preferred sex with the lights off and his socks on. Sandra would have preferred him to have kept his pants on too.

With Ben asleep on the sofa, she felt like a lovelorn teenager as she imagined what it must be like to make love to someone so full of hate he had slit another man's throat.

The bloody image brought her back to reality. What was she thinking, letting him stay in her house? The decision defied logic yet made perfect sense. Who better to protect her? Yes, he could turn on her any minute but had he wanted to do that he would've done it by now, wouldn't he? There was a wine bottle within arm's reach beside her bed. If she had to, she would use it as a weapon.

Who was she kidding? She could no more attack Ben than raise a hand to her son. There was one time when she came close.

Carl was at school and she had taken the opportunity to clear out his wardrobe. Amidst the discarded trainers and tee-shirts, she discovered a haul of hand-held game consoles.

'Where did you get these?' she asked when he arrived home.

'Mind your own business, bitch.'

He was just eight-years-old. She had taught him 'B' was for 'ball' or 'baby' but never 'bitch'.

His voice, as yet unbroken, so pure and innocent, was not ready to say such a word. Let alone to her.

Shocked, her first reflex had been to silence him. Punish him. Teach him a lesson. She had raised her hand to hit him but instead used her palm to wipe away her tears. Carl was not to blame. She was. She had broken up the family home, told his father to leave and forbidden him from having any further contact. Was it any wonder the little lad was confused?

The memory had been locked away for years. She turned the key on it again but not before the word slipped out again to taunt her.

'Bitch.'

Suddenly, the floorboards creaked on the landing outside her bedroom. Sandra gasped. Her body stiffened as she held her breath and listened to the sound of the bathroom door being opened. She waited a few moments for the noise of the flush. But it never came.

If she was honest, she was disappointed Ben hadn't tried her door. Perhaps he didn't fancy her after all and it was just wishful thinking on her part, a middle-aged woman's fantasy, nothing more. After all, he had to be at least ten years her junior, what would he want with her? With his looks Ben would have no trouble attracting girls half his age.

She reminded herself she was in good shape, years at the gym under the watchful gaze of her personal trainer had seen to that. Blessed with a naturally athletic physique, her body had responded well to the relentless regime.

Her confidence boosted she considered going downstairs and surprising him? The more she thought about seducing a younger man, the more exciting the idea became. In preparation, she unscrewed the top on the wine bottle and took a slug.

Fortified, she got up and quickly began to apply some mascara. She went for the lipstick, then changed her mind; too messy with all that kissing.

Unable to contain herself, she went over to the door and pushed away the chest of drawers. As soon as she had created a big enough gap, to open the door, she was off. The whiskey and wine made the decision for her. She was going to have him. Her body shivering with anticipation, she raced downstairs and into the living room.

Moonlight flooded the room enabling her to see Ben feigning sleep. Clearly, this was a game. He had obviously gone up to the bathroom as a ploy to lure her downstairs. His eyes were closed and his breathing shallow; he was very convincing, she would give him that.

From where she stood, she could just make out the handle of the knife underneath the sofa. Tentatively, she went over to him and stood in the way of the knife, just in case.

'Ben,' she whispered softly. 'Ben, it's me, Rose.'

No response. She smiled. He was a good actor. Using her toe, she slowly and carefully edged the knife further under the sofa.

She looked down at his face. He was beautiful in an ugly sort of way, his bold features perfectly symmetrical.

'Ben,' she said, louder this time.

'You fucker!' he shouted, reaching under the sofa.

'Ben!' she cried, leaping backwards. 'It's me, Rose.'

She watched his expression change as his eyes adjusted to the light.

'What the fuck are you doing, creeping up on me?' he demanded his hand feeling around on the floor. 'I could've killed you. Where the hell's the knife?'

His voice was still thick and heavy with sleep. He got off the sofa, wearing nothing but a pair of boxer shorts.

'What's it doing here?' he asked lying face down, his right arm extended under the couch.

She shrugged.

'What's up? What did you wake me up for?' he asked, getting back onto the couch.

'You were already awake,' Sandra persisted. 'I heard you in the loo a

113

few minutes ago.'

'No, you didn't.'

'Don't lie. You were outside my room. I heard you,' she said
nervously stepping away from him.

He shrugged.

'I was sparko, you're imagining things; must've been the whiskey,' he
said pointing to the empty bottle.

'If it wasn't you, who the hell was it?' she cried.

He pulled her towards him and stroked her back. She pushed him
away.

'Supposing whoever it was is still here?'

'Ssch,' he said slowly drawing the knife out from underneath the sofa.

Motioning her to stay where she was, he stood up, the blade glinting
and stole upstairs.

To survive the next few minutes, Sandra's body balled into a tight
knot of fear as she wondered how much more she could take.

Ben reappeared a few moments later to check the cupboard before
going into the kitchen.

He came back, shaking his head,

'Someone's been and had a piss. Dirty bastard didn't flush.'

'In God's name, no!' exclaimed Sandra close to tears.

'What?'

'That's what happened before, he used the loo.'

'Nice,' muttered Ben.

He knelt down and replaced the knife under the sofa.

'I'll get the bastard. Promise,' he told her, stroking her cheek with the back of his hand.

She grabbed his wrist and pulled his hand away from her face before releasing her grip.

'So you keep saying but you had your chance. He was here. You could've got him. He must've walked right past you.'

'We don't know that.'

'Of course we do.'

She looked at him coldly, angry with him for leaving her open to attack.

'You said yourself the windows are too small to get in. So whoever it was would have had to come in the front or back door. Either way, he had to walk past you.'

'So how come I never heard him?'

'You were too pissed to notice,' she yelled, collapsing into tears. 'We've got to call the police, we can't go it alone.'

Ben sat beside her.

'The police are only goin' make this worse. If they fuck up, it's your life on the line.'

It was not her life she was worried about it was Carl's. She was not about to entrust his safety to an incompetent police officer. Someone had to watch Carl's back and that person was Ben.

He held her face in his hands.

'Whoever it was, has gone now. If they come back, I'll be waiting for them.'

'Bit late for heroics. I could've been killed,' she said.

Before she could stop him, he drove his fist into the wall. Once, twice, three, four times, punctuating his blow with the words,

'I… let… you… down.'

'Stop it! For God's sake,' she cried reaching out for his wounded hand. Ben pulled away and forced his bloodied fist into his mouth.

'Let me look,' she said, taking hold of his wrist.

She caressed the flesh closest to the cut, tracing around his knuckles with the tip of her forefinger.

Permanently terrified, just existing exhausted her. She wanted to be obliterated but settled for a moment of oblivion. Desperate to be engulfed, she pulled Ben onto the couch, on top of her, allowing herself to be consumed until all that remained of her was her essence.

Ben was happy to oblige, his urgency overpowering her every sense until she felt nothing, not even the fear that until just a moment ago had clogged every artery.

Chapter nineteen

[Isle of Wight 2013]

Sandra had had thirteen lovers, but only one god. She worshipped him, no-one had ever made her feel the way he did. Certainly not her ex-husband whose idea of love-making was jerking about on top of her like an agitated goat.

'What's up?' Ben asked as he lay in her bed waiting for her to respond to his touch.

'Sorry, I just …'

She trailed off, inwardly cursing herself for allowing the past to spoil the present. Moving on was hard for her; she preferred to walk in yesterday's shadow.

Ben reached out to her but she looked away.

'I don't get you, Rose,' he said flinging the duvet back and getting up.

'Neither do I,' she whispered as he slammed out of the room.

She called after him but doubted he heard; the shower was on full blast.

Typical, she had a real man in her bed for once but was unable to keep him there. Her ex-husband had no interest in sex; it was a wonder he ever managed to get her pregnant.

They had several bottles of Chablis to thank for Carl's existence. The frugal meal eaten on their first anniversary had been woefully insufficient to absorb the alcohol. As a result, her husband had been uncharacteristically frisky in the back of the cab on the way home, his hand shooting up her skirt and clumsily grabbing her gusset. Not exactly romantic, but Sandra was no prude and, given it was something of a one-off, she decided to go with it.

Her eyes flickered up to see the taxi driver, one hand on the wheel, adjusting his rear-view mirror to get a better view of the goings-on. Being the worse for wear, she allowed herself to become a participant in this unconventional ménage a trois. To her surprise, knowing a stranger was watching, made her less inhibited. If anything, she liked having an audience. Her husband seemed oblivious that while she was having sex with him, she was simultaneously making love to another man.

Not surprisingly, the driver took the long way round, racking up the fare to almost twice what it would have been had he gone the usual route. The cheek of the man, he should have been paying her.

The ride well and truly over, Sandra had stood on the pavement, with her knickers stuffed into her handbag. Embarrassed, she had pushed two twenty-pound notes into the driver's outstretched hand, desperate to get away from him. She just wanted to go to bed. Alone.

The night air had sobered her up but evidently not her husband who had activated the security light and was attempting to unlock the front door by turning his key in the letterbox.

Once Sandra had succeeded in letting them both inside the house, her husband had grabbed her and pushed her down on the staircase. Somehow he managed to take down his trousers with one hand and snatch her left breast in the other. As she lay there, bored, with him bobbing about on top of her, all she could think of was how relieved she was to have vacuumed before leaving the house.

Two months later, it came as a shock to discover she was pregnant. She had stopped using contraception years ago having been told by doctors she would never be able to conceive.

At first, it was easy to conceal her pregnancy from her colleagues but within a few months, her belly had swollen to such an extent there was no denying it.

Eventually, she learned to love her new womanly shape. She even liked the way her protruding tummy got in the way of everything she did, excited this new life was already making its presence felt.

Motherhood terrified her. As an only child she had never had to care for anyone other than herself and had no idea what to expect.

Her husband was a pedant, devoid of emotion and she could be over excitable and controlling. What would this uneasy mix of genes produce? Eschewing the worst-case scenario, she told herself the baby would inherit the best characteristics from them both although she struggled to define what they might be.

Having stopped work in the final months of her pregnancy, she discovered she enjoyed playing house even if her husband was reluctant to join in the game. After all, it was only ever going to be a temporary arrangement and she would soon be swopping the play-room for the more familiar territory of the board-room.

'Hello, darling,' she had called from the kitchen where she was dutifully making his favourite meal, smoked salmon and scrambled eggs. 'Good day?'

At eight and a half months pregnant, the fishy smell made her want to heave but she persisted in layering the transparent oily strips onto the plate before cutting a wedge of lemon and placing it on the side.

As her husband had gone to kiss her, she noticed him give the food what she took to be a disapproving glance. Annoyed at his ingratitude, she had deliberately turned her head causing his lips to miss her mouth. He seemed taken aback. Suddenly aware she may have read him wrong, she tried to make amends.

'The dinner won't spoil, fancy popping upstairs?' she had asked.

'Must be careful not to harm the baby,' he told her, plucking her hands off his chest.

He was an intelligent man; he would have known his fear was unfounded. Sandra felt he had used her pregnancy as an excuse to get out of having sex with her. Much to her chagrin, she had noticed how repulsed he seemed by the sight of her burgeoning body as she sailed around the house, like a galleon in her vast maternity frocks.

Whatever the reason, she felt rejected when night after night, he chose to lay in the bath with his beloved Mahler rather than in bed with her. Out of spite, she bought a Westlife CD to play at full volume in retaliation.

'Wine?' she asked gesturing to the bottle on the side, hoping a glass of something cold and expensive might put him in the mood.

He nodded. Of course, he wanted a drink. He was borderline alcoholic. Another of the many character traits he had kept under wraps until after he had ensnared her.

She watched as he pulled the cork and filled his glass, holding it up to the light and sniffing the wine in that irritating way of his. The elaborate charade out of the way, he got down to the business of drinking.

Seeing him lurch towards her, his eyes unable to focus, she wondered why she had thought going to bed with him was a good idea. The closer he got, the stronger the smell of whiskey on his breath. Doubtless, he had stopped off at the pub on his way home from work, just like he did most nights. The man was rarely sober although most people would never guess. Even when he was completely shot, no-one would ever guess; he seemed so normal. And that was the problem. He was ordinary when she wanted extraordinary.

Just as he reached her, she turned away.

'Dinner in two minutes,' she told him.

Breaking four eggs into a bowl, she whisked them with a fork. The sight of the prongs piercing the yolks made her feel sick and she was suddenly aware of her own egg, fertilized by her husband following a freakish, drunken grope. God help the poor kid. Then and there, she decided it was her job to ensure the child did not turn out like its father.

She added a knob of butter to the pan. As it bubbled golden brown, she poured in the eggs. Their slimy viscosity made her wretch and she was relieved when the heat set them quickly into big yellow lumps that she spooned onto a plate, next to the fish.

'Dinner's ready,' she shouted before running to the bathroom and throwing up.

This wasn't morning sickness; this was self-disgust. Where was the integrity and honesty she prided herself on?

She was tired of living a lie with a man who blotted out the truth by being blotto. It was bad enough when she discovered he had a drink problem, but when she found out he had been running up huge credit card bills behind her back, she had despaired of him. It was the underhandedness that got to her. If he could deceive her so effortlessly what else was he lying to her about?

'I think we should get a divorce,' she told him when she came back downstairs

'Don't be so ridiculous, you're having my baby.'

'All the more reason, not to stay together,' she said hanging her head over the sink and turning on the cold tap.

She gulped some water before wiping her mouth deliberately on the tea-towel. He was a clean-freak; it would wind him up and she enjoyed seeing the disgusted look on his face.

'Do you have to do that?' he asked.

She nodded.

'We can't bring a baby into this,' she told him.

'What's that supposed to mean?' he asked as the eggs congealed.

'We're not happy so the baby won't be happy. It'll pick up the bad vibes,' she replied grabbing his plate and scrapping the food into the bin.

'For God's sake, Sandra, I was eating that. What the hell's wrong with you?'

She put the plate in the sink and turned the hot tap on full blast.

'Here we go again, you and your bloody hormones,' he moaned. 'It's like living with a mad woman. For God's sake, go to the doctor and get him to give you something.'

'Surely even you know we can't bring a baby into this mess,' she said.

He looked around and perused the opulent art works adorning the walls, the lavish interior design and expensive antique furniture.

'Looks alright to me,' he said. 'The kid will want for nothing. It'll have a better start in life than I did.'

'It's all about the money with you, isn't it? Sadly, you can't measure happiness by a bank balance. If you could, I'd be delirious,' she told him.

'I'm not having this conversation. Go and talk to the doctor,' he said before opening the fridge and taking out another bottle of wine.

'Why don't you go and see him?' she asked. 'I'm sure he knows a good rehab centre.'

Before he could stop her, she had taken the dirty plate out of the sink and smashed it on the floor.

'Look what you've done,' he said stepping over the broken crockery, still clutching the wine.

Sandra stared at him defiantly. He raised his glass with one hand and pointed to her protruding belly.

'Cheers. Here's to you, kid. Have a wonderful life.'

'Oh, don't worry. I'll make sure of that,' she replied.

Then, she went upstairs and packed her husband's bags.

She should have done it a long time ago but work had always provided the perfect distraction, never allowing her time to dwell on the state of her marriage.

She had hoped impending fatherhood would persuade him to face his demons.

As the months wore in, it became obvious he had no intention of changing.

His selfishness hardened her. He could drink himself to death; she would soon have a new life to care for.

She dragged his stuff onto the landing and launched them down the stairs.

'Christ,' he slurred racing into the hall. 'You've finally lost the bloody plot.'

'And you've lost me and your baby,' she replied.

'You're having a baby; women do it every day. It's no big deal.'

'Get out! And take your bloody chess set with you.'

She walked purposefully towards the table where the glass pieces were laid out.

'No!' he shouted, his arms outstretched. 'Don't you dare. I'm warning you.'

She took hold of the edge of the board and tilted it at a forty-five degree angle and watched as the figures slid onto the tiled floor. The king fell first, his head breaking off his body and rolling under the chair.

Sandra calmly opened the front door. 'I'd like you to leave now. I need to consider my next move.'

'I'm not going; this is my home.'

'But it's my house.'

'Really? I don't think so.'

'I don't care what you think.'

'I'll fight you. I'll make sure you get nothing. Nothing.'

He was right up in her face, jabbing his finger at her.

'Go ahead. You'll be laughed out of court,' said Sandra.

'We'll see what my solicitor has to say about that.'

'Be my guest.'

He went to hit her but she stood her ground, looking him in the eye, daring him to strike her.

'You bitch!' he cried.

He spat the words with his face just inches from hers. Picking up his bags, he slammed out of the house. Sandra stroked her stomach and silently thanked her unborn baby for saving her from a beating.

The letterbox flapped open.

'Fuck you!' he screamed, kicking the door.

She jumped back, her heart pounding. Still reeling from the finality of what had happened, she steadied herself against the wall. What the hell had she done? Becoming a mother, especially not a single one, had never been on her agenda. Nothing would ever be the same again. Thank goodness. She had done the right thing.

From the moment her baby was born, Carl captured her heart. This love was like no other, whole, beautiful and perfect. He was her son. She was his champion. She would look out for him, always and forever.

How could she love another man? She had none to give. Carl had taken the lot.

Chapter twenty

[Isle of Wight 2013]

Ben reappeared in bedroom doorway, naked.

'Aren't you cold?' she asked.

'No, can't you tell?' he said thrusting himself in her direction.

'Like I said, 'Aren't you cold?' she smiled.

'It's the best you've ever had.'

It was. But she wasn't about to tell him. For one night, she had been able to shut out the overwhelming pain and fear with devil-may-care excitement. She shivered with joy remembering how he had led her upstairs, in the midst of their love-making, after they had tumbled as one, off the sofa and onto the floor, a jumble of awkward limbs and banged knees. She had slept with Ben. She had slept with a murderer. One to tick off her bucket list, she thought ruefully.

Sadly, it could never be more than a one-night stand. Ben seemed the sort to take what he wanted and to hell with the consequences. He didn't do deep and meaningful; when it came to sex, he was happy to keep it shallow.

'Good news or the bad news?' he asked.

She wrinkled her brow, urging him to continue.

'Well, we're still alive, no-one murdered us in our sleep but the bad news is I still can't work out how the bastard's getting in.'

Recent events left her void of rational thought and she could see no end to the torment. Even with Ben in the house, the stalker still played his sick games.

'What would you do if he came back?' Sandra asked.

Without hesitating, Ben drew his forefinger across his throat.

'God no,' she said, alarmed.

'Calm down. I'm a good boy now.'

'Okay, well, you've got all day, I'm sure you'll work out what's going on,' she said pulling the duvet up around her shoulders. 'You are still fitting the locks, aren't you?'

He nodded, running his hands over his short hair.

'Yeah, should have it all done by this evening.'

'Thanks. Now please go, I've got to get dressed for work.'

'Bit late for modesty, Rosie,' he said stepping out onto the landing and pulling the door to.

Sandra got up, opened the drawer and grabbed the first pair of knickers that came to hand.

'Not those, Rosie, your lacy ones,' he laughed through the crack in the door.

'Mind your own business.'

Nevertheless, she decided on her red silk pants and the skirt and cream top, the one she had worn on the train the first time they met.

She checked her phone. No messages or missed calls. It was seven-thirty.

'Dying for a cuppa. My stomach thinks me throat's been cut,' he called.

'Not funny,' she told him as she heard him go downstairs.

Her head was foggy. That was whiskey for you. Her ex-husband was to blame for introducing her to the properties of a good single malt, his way of justifying the copious amounts he drank.

'I'll make the tea,' he called out. 'Then me and you are goin' 'ave that little chat.'

The thought of telling Ben, a murderer, about Carl, a grass, made her

126

stomach churn.

'Sorry, got to go to work, haven't been in for days,' she called as she went out onto the landing.

'Phone in sick,' he shouted up the stairs. 'We can play doctors and nurses.'

Sandra knew that would be a lot more fun than working at the hospital.

'Fancy a Rosie Lee, Rosie?' he asked.

'Rather have tea,' she said, going along with the joke as she went into the bathroom. After her shower and, for the first time since Carl had left, she put on make-up. It made her feel better about herself even though she knew it was just a quick fix and did nothing to assuage the fear that clawed at her stomach.

She got dressed and went downstairs, where she derived pleasure from watching Ben make tea. He was wearing just a pair of jeans affording her a view of his back muscles moving beneath his flesh like fish under water.

'Here,' he said handing her a mug with one hand as he opened and closed the window with the other. 'Still can't work out how they're getting in.'

She took a sip of tea before throwing the remainder down the sink.

'Euw! How can you drink it black?'

'Get used to all sorts inside,' he told her.

'Oh please; everyone knows prison life is cushy,' she said playfully.

He gave her an odd look, a cross between a smile and a snarl.

'Toast?' he asked turning away, his head in the fridge. 'Forget it, no bread.'

'Don't worry. Haven't time for breakfast.'

He was at the front door before her, barring her way.

'No you don't Rose. We had a deal. I agreed to stay the night and you promised to tell me your little secret.'

'But I'll miss my bus.'

'No you won't. When you was asleep, I reset the clock on your phone. It's an hour fast,' he said.

'You did what?'

He pointed to the display on his mobile, 'See, it's not even seven yet.'

He had deceived her and made her feel a fool. It made her even more determined to go. She picked up her bag.

'Can't believe you did that,' she told him. 'Move.'

Ben reached out and placed his hand on hers.

'It was just my way of making more time for us.'

'Don't play tricks.'

'Don't get the hump. Talk to me, Rose.'

She took a deep breath. Her life had become a matrix of lies. It was time to tell the truth.

'I have a son, Carl,' she said as they sat down on the sofa.

It was a relief, being able to say his name again.

'I know,' said Ben nonplussed. 'You told me on the train.'

She looked aghast.

'I didn't think you were listening?'

'Of course I was.'

She looked at him. How could she resist? He was not just some brute. He had a brain. And if last night's love-making was anything to go by, a heart. If only things were different and the thread that bound them was woven from silk not barbed wire.

She rifled through the quotes, faces and names she had spent years trying to forget.

The police-officer's words came instantly to mind: 'Carl, remember, everyone you tell is a potential grass. The fewer people who know, the fewer people can hunt you down.'

She imagined he returned home every night to an empty house. She could practically hear him belching on his way up to bed having downed yet another microwave meal.

'Carl was on a Witness Protection Programme.'

Ben reached for her hand and she felt safe. Admittedly, holding a knife to her throat had been an unorthodox way of gaining her trust, but it was effective.

For the first time, she wanted to tell her story and she wanted to tell Ben.

'I can still picture that policeman in my living room, totting up the paintings and the sculptures, calculating my worth. Cheeky bastard. Then, when he was confident he had me pegged, he ordered Carl to pack a suitcase for his first move to a hotel. It was actually happening; Carl was leaving.'

Ben got up and ran his finger over the cigarette burn on the picture of Totland Bay.

'My son was being sent away and all that bloody police officer could do was stand in my house and yawn like a bloody dog.'

Ben nodded.

'I keep telling ya, the police ain't your friends, Rose. Wanna another drink?'

'Whiskey,' she said automatically.

'It's not even seven yet,' he laughed but got up and poured her a triple measure. 'There you go. You look like you need it.'

'It's the old story. We get the life sentence and the killer gets away with murder. What a joke.'

'Not funny, is it?' said Ben sympathetically.

His expression gave nothing away but she wondered how he felt, as a one-time perpetrator himself, hearing about the pain he would have caused.

'You okay?' she asked.

He shrugged.

'Better alive than dead. Carl had to go, Rose.'

'I know. He did the right thing. But often, the right thing, is the hardest thing to do, isn't it?'

Ben thought for a moment.

'I've never done the right thing,' he whispered.

'You're here, aren't you?'

He squeezed her hand tightly. Too tightly. She pulled away. Her fingers were willowy enabling him to crunch them in his fist like newborn mice.

'Sorry,' he said immediately letting go when he saw her wince. 'You don't deserve any of this shit; you've done nothing wrong.'

'Neither has Carl,' she said defensively.

'I know.'

'What d'you know?' she railed. 'You don't know what it feels like to have your child taken from you.'

Ben tore at one of his cuticles with his teeth, creating a bubble of blood. She watched as it inflated like a tiny balloon.

'Oh God, I'm sorry,' she said realising her mistake.

He sucked at the wound before firing words at her like bullets.

'Their Mum won't let me see m'girls. She's right. I ain't no good. I ain't their Dad, I'm never there, not birthdays or Christmas. Always in the nick, aren't I?'

He pumped his fists, making the cut bleed again. She took a tissue from her bag and gave it to him.

'Here, press hard,' she instructed.

She could deal with the practical stuff; it was emotions that foxed her. It was no mystery why, of all the fish in the sea, she had picked the coldest one to marry. At least there had been no messy feelings to navigate.

Neither of them spoke for a while. Sandra broke the silence.

'When Carl was born, he nearly died. I spent fifteen days with him in the Special Care Unit at the hospital, trying to ignore the frightening mass of tubes and monitors, praying he would survive. By some miracle, he pulled through. His father never visited, not once. The bastard.'

'What a shit. I was there when both me girls was born.'

Ben put his arms around her.

'Carl's lucky to have you as a mum.'

'How's your Mum?' she asked pulling away from him and changing the subject.

'Fine, thanks. You only get one Mum and Dad, don't ya?'

He looked lost and she made the mistake of trying to guess what he was thinking.

'Don't worry, Ben. Your girls knew how much you cared about them.'

He pulled away with such force, she gasped.

'Don't say that,' he spewed. 'Like it's all in the past and they don't love me no more.'

'Sorry. That came out wrong. You're their Dad; they don't have to see you to love you.'

When it came to absent children she knew how only too well how it worked.

'I ain't with 'em and that's that. I've just gotta get on with it, like you 'ave.'

He got up and went upstairs and she jumped as the bathroom door slammed behind him. She checked her phone for messages then corrected the time, adding on the hour he had taken off. When he returned he had lost his swagger.

'Thought you were going to work,' he said softly.

She shook her head. She wouldn't be able to concentrate with all that was going on. She texted Rob a lie.

'Won't be in. Not well. X'

'There, all sorted. I'm staying with you today.'

Ben barely smiled.

'If the past doesn't exist, how come it hurts so much?' she pondered.

'Because we can't leave it behind. We keep raking it up,' Ben replied.

Ben reached into his trouser pocket and pulled out his wallet. He flipped it open to reveal a photograph of two blonde girls, both with happy, gappy smiles.

'Carly and the little one's Kim,' he said affectionately as he pointed proudly to each in turn.

'Very pretty,' she said tactfully, desperate not to offend him again. 'They've got your eyes.'

He smiled, then his face clouded over.

'Kim don't remember me being at home. Just six-months-old the last time the police come for me. Carly had seen it all before. Just sat peeping through the banisters. The police-woman tried to distract her but she weren't having none of it. Didn't say nuffin, just stared. I'll never forget that look.'

Sandra watched him replace the photograph back in his wallet, behind two Oyster cards. Doubtless the same ones he had offered her on the train.

Only time would tell whether meeting Ben was a blessing or a curse. She got up and made them both them a black coffee.

'You must miss them,' she said, sitting back down and setting the cups down by their feet.

'They're better off without me,' he said without a hint of self-pity as he sipped his drink. 'Anyway, they're doing all right. But this ain't about me. You've got an uninvited guest and if your coffee's anything to go, he ain't 'ere for your full English.'

'Is it that bad?' she asked.

'It's shit. Same colour an all.'

They laughed, harder and longer than his comment warranted but they both seemed determined to bring some joy into the room.

'Come on, Rose. Stop Stalling. They didn't stick Carl on a Witness Protection Programme and hand out a new ID for nuffin'. What happened?'

Chapter twenty-one

[Isle of Wight 2013]

'Carl gave evidence at a murder trial,' explained Sandra sickened at the memory. 'Some thug called Elliott.'

'Elliott? That rings a bell,' Ben said. 'Yeah, that's right. A few years back, I heard the old man took a couple of his boys on a job. All three of 'em was tooled up, knives the lot. Apparently, the youngest was only twelve.'

Sandra raised her eyebrows.

'This time it was the oldest, Lee Elliott. From what I gather, not the sharpest tool in the box.'

'Just a tool then?' sniggered Ben.

She ignored him.

'He slit some man's throat,' she declared before fidgeting uneasily in her seat, realising Ben was no stranger to a spot of knife-wielding himself. Luckily, he didn't seem to notice; he was too busy digging like a dog for the next clue.

'Where was the murder?'

'The park behind our house,' she replied with a shudder remembering the strip of grass where she had taught her seven-year-old son to ride his bicycle and the day when she had finally let go and watched him pedal off.

That same week, Carl had careered into a puppy. She had shouted at him to stop but he took no notice. As the owner had knelt tearfully beside her pet's lifeless body, Sandra had tried to shield Carl but he had pulled away.

'I want to see the dog lying dead on the ground,' he had told her with a smile.

Shocked, she had refused to let him cycle home, insisting he walk his bicycle back with the dog's blood still splattered on the white-wall tyres.

Ben was leaning towards her, his face just inches from hers. The notion of personal space was an anathema to him. She put it down to all those years in prison, being surrounded by other people.

'So no-one else came forward?' he asked. 'Surely, someone saw something?'

In no mood to be cross-examined and certainly not by a murderer, she snapped.

'In the name of God, Ben, what's with all the questions?'

His eyes widened but he said nothing.

'I'm trying to tell you what happened, why don't you listen? All this probing, you're worse than the police,' she shouted getting up and walking over to the window, her back towards him.

'If I were you I wouldn't fuck with me, Rose.'

His words entered her brain like a bullet. Not daring to turn round, she gripped the window ledge. What a fool she had been. Why was it so hard to accept the man was a criminal? Suddenly, he was beside her, smiling.

'Sorry, didn't upset you, did I?' he asked. 'I just don't like being spoken to like that.'

It was best not to cross him. She knew that much. Besides she needed him. Who else would help her? All the same she remained on her guard and her body stiffened. They both stared ahead, addressing their remarks to the window.

'Y'see what I don't get is how no-one saw nuffin', what with all them people about. It's a bit odd, innit?' persisted Ben.

She thought very carefully before replying.

'I suppose they were all too frightened to come forward. A jogger gave evidence but it didn't prove much. All he saw was Elliott running away, covered in blood. Carl was just unlucky, I suppose. Wrong place, wrong time.'

'You can say that again,' mused Ben.

Sandra turned to look at him, her fear replaced with indignation and annoyance.

'Thanks to Carl the victim's family got justice. They heard the judge hand down a life sentence and saw their son's killer jailed. I know it's no compensation but at least it was something.'

She chewed the inside of her mouth, anxious she may have overstepped the mark again. The trouble was, she had no idea where the mark was; Ben moved it to suit.

'So Carl was the only one to grass up Elliott,' said Ben, a hint of incredulity in his voice. 'Brave boy. I wouldn't mess with that lot. Last I heard, the old man and one of his boys had been done for armed robbery.'

'I daresay. He's got seven sons, all of them bad.'

'All bad? Really? You sure about that?' asked Ben.

He was really beginning to get to her. How dare he cast aspersions on her son?

'The Elliotts are scum. Carl did the right thing. How many more times? He could've chosen to play dumb but he didn't. I...'

Very gently, Ben took her arm. She flinched.

'I ain't goin' hurt you. And I ain't 'aving a pop, Rose. I was just goin' say what Carl done took guts.'

Finally, Ben got it. He could see her son had been a hero.

'Yes, he was courageous,' she whispered hoping that was an end to the conversation.

But Ben was not finished. Not by a long way.

'So why did Lee Elliott cut the bloke?' he asked sounding more like a police-officer than an ex-con.

'Drugs. Apparently, the guy owed him money. Lots of money.'

Ben chewed savagely on his cuticles before spitting a piece of dead skin onto the floor. She winced recalling that afternoon when Carl appeared, spattered in blood, providing an unwelcome splash of colour in her white and chrome kitchen.

'That's it, I've told you everything,' she concluded, tired of talking and sick of remembering. 'Carl came home, told me everything and I called the police. End of.'

'What? You called the police? Why didn't Carl ring them? Surely, that's the first thing ...'

She rounded on him.

'Killing might be an everyday occurrence for you but not Carl. The memory of what he saw will never leave him. So Ben, tell me, exactly what point are you trying to make?'

She was shaking.

'Well?' she yelled.

'Whoa!'

He lifted both arms above his head in mock surrender.

But Sandra was the one feeling defeated. Exhausted, she cried tears of undiluted misery. Ben disappeared upstairs and came back with a toilet roll.

'Here,' he said unravelling a few sheets and handing them to her. 'Sorry, Rose, but you've gotta admit, it don't add up.'

'Do the maths Ben,' she shouted. 'The case was tried at the Old Bailey. Elliott got twenty-five years for murder. My son got a life sentence for telling the truth. What part of that don't you understand?'

For a moment she thought he might hit her but he just walked towards the door.

'Go on, go. I don't need you, you bastard,' she cried, running at him, raining her fists on his back. 'I must've been mad asking you for help. You're as bad as they are.'

He spun round and grabbed her by the wrists. She twisted and turned, kicking his shins.

'Get off me, you bastard!' she screamed trying to bite his hand to free herself.

'It's okay, Rose,' he said releasing her. 'Calm down.'

She rubbed her wrists. 'You …'

'You're right, Rose. I was a bastard. I killed a bloke and I didn't give a shit. He had a kid the same age as Kylie for fuck's sake.'

He sunk down onto the sofa. Sandra sat beside him. She could feel her anger ebbing away. She felt almost sorry for Ben. It was ridiculous. Neither spoke for a while.

'Why did you do it?' she asked tentatively.

He looked at her and slowly shook his head.

'You must've had a reason. You wouldn't have just done that. I know you wouldn't.'

Her voice was soft and reassuring.

'He'd met me wife when I was in the nick. Came 'ome and found 'em in bed. My fucking bed, if you please.'

'You slit his throat for that?' she asked trying to keep the shock out of her voice.

He glanced at her and she wished she could take back her last comment or at least erase her incredulous tone.

Ben shook his head.

'Please, you can tell me.'

His features twisted into a snarl.

'The bastard raped her.'

'But you said they were in bed together.'

'I didn't say she was enjoying it.'

Sandra covered her mouth with her hand. Feeling shocked and slightly awkward, she got up and poured them both a drink. As usual, Ben downed the whiskey in one. When he eventually spoke, something had changed between them.

Truth did that; it shone a light on what really mattered.

'Sorry, didn't mean to upset you, Rose.'

'Oh, no, you didn't, I'm fine, really.'

And she was. She understood. Not fully, but enough. Enough to still want him.

'Ben, I ...' she began but he cut in, changing the subject.

'Can't have been easy bringing up Carl on yer own?'

Twisting the damp tissue between her fingers, she watched as it disintegrated onto her lap like snowflakes. She brushed the pieces onto the floor.

'I love my son but being a single parent was the toughest job in the world,' she laughed bitterly. 'Work was a breeze by comparison.'

'Was you the boss?'

She nodded.

'Miss your old job?' he asked.

'I miss the money, but not the stress,' she smiled, relaxing a little.

'Was you a Yuppy?' he asked trying to lighten her mood.

She hated that label. Carl used it whenever he wanted to push her buttons. The older he got, the more he enjoyed winding her up. When she did not reply, Ben changed tack.

'Carl see much of his Dad when he was growing up, then?'

A guttural snort shot out from the back of Sandra's throat.

'Carl's Dad isn't exactly the fatherly type.'

'Oh well, Carl hit the jackpot having you for a mum.'

She laughed, wildly.

'He used to say I 'smothered' him when he was a teenager. I was only trying to protect him for God's sake.'

'That's kids for yer. I was a right little shit after me old man left. I blamed me Mum. But it weren't her fault he was a cheating bastard who couldn't keep it in his trousers.'

They shared a faint smile. Sandra was happy. She was on her pet subject. Her son.

'Carl did well at school and never got in with a bad crowd. Just the opposite…'

'What no mates?' Ben asked with renewed interest.

She shook her head and went into the kitchen.

'Want something to eat? I'm starving. There's some ham. I think it's still okay,' she said taking a joint of boiled bacon from the fridge and sniffing it suspiciously. 'I've got some pickle somewhere, too.'

'Lovely,' he shouted.

She sorted through the jars in the cupboard until she found some chutney. She squinted at the sell-by date before unscrewing the lid and examining the contents.

'No fat on me meat,' Ben called.

His grammar simultaneously irritated and delighted her. No-one could accuse him of trying to be someone he wasn't. He was refreshingly black and white just like the chessboard her ex-husband had spent hour after wasted hour pawing over, rarely deigning to look up, let alone make conversation with her. When he did it was in a dull drawl. Ben was many things, but never boring.

She set the meat on a wooden board and hunted for the carving knife. It was not in its usual place in the block.

'Why did you say Carl left the Programme?' Ben asked, appearing in the doorway.

'I didn't. He told me he couldn't live a lie anymore and his new job wasn't exactly stimulating,' she said, checking the sink and the drawers.

'Better bored than dead though, eh?' asked Ben wryly.

The knife had gone. Confused and terrified, she looked at Ben. Not a flicker. Then, with a sudden pang of relief, she remembered him putting it back underneath the sofa. It must still be there. Although she thought she trusted him, something made her not tell him what she was about to do.

'Excuse me, just getting my glass, I could do with a refill,' she said, squeezing past him.

She could see he was too busy ripping off chunks of ham and eating them to follow her. Quickly, she went into the living room, bent down and peered under the settee.

'While you're down there?' he leered, suddenly appearing in front of her.

Where the hell was the knife?

'Come on, Rose, I was just joking.'

When Ben offered to help her up off the floor, she pulled away. He looked concerned, like he genuinely cared. He was a good actor; she would give him that. He was towering above her; all the self-defence techniques he had taught her would not help her. She needed to say something to distract him.

'Carl's girlfriend is pregnant.'

'Bloody hell!' exclaimed Ben.

Sandra scrambled to her feet then edged slowly towards the front door.

'Exactly, I couldn't believe it when I read his letter.'

'Why didn't he just text yer?'

'Letters are more secure,' she said, her hand on the latch as she looked towards the sofa.

'Where you goin'?' he asked.

To her horror he followed her gaze.

'Where's the knife? Where's the fucking knife, Rose?'

Her mouth was dry and her fingers shook as she tried to free the bolt.

'Oh, Jesus, Rose, you think, I've got the knife, don't you? You think I'm going to stab you first chance I get?' he asked sounding hurt. 'Perhaps you've got it? Come on, Rose, don't play games, where the fuck is it?'

He thrust his arm urgently underneath the sofa and felt around. He looked terrified. If his reaction was genuine, he was no wiser as to the whereabouts of the knife than she was. It suddenly struck her, Ben not having it was more terrifying than if had he been brandishing the blade.

As ever, Ben's criminal mind was one step ahead.

'Well, Rose, now we know two things.'

'What?'

'We guessed your visitor is an Elliott but now we know he's armed.'

Her insides turned to chicken stock and she covered her face with her palms.

'I'm calling the police.'

Ben grabbed the mobile from her.

'No! They ain't goin' help, Rose. Believe me.'

'But I can't stand this anymore.'

'Why don't you go and stay with a mate, just until all this blows over. I'll stay 'ere so when the bastard turns up, I'll be waiting.'

'I want to be with you,' she told him emphatically.

'You trust me then?'

She nodded and he smiled.

'Good girl, it's time to do the right thing, Rose. What was it you told me? 'The hardest thing to do is often the right thing to do'.'

I'm confused. 'What do you want me to do?'

'Nuffin, Rose. Don't do nuffin'. Tomorrow, I'll sort the locks and you go to work, just like normal. You'll be fine.'

He kissed her hard on the mouth and forced her back onto the sofa. She didn't resist. Why would she? She let him overpower her. It meant she didn't have to think. It meant she didn't have to do 'nuffin'.

Chapter twenty-two

[Isle of Wight 2013]

Being stalked by a man keen to sharpen his skills using her Sabatier knife made her all the more desperate to keep reality at bay. Nestled in the safe haven of Ben's arm, her body buzzed with joy even though she could not escape the notion they could be run through with a knife at any moment. She turned her head to talk to Ben but he was asleep. How could he relax when she was forever on her guard?

She looked towards her bedroom door and noticed it was ajar. Strange as she always made a point of closing it before she went to bed. She was very particular about that, especially these days. Perhaps Ben had used the toilet in the night. If he did it was the first time he had managed to get out of bed without waking her. She thought she saw the door move, just a fraction. Or did it? She screwed up her eyes and squinted at the gap between the door and the frame. Was it bigger than before? It was impossible to know. Telling herself the movement had probably been caused by a draft, she closed her eyes but sleep proved elusive. A drink might help but there was no way she was going downstairs to get one.

Then, she heard scrabbling and scuffing.

'What was that?' she asked, elbowing Ben awake.

'What? I didn't hear nuffin',' he mumbled. 'Go back to sleep.'

'Ssch! Listen,' she said. 'There it is again.'

Reluctantly, Ben eased himself up against his pillow.

'What?' he asked.

'It's stopped now,' Sandra tutted. 'What d'you think it was?'

'A mouse,' suggested Ben sliding back under the covers.

'A bloody big one,' said Sandra. 'I know what I heard. Please, go and see if someone's downstairs?' she implored, pulling back the duvet.

144

Still half-asleep and consequently lacking any sense of urgency, he got up and pulled on his jeans.

'Hurry up,' urged Sandra as he padded softly towards the door and out onto the landing. 'Check the bathroom and the wardrobe on the landing. Be careful!'

As she listened to him creep across the floorboards, opening and closing doors, before walking downstairs, she imagined a murky figure lurking in the shadows, knife poised, ready to pounce. When she heard footsteps ascending the stairs, she called out, just to make sure.

'Ben?'

Her voice was laced with anxiety.

'That is you, isn't it Ben?' she cried unable to control the rising panic.

Silence.

Oh God, supposing someone had been down there, waiting for Ben? Perhaps he was already dead? Very quickly, that notion became a reality. He was dead, no doubt about it. Stabbed, probably. Oh God.

Within moments, she went from mourning Ben to fearing for her own life. After all, without him to protect her she did not stand a chance. She let out a terrified whimper before instinctively covering her mouth with her hand. Paralysed with fear, her body had simply stopped working. She could not run away even if she wanted to. She was barely breathing as she watched the door open very slowly.

She screamed.

'Rosie!' cried Ben, flicking on the light and putting his head round the door.

'You bastard! I thought you were dead,' she got up and flew at him, screaming, crying, raining her fists against his chest.

He grabbed her wrists.

'Hey, hey, stop. I'm sorry. I thought you knew it was me?'

'How, how would I know? Why didn't you just answer me?' she shouted.

He said nothing.

'I said, why didn't you answer me?'

'Calm down.'

'Why did you do it? You terrified me.'

She eyed him suspiciously. Could she trust him? Or would he revert to type?

'I've checked everywhere. All the doors and windows are locked. There's nuffin' to worry about. Told yer you imagined it.'

Sandra shivered and got back into bed. Ben leapt in beside her.

'Now, we're both awake we might as well make the most of it,' he said leaning in to kiss her.

She pulled away. Even though she was shivering; she did not want Ben near her.

'Get off me! For God's sake, Ben, there's a man with a knife stalking me and you want to have sex.'

'Well, he ain't here now; we might as well enjoy ourselves.'

'Are you sure you looked properly?' she asked.

'Yeah. Come on, Rose. It's okay. Just relax,' he said stroking her face.

She pushed away his hand but there was no fighting his kiss. It acted like a full stop on the conversation. His embrace was soft yet powerful enough to momentarily suffuse her fear. Yet, all the while, the anxiety smouldered within her, just waiting to be reignited.

She sighed, moving down the bed to rest her head on his stomach, ideally tracing with the tip of her forefinger along the intriguingly familiar line of dark hair that ran down from his navel. Instead of it rekindling her desire, like it always did, it had the opposite effect. Worrying was second nature to her these days, permeating every aspect of her life and before long, she found herself obsessing about how many other woman had touched him before her. Sandra knew of two lovers for certain: his ex-wife and the prostitute. The notion Ben had been with a tart repulsed her. Why would such a good-looking man need to pay for sex?

She sat up.

'Do you still see her?'

'What the fuck?' asked Ben opening his eyes. 'Who? I can't keep up with you, Rose. One minute you're going on about some bloke stalking yer, the next you're talking about some mystery woman.'

'You know who I mean. The …'

Sandra could not bring herself to say 'prostitute' or any of the other unsavoury names used to describe the sort of woman who went with men for money.

'That… that girl, the one you told me about, the one you met in Portsmouth?'

Much to her annoyance, he laughed.

'No, cos not. For God's sake, Rose. When have I had chance to see her? I've been with you.'

'That's not what I asked,' said Sandra bridling.

She silently cursed herself for letting him see how jealous she was.

'Well, do you want to see her?'

He smirked in that annoying way of his; a response Sandra felt was deliberately engineered to tell her absolutely nothing.

She wished she had never mentioned the bloody woman as she inwardly winced at the image of an over-made-up whore, decked out in her grandfather sailor's suit riding Ben on a stormy sea of tangled sheets.

Well, it was high time she brought an end to all that nonsense. She pulled him down on top of her, allowing his weight to pin her to the bed. It was a wonderful sensation not least because it was the only thing powerful enough to numb the fear that engulfed her. Ben was hers. All hers. The call girl could turn tricks but this was Sandra's chance to perform magic. When she had finished, Ben seemed suitably impressed.

'Where did you learn to do that?' he asked as he lay back, satiated. 'My mates would pay good money for that.'

She jerked away from him, disgusted. Not so much with Ben's comment but more with herself.

'Thanks for making me feel cheap.'

'I was only joking.'

'Ha bloody ha.'

She pulled the sheet around her and turned her back on him. What was she doing with a crass, crude ex-con like him? Had her life really unravelled to such an extent she was reduced to sleeping with a no-mark murderer? Shivering, she got up and pulled on her dressing gown, securing the belt around her waist.

'Come back here and let me warm you up,' he said, his eyes never leaving hers, lasciviously sliding across the bed.

'No, I don't want to,' she told him emphatically. 'There's a man with a knife after me. I can't keep pretending this isn't happening even if you can.'

'So now you know he's got a knife, so what? He could've been armed all along. Let's face it, he ain't come 'ere to have a nice cup of tea and a fuckin' biscuit, has he?'

He reached out and caught hold of her hand.

'I've told yer. There ain't nuffin we can do, Rose. We've gotta wait for him to make a move. You worrying ain't goin' help.'

'It's not fair. He holds all the cards; he knows the police can't touch him.'

'Yeah, because he ain't done nuffin'. They can't 'ave him for summit he ain't done.'

'Yet,' added Sandra tartly.

'I told you, he's just trying to scare you. No-one's goin' hurt you, Rosie. You've got my word.'

The word of a murderer? What that was worth? Not much. As soon as the thought formed in her mind, she felt guilty. Without Ben to protect her, where would she be? Her life would be unbearable. She should be grateful. Softening, she smiled at him.

'Come 'ere, you silly cow,' he said with a smirk.

One deft movement of his hand was all it took to undo her dressing gown cord allowing the folds of fabric to part.

'Fuck me, you're gorgeous,' he exclaimed approvingly as he ran his eyes over her naked body.

He threw back the duvet and proudly showed-off his erection.

'Shame to waste it, Rosie.'

Again, the bawdy remark. For once, she wasn't even tempted. Unfortunately, her libido seemed to have shrunk in equal and opposite proportions to the rising terror that constantly consumed and exhausted her.

'Sorry, nothing personal,' she said gathering the dressing gown back round herself and knotting the belt tightly.

'Ah Rosie. Don't do this to me.'

She raised her eyebrows in disapproval at his attempt at guilt-tripping her into having sex with him and watched his erection deflate. What was she playing at? But that was the trouble, she wasn't playing at anything; she had forgotten how to have fun.

'I'll make it up to you. I promise. But right now, I need to get out of here. This place is too claustrophobic; it's getting to me. I'm hearing things, imagining stuff. I don't know what's real and what's not anymore. You must think I'm crazy.'

'No, you're not mad. You're lovely,' he told her.

Sandra gasped. 'Lovely?' What an odd word. Two letters more than 'love', yet it meant so much less. 'Love' is to 'lovely' as leather is to plastic.

'I told you, Ben, I'm not in the mood. Besides, I need to get out of here. I need to get back to work.'

'What? You're really going back today?' he asked sounding surprised.

'Yes, I've been thinking about what you said and given everything that's happened recently, you're right, I need to carry on as normal. I'm dreading it but if I don't go back to the hospital now, I never will.'

'Well, look on the bright side, if he does turn up and stab yer at least you'll be in the right place.'

Ben was laughing at his own sick joke. Sandra wanted to kill him. It had taken all her courage to get to this point and he had to make one of his stupid remarks.

'What time is it?' he asked, suddenly reaching out for his phone. 'Half-seven. I don't feel like I've had no sleep. You must be knackered too.'

'Not that old trick again, is it? You haven't altered the clock again, have you?'

'Not this time,' he said and then started to laugh.' Did you see what I did there?'

Ignoring his attempt at humour, she went to the chest of drawers and sorted through her underwear.

'My black pants have gone,' she said looking at Ben.

'Not guilty. They wouldn't suit me!' he joked leaning out of the bed to watch her.

Again, the inappropriate quip.

'It's not funny,' she shouted.

Her voice began to falter. He got up and stood behind her, wrapping his arms around her. This simple act of kindness was all it took to reduce Sandra to tears.

'Oh Ben, I'm sorry. I can't stand all this. I am so frightened. How much more am I supposed to take?'

Gently, he kissed the back of her neck before turning her around to face him.

'I'm sorry, Rose. This should never have 'appened. I shouldn't 'ave let it. He's one sick bastard and I'm goin' 'ave 'im,' he said tightening his grip on her. 'The sick, dirty bastard.'

She stepped away.

'When? When will you have 'the bastard'?' she demanded angrily, mimicking his accent. 'You keep saying it but he's still one step ahead of you.'

Ben seemed flustered, shifting his weight from one foot to the other and repeatedly lifting his hands to his head. He reminded her of a polar bear she had seen once at the zoo when she was a child. Imprisoned behind the bars of its steel cage, stripped of its natural habitat, the wretched animal padded ceaselessly back and forth.

'You're right. I'm sorry. You're right. I'm sorry.'

'Ben! Stop! It's okay,' she reassured him, gently stroking his arm in an attempt to calm him.

'I've let you down, Rosie. I've let you down.'

Again she cut in before the mantra could be repeated.

'Ben! Forget it! You're doing your best.'

'I don't know what to say, Rosie. It ain't right.'

It was no comfort but at least he was being truthful and she admired that. Given his past, honesty was probably not his default setting.

'I think we both need a break. This place is driving us insane. Okay, I'm going to get ready.'

She enjoyed her shower, imagining the water was washing away the fear that clung to her like spores.

Eventually, she stepped out and towelled herself dry. The mirror above the sink misted over. She was about to wipe it with her hand but something stopped her. Suddenly gripped by an all-consuming fear, she yanked open the door.

'Ben?' she shouted

Much to her relief, he replied immediately.

'Yeah?'

'Nothing.'

She secured the towel around her and ran back across the landing, into the bedroom where Ben was looking out of the window.

'You goin' be alright, Rosie?' he asked turning to stare at her.

She nodded.

'Tell you what, why don't I get the bus into Newport with yer and get them locks? I can fit them while you're out. Once they're done, I reckon you'll feel a lot safer.'

'What's the point?' she asked sourly. 'You said there wasn't a lock that could keep you out. Why would Elliott be any different?'

'You can't compare me to him. The bloke's a nutter, a little shit who goes round frightening women and nicking their knickers. I don't like cowards and I don't like perverts. If I see him, I'll kill him.'

The word 'kill' leapt out of the sentence and grabbed her by the throat. She could barely breathe; the thought of being mixed up and implicated in a violent, amoral act was an anathema to her and she wanted no part of it.

'Ben, no!' she cried.

If he had heard her, he gave no indication.

He frightened her. He was a loose cannon, capable of anything. It was time to take back the reins. But, it was too late. A murderer was calling the shots and if he had a mind to take someone's life, he would. He had done it before.

'Ben, you can't…'

'You can't stop me. I will, Rosie. I will kill him.'

Chapter twenty-three

[Isle of Wight 2013]

The journey to work was fraught was fear. She had even deliberately chosen her clothes to ensure she looked as anonymous as possible. In her dull grey cotton dress, flat shoes and sunglasses, she could have been anyone. It was probably too late for subterfuge but it made her feel safer. Much to her annoyance, Ben made no effort to disguise his appearance and would have been instantly recognisable to anyone who knew him.

On their bus journey into Newport, Sandra insisted they sit on the top deck so she could see who was getting on. Every time they reached a stop, she would glance nervously out of the window to check Elliott was not lurking in the queue, about to get on.

By the time they reached town, she was down the stairs and at the bus door well before they pulled into the terminus.

'I'm going to get a cab to work,' she announced, her hand shaking as she reached into her bag for her purse.

'But the hospital's only up the road,' protested Ben, glancing across at the Number 2 bus that stopped right outside the main entrance.

'I'm frightened.'

'D'you want me to come with yer?'

'No, I'll be fine,' she said opening her purse and checking she had sufficient cash for her fare.

She leant forward and held him like she never wanted to let him go.

'Steady on, Rosie,' he laughed, gently easing away and taking her by the arm. 'Come on.'

He guided her around the corner to the taxi rank and put her in a cab. Fortunately, the driver was not the talkative type but she was unnerved when he adjusted his rear view mirror and caught her eye. Immediately, she looked away, took out her phone and scrolled through her address book, anything but look at him. The journey was mercifully short. When they pulled up on the hospital forecourt she could not wait to get out.

She handed him a note and told him to keep the change. She just wanted to get away from him as fast as she could.

The reception area felt warm and welcoming. She sighed audibly and walked quickly up the stairs and to her office.

If anonymity was what she was after, her colleagues did not disappoint. Not one of them looked up from their screens when she walked in. She took off her sunglasses, desperately hoping to avoid her line manager, Kim who was standing with her back to her. Unfortunately, she turned just as Sandra walked past.

'Oh, you're back. I'd like a word with you.'

Sandra followed her into her office and shut the door.

'How are you feeling after the accident?' Kim asked tilting her head to one side and trying to look concerned. 'Rob said it was quite serious. You were admitted overnight, weren't you?'

'I think the doctor was being cautious. There was nothing to worry, just a few bruises.'

'Oh I assumed it was more serious than that; you've been off a while.'

In all the time Sandra had worked there, she had barely spoken two words to the woman and had no intention of confiding in her. She said the first thing that came to mind.

'I've had gastroenteritis for the past couple of days.'

Yet another lie but she knew it was guaranteed to avoid awkward questions. The last thing any hospital needed was an outbreak of diarrhea or worse.

'I hope you're fully recovered?' Kim asked suspiciously. 'We don't want you here if you're unwell.'

'I'm fine now but I spent most of yesterday in the loo.'

With recent events leaving no time for levity, Sandra seemed determined to find some humour in the situation however inappropriate. Kim looked suitably taken aback.

'Sounds horrendous. How did you cope on your own?' she asked giving her hands a squirt of sanitizer from the wall dispenser.

Sandra couldn't help herself.

'I lived on water and apples.'

Again Kim looked shocked.

'Apples? But they're full of acid. Surely, they're the last things you should be eating with an upset stomach?'

'BRAT,' said Sandra.

She was behaving as if she had Teurette's, compelled to say embarrassing things. If she was honest, she enjoyed it; freedom was power. A power denied her for too long.

'I beg your pardon?' asked her boss, her tone both haughty and horrified.

Sandra enjoyed being away from the confines of the cottage and her tormentor. The sudden freedom had an unnerving affect. No longer shackled by fear, she felt disturbingly out of control.

'BRAT. It's a mnemonic, stands for bread, rice, apples, tea, all good for an upset tummy.'

How could she forget? She had taken Carl to the Science Museum where they had queued for over an hour to discover the inner workings of the human body through a series of child-friendly exhibits. Sliding out of a giant nostril, Carl had thrown one of his tantrums when Sandra, exhausted after yet another stressful week at work, had had the temerity to suggest they should go home. Carl was having none of it, screaming and shouting, throwing himself on the floor and refusing to budge. She had manhandled him out, past the hoards of horrified onlookers who made no attempt to disguise their disapproval. He had played up all the way home, even giving her a nasty bite on the arm, drawing blood. He was eight-years-old. Hardly any wonder BRAT was forever engraved on Sandra's brain.'Right,

I'm going to have to go or I'll be late for the planning meeting. If it's anything like the last one, it'll go on for hours. Just make sure you have a word with payroll, there may be some paperwork to fill out.'

'Hey Sandra! Lovely to see you. Feeling better?' asked Rob suddenly appearing in the doorway.

No matter how difficult life became, Rob had a way of making everything seem better. He was just one of those people. Without thinking, she reached out and embraced him. He hugged her back.

'Careful, Rob, don't get too close, Sandra's had gastroenteritis. Can you email everyone and remind them to use hand sanitizer? Don't want to be held responsible for an outbreak of Norovirus and be blamed for putting the hospital in lock down. Again,' Kim said running out of her office.

'Well, she should know all about gastroenteritis, she suffers from verbal diarrhea,' whispered Rob with a wry smile. 'God forgive me but I wish she would go down with something and be off for a few weeks. She had me doing all your stuff as well as my own. Worked me to a frazzle. Look at me. The last time I was this thin, I was six.'

Sandra noted he was as robust as ever.

Suddenly Rob laughed which gave Sandra an excuse to do the same. She had no idea what she was laughing at. All she knew was that it felt good and for a brief, blissful moment, there was no stalker. Ben was right about coming back to work; it was a good idea.

'Were you really ill?' whispered Rob with a sly wink as the left Kim's office and went over to Rob's desk. 'Or was it just too much bed and not enough sleep?'

Sandra blushed as she remembered being with Ben.

'Ohmygod, you've gone red! You did, didn't you? You slept with The Brute,' Rob said thrilled with himself.

Sandra was not keen on Rob's nickname for Ben but knew he meant no harm. He purloined a chair from an empty desk and motioned her to sit down.

'Tell me more,' he insisted.

'Mind your own business,' she replied.

She did not want to be rude but they were her memories, perfect, private moments to cherish. They were lovingly preserved in her heart, enabling her to take them out and relive them whenever she liked. It was important they stayed intact and untarnished.

'Oh come on. Let me live vicariously through you. I can't remember the last time I got any action,' he pouted, clasping his hands together as if in prayer.

She had no intention of letting Rob in too far.

'Ben's lovely,' was all she would say.

'Lovely'. There was that word again. What did it really mean? Was it a way of saying 'love' without the associated complications and implications? Surely, she couldn't be in love with Ben, could she? The notion was ridiculous; she hadn't known the man five minutes. Yet, being without him was unthinkable. Was that because she liked him, really liked him or just because she needed him as her protector?

Nothing and no-one frightened Ben and, if his murderous tales were anything to go by, he knew how to handle himself. How odd, the one person she felt safest with was also the most dangerous man she had ever met.

The idea she had subconsciously substituted the word 'lovely' for 'love' was ridiculous.

'Yes, he is lovely, isn't he?' Rob said, resurrecting the notion without even knowing it.

'Yes, he's very …' she paused as she searched for a word to describe Ben. '… helpful. He's very helpful. In fact, he's probably back at the cottage right now fitting new locks. That place is so remote, I thought it was a good idea.'

More dishonesty. She was shocked at how adept she had become at pedalling lies.

'So, you've left The Brute screwing at your house and you've come to work? You really must be ill.'

His innuendo sounded cheaper than ever yet it proved the perfect antidote to the horror that clogged her veins like infected blood. Allowing herself a moment, she continued the joke, resting the back of her hand against her forehead.

'You're right, my temperature is sky-high, I should be in bed,' she smirked.

Rob smiled, he looked delighted to see her happy.

Where would she be without him to lighten the mood? He took her back to a time when she hadn't always been this on edge, this jumpy. Once, she had been normal: a boss who enjoyed a laugh with her team but was never the butt of the joke, a party girl who liked a drink but was never a drunk and a Mum who loved her son more than life itself but didn't spend every day worrying he might die.

How times had changed. She had gone from carefree to careworn overnight, the old Sandra had disappeared for good, swallowed up in a black hole. Surely, there had to be a way back for her, in time?

'Come on, Sandra, we better do some work or we'll be on sick leave, permanently.'

'Okay. Can you fill me in?' she asked reaching for a pad and pen.

'Sorry, if you want 'filling in' you'll have to ask The Brute to do the honours.'

Enough, his endless stream of double entendre had become tiresome. She went over to her desk and took a batch of files from the drawer.

'Oh, you're no fun,' Rob said trailing after her. 'What's wrong, Sandra? You don't seem yourself.'

His sudden concern made her want to cry but she couldn't, not here. She wanted to tell him everything but what was the point? There was nothing he could do. Why embroil him in her mess? It wasn't fair. Besides, Rob was fun; he didn't do serious.

He put his arm around her.

'Seriously, Sandra, I was really worried about you when you didn't come in.'

She could see from his face he meant it.

'Sorry, Rob, there's been too much going on.'

'Like what?'

She shook her head and avoided his gaze.

'Come on, Sandra. You can tell me. What's wrong? It's not Ben, is it?'

'No.'

It was true. Ben was the last person who should shoulder the blame. Rob watched her closely before changing the subject.

'Wanna hear some good news? Apparently, Kim's leaving, she's pregnant.'

He waited for Sandra's response. Seeing her shocked expression, he added, 'Just try to erase the image of the actual conception bit from your brain. It'll give you nightmares.'

Sandra was only half listening. Kim was married to her job; everyone knew that. In all the time Sandra had worked for her, she had never mentioned a boyfriend, let alone wanting a baby. Her curiosity piqued, she wanted to know more.

'Who's the daddy?' she enquired.

'Not me!' Rob retorted. 'The smart money is on the new neurologist but I reckon it's the porter. He's always up here, asking if she fancies a ride on his trolley.'

Sandra laughed for far longer than Rob's smutty joke warranted but it didn't matter, she was enjoying herself.

'Oh thank-you, Rob. You are the only person who could've made me laugh today. Life has been hell recently.'

'Wanna talk about it?'

She hesitated.

'No, I'll be fine,' she lied. 'Like all things, it will pass.'

She hated herself for trotting out two clichéd lies in a row but what else could she say? Deception had become her truth. She shuddered and changed the subject back to Kim.

'Have they got someone to cover for her while she's on maternity leave?' Sandra asked.

'You don't want her job, do you?' asked Rob incredulously.

She shrugged.

'Are you mad? The woman is living proof all work and no play gets you nowhere.'

'Well, judging by her current condition, she's definitely had her fair share of play recently,' replied Sandra.

Bringing an end to the conversation, Sandra turned away. She switched on her computer and tapped in her name and password. Her heart sank when she saw her inbox full of unanswered emails and set about the unenviable task of dealing with them. Resigned to the tedium, she felt safe with the rigidity of wall-to-wall tasks, leaving no time for reflection.

Lunch was a sandwich Rob brought her up from the canteen and the afternoon an onslaught of spread sheets, endless facts and figures that had no bearing on her own life but she knew were life and death to the patients involved.

'Can I borrow you for a moment, Sandra,' Kim ordered, suddenly appearing at Sandra's elbow before turning on her heel and walking away.

Convinced Kim knew she had been lying about being sick, Sandra was shaking by the time she reached the office.

'Come in and sit down,' Kim said.

She said it so kindly, Sandra was fooled for a moment into thinking she was chatting with a girlfriend.

'When's your baby due?' she asked.

Seeing Kim's shocked reaction, Sandra was suddenly struck by the sickening thought Rob may have got it wrong and the woman wasn't pregnant at all, just a bit fat.

'Four months to go,' Kim replied looking down at her distended stomach. 'Yes, somehow I have managed to become both peri-menopausal and pregnant. How the hell did that happen?'

What was Kim doing opening up to her? It was embarrassing especially as they had never discussed anything other than work.

'Yes, one minute, I was contemplating HRT, the next I'm in Mothercare buying one of those stupid Baby-on-Board stickers. Because, let's face it, if I don't let other drivers know I've got a kid in the car, some idiot will plough into the back of me, then say, 'It's your own fault. You weren't displaying your sticker. How was I to know you had a kid in the car? I thought it was just you so fine to stove in your rear end.'

Sandra was stunned. Not only was the woman confiding in her, she was also trying to be funny.

'Sorry, was that too much information?' Kim asked. 'I didn't mean to make you feel uncomfortable? Just thought I could talk to you, what with you being a mum.'

Sandra froze. At first, she thought she must have misheard. No-one on the island, apart from Ben, knew about Carl. She had always been very careful to protect him and not mention him. She stared ahead, not knowing what to say. Should she admit it? Or was Kim just fishing for information? Perhaps she was involved. Perhaps she knew the Elliotts? Sandra's mind somersaulted and tripped-up over some of the horrendous possibilities.

She told herself to get a grip.

'You have got a son, haven't you?' asked Kim.

The words wormed their way into Sandra's heart and formed a hook, extracting the very thing she should have kept hidden. Carl. But how could she keep denying his existence? She was a mother. She was Carl's mother.
'Yes,' she said proudly. 'I've got a son.'

It felt wonderful to acknowledge him after all these years.

'Yes, I know, I've met him,' said Kim. 'He popped in to see you when you were off sick,' she said finishing her tea and smiling warmly at Sandra. 'He's charming,'

Sandra thought she might be sick. What the hell was going on? Why would Carl suddenly visit the island, let alone her office?

'Here? He came here?' she asked careful not to mention his name.

'Yes,' said Kim breezily, running her hand over her belly.

Sandra tried to stay focused.

'When was this?' she asked, pressing the tips of her fingers to her forehead, trying to ease the sudden stabbing pain.

'Monday, about one-ish. Yes, I remember, I worked through lunch so I could leave early for my scan. Sandra, are you alright?'

'What did he look like? I mean how did he look? Did he look well?' she asked, desperate not to give anything away.

'He seemed fine but surely, you've caught up with each other by now?' she said. 'Not a problem, is there?'

'No, not at all,' lied Sandra trying to keep her voice steady. 'Thanks for letting me know.'

Her hands began to shake so much she had to sit on them forcing her knuckles to press painfully into her buttocks.

'He caused quite a stir with some of the younger girls here. He's a very handsome lad. I would never have guessed he was your son, nothing like you, is he?'

Sandra ignored the insult and held her breath. With his long, gangly limbs and fair hair, Carl was the image of her. People had always commented on how alike they were and she had always been delighted her son bore no resemblance to his father, physically at least.

Whoever had come to the hospital did not sound like her son. She felt sure the identity of the mystery stranger was no mystery. It had to be an Elliott.

'I'm sorry, I don't feel well,' said Sandra getting up and leaving the office, her hand clamped over her mouth.

She ran into the toilet where she collapsed over the hand-basin, her palms sweating and her heart pounding. She turned on the cold tap and splashed cold water on her face. Catching sight of her reflection in the mirror, she could see her features had become a study of despair and fear.

Texting Ben, she was careful not to give too much away and keyed in just four words.

'The enemy is close.'

She gripped the phone, staring at the screen, willing him to reply.

'Come on, come on,' she whispered.

She waited another few minutes and when he still hadn't replied, she reluctantly returned to the office where Rob was waiting for her, a mug of coffee at the ready.

'Here, drink this. You look awful. That cow hasn't fired you, has she?' he asked genuinely concerned.

Sandra shook her head. Losing her job would have been preferable to what had happened.

'I feel ill. I've got to go.'

She ran out and down the stairs, through the front doors and across the car park not stopping until she got to the road. Standing on the pavement, her breath came in short little gasps, her throat burning. She felt hunted. Where was Elliott? In one of the passing cars maybe or across the road, lurking? Or was he watching her from a hospital window? There was no knowing but one thing she had discovered; he was usually wherever she was.

Her headache no longer troubled her, terror brought its own unique agony, far more painful than any physical aberration.
Suddenly, her phone vibrated in her pocket. Her hands shaking, she struggled to click on Ben's response. As soon as she saw it she wished she hadn't.

'The enemy has paid us another visit.'

Chapter twenty-four

[Isle of Wight 2013]

'Straw? Are you serious?' asked Sandra when she arrived home to find Ben in the living room brandishing a few bits of hay. 'I've rushed home, frightened out of my life and all for a few bits of straw you found on the living room floor. Tell me you're joking?'

'No, I'm not fucking joking. It weren't here when we left but it's here now. The bastard trod it in. I'm telling yer, he's been back.'

'Or the wind blew it in when we went out,' said Sandra grabbing the stuff from his hand and throwing it into the fireplace. 'For God's sake, Ben. I don't need this.'

'Well, I think…'

She cut in; she didn't have time for him and his nonsense.

'I don't care what you think. I'm going to tell you what I know. I know someone went to my work on Monday and whoever it was told my boss he was my son but from her description, he certainly wasn't Carl.'

Her mouth dry, her stomach raw, she thought she might be sick.

'Shit. D'you reckon it was an Elliott?' asked Ben, rather too excitedly for her liking as he ripped at his cuticles with his teeth.

'Who else?'

Ben ran at the front door and kicked it. Sandra jumped.

'Fuck it! Fuck it! Fuck it!'

His hands flew to his head, repeatedly slapping at his skull.

'No! No! No!'

'Ben, please,' she said calmly in a vain attempt to counter his agitation. 'Perhaps it's time to tell the police. Now that Carl's left

Witness Protection, they need to know what's going on.'

'No!' he shouted! 'No police. I've told yer, Rose. They ain't yer friends. You don't know 'em. I can handle this.'

'But Ben, I …'

'No!' I've got this place all sorted, locked up nice and safe, so he can't get to yer. I won't 'ave the bastard turning up at yer work. I won't 'ave it.'

The door took a second battering as he repeatedly kicked the lower panels.

'Calm down, Ben. You did your best but we both know he's not going to give up. Wherever I go, he'll be there, waiting.'

She regretted voicing her fears. She hated giving them oxygen.

'Not if I've got anything to do with it, he won't,' Ben fumed, curling his upper lip.

'Be realistic. You can't be with me 24/7. Even the police couldn't offer Carl that level of protection. We both know Elliott will just bide his time until he gets what he wants.'

Again her tone was calm, as she tried to distance herself from the situation. Like an actress tiring of a taxing role, she occasionally let her eyes travel down the script until she found a less demanding part, something she could play twice nightly without it taking too much toll.

'I'll kill 'im, Rose.'

Ben's voice was tight as if conserving his energy for the actual murder. Sandra imagined taking someone's life took considerable effort.

'And if you do, you'll end up back in prison. You don't want that. Think of your girls. We ought to let the police deal with this now.'

Her words were petrol to his flame. She watched as his hands balled into fists of bone and muscle, lethal weapons ready to strike at any moment.

Sandra shook like a tree in a storm, threatening to bend and break. There was no stopping the tears when they came. To her surprise Ben reached out and held her. Eventually, she relaxed into him, letting go of the strong, upright posture that, for the past few years, had fooled her into thinking she too was strong and upright.

'Come on, Rose,' urged Ben. 'Someone's goin' cop it but it ain't goin' be you. I promise you that.'

'So you keep saying.'

Her tone was suddenly accusatory. What was she doing? Why attack the one person who was trying to protect her? It made no sense. She had become as screwed up as her life. Whatever Ben's past, he had shown her nothing but kindness. Admittedly, it was his own unconventional brand but he meant well, she was sure of that.

'I think I should warn Carl. He needs to know what's been going on.' When Ben spoke again he all but breathed fire.

'There's no need to tell the police or worry Carl. I told yer I'd kill the bastard and I will.'

He meant what he said. She could tell it wasn't just some idle threat to make her feel better. Could she really put her son's safety in the hands of a man she barely knew? Supposing one of the Elliotts got to Carl before Ben could get to them?

'Maybe I should just go.'

'What d'you mean?'

'Leave the island. Just get away.'

'Don't be silly. You don't wanna do that. You can't keep running. Where would you go? Besides, you've got me now. I'll protect you.'

Adrenalin flooded her body. She had worked at the hospital long enough to know the hormone, in sufficient quantities, could either start or stop the heart. She closed her eyes. Death would be a welcome release.

When she eventually opened her eyes, Ben's whole body seemed to have erupted into a smile. She found his happy face more disturbing than his angry one.

He was murderous and mercurial. Who in their right mind would chose to be with a man who had both traits in equal measure? Yet, given the situation, both were essential qualities especially if Ben was to keep his word and keep her and her son safe.

She watched him, trying to anticipate his next move but had yet to master the art. He was impossible to gauge.

'Well, go on then, Rosie, bolt the doors and break out the booze,' he told her with a grin. 'You and me are goin' 'ave a lock-in, just the two of us. No uninvited guests, eh? I've got us some food in. Let's have a party.'

His erratic suggestion upended her. Before locking the door, she contemplated the pros and cons of holing up with one killer in order to shut out another.

She looked at the chipped, dented paintwork on the lower half of the door, evidence of where Ben had kicked it. Violence, even when it wasn't directed at her, unhinged her.

Avoiding Ben's gaze, she went into the kitchen and took out her phone. She scrolled down and found the number for the police – not the local station but the number she had been given by Witness Protection. Carl's life could be at stake, she had to do something.

She clicked on the number. Ben's shopping was in two bags by the sink. She couldn't be bothered to unpack it and instead went to the fridge, took a small, dry piece of cheese from its already-opened wrapper and forced it into her mouth. It was how she imagined the hard skin on an old lady's heel might taste. She spat the lump into the bin and switched off her phone just as Ben swaggered in.

'You okay?' he asked.

She nodded. A lie.

'Who you calling?' he asked seeing the phone in her hand.

'No-one. Just checking my texts.'

Another lie.

Not wanting to upset him again, she slipped her phone in her pocket.

'Them locks are industrial,' he assured her pointing at the windows. 'Use them ones on banks. This place has got more locks than Wormwood Scrubs. And more screws.'

He smiled at her as if waiting for her to applaud. In no mood for his puerile jokes, she ignored him. What he had fitted was so high-spec and expensive-looking, it had to be dodgy. Time was when she would not have had stolen goods in the house. But these days, it didn't bother her. To hell with integrity, having morals had not done her or Carl any favours.

'Come on. Let's 'ave a drink,' said Ben. 'I bought some cider when I was in town.'

He opened the cupboard, took out two glasses and a large plastic bottle, just like the one he had been drinking from the first time she had met him on the train. The memory made her feel uneasy.

'But I don't like cider...' she began but he had already poured her a glass.

'Here,' he said thrusting it into her hand.

The cloudy amber liquid looked like a urine sample.

'What's that face for? Bet you've never tried it, 'ave yer? Go on, drink it then,' he said with an encouraging smile.

Reluctantly, she lifted the tumbler to her lips. It smelt vinegary.

'I'd rather have wine,' she said, wincing. 'I've got a nice bottle somewhere.'

But Ben was having none of it.

'Just drink it. *'Cider with Rosie'*!' he laughed, chinking his glass forcefully against hers.

The literacy reference threw her.

'You've read *'Cider With Rosie'*?' she asked making no attempt to disguise her obvious disbelief.

His eyes shone as he took another glug.

'That shocked yer, didn't it? You ain't the only brainy one, yer know. *'Cider With Rosie'* – nice name.'

Too shocked to speak, she could hardly imagine a more reluctant reader than Ben.

'Did you enjoy it?' she asked unable to imagine him curled up, engrossed in the book's lyrical prose.

'I did as it goes. My Dad's girlfriend used to read it to me. Stella her name was. I'll never forget her. Well fit and a real brain-box. She was in the Upper Sixth and used to come round to our house after school and perch on the settee with her legs crossed. I sat on the floor so I could look up her skirt.'

'How old were you?' asked Sandra horrified.

'Dunno, twelve, thirteen? She used to wear these ...'

'Okay, too much information, I've got the idea. Anyway, let's drink to Laurie Lee,' she said raising her glass.

'Who? I don't know no Laurie Lee.'

'He was the author,' she explained trying not to laugh.

Ben looked confused, hurt almost.

'Well, I dunno, do I?'

She felt bad, mocking him in that way. It was unkind and unnecessary.

Laurie Lee' wrote *'Cider with Rosie',*' she explained.

'Good bloke. I'll drink to Laurie. If it hadn't been for him I'd never have seen Stella's black lacy knickers. Bottoms up!'

He chinked his glass excitedly against hers.

Sandra went cold. Black lacy knickers? Her missing knickers had been black lace too. Perhaps Ben had been lying and he had taken them after all, a trophy, secreted away. Oh no, please God no. She wanted to believe him but was she being naïve in thinking he was telling her the truth?

She glanced over at Ben but his expression gave nothing away; he was too busy draining half a pint of cider in one long slug. Sandra tried to convince herself she was being silly, making connections where there weren't any and took a tentative sip of her drink. It was urine.

'What you lookin' like that for? Don't be a snob. Wine, whiskey, cider - it's all the same, all gets yer pissed. The only difference is your hang-over costs more than mine.'

She frowned. She didn't like being told off but what she really hated was Ben being right.

'Whatever we're drinking, we mustn't get too carried away. If Elliott does come back we need to be sober,' she said putting her glass down.

'Don't worry about it, Rosie. I can kill, drunk or sober,' Ben laughed refilling his glass. 'Get it down yer neck. Go on. I ain't poisoned it or nuffin'.'

'Why would you say that?' she asked spinning round to face him.

'It was a joke. Calm down for fuck's sake.'

'It wasn't funny. You're not funny.'

She picked up her glass and threw the contents down the sink, watching with some satisfaction as it fizzed around the plug-hole.

'Oi! Don't waste it. I could've 'ad that.'

'Sorry, Ben,' she said unable to keep the sarcasm out of her voice. 'What was I thinking? Some madman wants to knife me to death. He knows where I live. He knows where I work. He's been to my home; he's been to my office. But, you're right, let's just get pissed so he can murder us in our bed.'

She grabbed the tumbler from his hand and threw it against the wall. Ben ducked and lifted his hands to protect his face from the shards of flying glass. Sandra watched as the cider inched down the cream paintwork in long witch-like fingers.

172

Without a word, Ben started picking up the bigger pieces of broken glass. Sandra went to help but he pushed her away.

'Mind! Don't touch it, Rose. Don't want you cutting yourself and have to cart you off to A&E. Got a brush?'

Flustered, she rummaged about under the sink, found the dust-pan and gave it to him.

'I'll do this. You have a drink and sit down.'

Her anger and frustration spent, she felt foolish, like a child after a particularly truculent tantrum. Ben's kindness only made it worse. Had he been annoyed she could at least have retained a sense of righteousness. She went to the fridge, took out the wine then burst into tears.

'I'm sorry, Ben,' she said putting her arms around him. 'You must think I'm mad.'

'Nah, you're alright,' he said kissing her cheek and wiping away her tears with the corner of a tea-towel. 'All this, it's too much pressure, innit?'

'Promise, you won't leave me? I couldn't cope without you.'

'Cos I won't,' he said embracing her. 'Cross my heart and hope to die.'

'Don't say that,' she said. 'It's a horrible expression.'

'I'd never leave yer, Rose. You know that; you've got an arse to die for.'

He reached round, cupped her buttocks in his hands and gave them a squeeze.

'I ain't goin' nowhere. I know where I'm well off,' he told her as he picked up the dustpan and shot the last of the broken glass into the pedal-bin.

Then he disappeared into the living room. She followed him then watched as he swept up the few bits of straw she had thrown into the fireplace earlier.

173

'There, that's better,' he said with some satisfaction as he got up and smiled at her.

She nodded towards the photograph of Totland Bay, perfect but for the burn hole where the setting sun should have been, yet another ugly reminder of their intruder.

'Want me to get rid of it, stick it in the cupboard, out of sight?' he asked.

Sandra thought for a moment, reluctant to relinquish something that had once meant so much to her. She felt for the rose locket at her throat. At least she still had that as a keepsake from Carl. The picture had been defaced, no good could come of keeping it. Once the photograph held only bitter-sweet associations of her son, recently it had acquired sinister connotations and was evidence of malicious intent. She wanted no part of it and handed it to Ben.

'Put it in the bin, with the rest of the rubbish.'

'Sure?' he asked.

She nodded and he broke it over his knee before throwing it away. Then he took two fresh glasses from the cupboard and poured them both some wine.

'There you go, the posh stuff. Right, drink up and follow me, young lady. We're going upstairs to finish what we started.'

He reached for her hand but she pulled away.

'Sorry, Ben, not now, not after everything that's happened. I can't just keep jumping into bed with you. Sex isn't the answer. It doesn't solve anything. It doesn't make all this go away, does it?'

'No, but it's a bloody good distraction, beats sitting around worrying. Fuck that. Come to bed and fuck me instead.'

It sounded less like a suggestion and more like an order, one she felt compelled to follow.

'Okay, I'll join you in a minute. I'm just going to freshen up.'

She smiled at him as she went upstairs and disappeared into the

174

bathroom. She turned the shower on full to drown out the sound of her conversation with Carl.

The room filled with steam as she listened to the ring tone.

What if Debs picked up? She'd just have to say she had dialled the wrong number by mistake.

Her heart sank when the answer machine kicked in and she heard an automated voice instructing her to leave a message. She didn't know what to say or how to say it. If she was too specific she would alarm Debs and with her being pregnant that was the last thing she wanted to do. If she was too vague, Carl would not know the imminent danger he could be in.

'Hi, Carl, only me. Hope you and Debs are okay. Just wanted to say if you were thinking of popping down to the island maybe leave it for a while. I'm having some work done on the cottage. Didn't want you having a wasted journey. But be lovely to see you soon. Just not right now. Okay, love you, bye. So don't come this week. Sorry, I ...'

The machine cut out.

Chapter twenty-five

[Isle of Wight 2013]

It was still dark when the knock came. Loud and insistent, it was obvious the caller had no intention of being ignored.

Sandra reached out and grabbed Ben's arm.

'Wake up, someone's at the door.'

'What the fuck?' he whispered, his hand reaching out to switch on the bedside lamp.

'Don't put the light on, they'll know we're here,' she told him. 'Just go downstairs.'

He pulled back the duvet and got out of bed. She could just make out his shadowy shape as he picked his jeans off the floor and pulled them on.

'Hurry up,' she urged her heart thumping.

Who the hell was down there? Her first thought was the stalker buy why would he knock, it made no sense unless this was yet another trick to torment her?

Then her blood froze. She knew who exactly who it was. The police. It had to be. Something had happened to Carl. Oh God no. All hope drained from her. No-one called in the middle of the night with good news. Fighting for breath, she balled the corner of the duvet up in one hand, as she wrenched the other through her hair. She knew the Elliotts would hunt him down. Whatever had possessed him to leave the Programme?

'Ben, answer the door, answer the door now.'

She was fighting for air, frantically clinging to the edges of sanity.

'Okay! Ssch!' whispered Ben. 'I'll go and see who it is.'

'It's the police,' she said, her teeth chattering. 'I...I...I know it is. It's the police. Tell them I'm not here. I don't want to know Carl's dead. I don't want to hear it.'

Ben went over to Sandra and held her, his fingers digging into the tops of her arms.

'Stop it, Rosie,' he said fiercely. 'We don't know who it is yet. Just shut-up and stay here.'

She slumped down onto the floor, where she lay hugging her knees to her chest.

She could just make out Ben zipping up his fly. He didn't waste time fastening his leather belt or putting on a top, he just strode over to the window where he parted the curtain fractionally.

'Is it the police?' she hissed.

'Can't see no-one,' he said, letting the curtain fall before making his way towards the door. 'No car, no flashing lights, nuffin'.'

As he stepped out onto the landing, the knock came again, this time it was louder and more rapid.

'Be careful, Ben.'

Sandra reached up for her pillow, pulled it down and hugged it to her as she heard Ben run downstairs and unbolt the front door. She had to go down and see what was happening.

She felt around for something to wear. Ben's shirt was first to hand. She got up and pulled it on as she tip-toed to the top of the stairs where she stood and held her breath, listening as the front door was unlocked and opened.

Immediately, there was shouting. Two voices. Ben was making the most noise but it was impossible to make out what he was saying. The other voice was too muffled to identify, just lots of yelling followed by a sickening thud.

Terrified for Ben's safety, Sandra skittered downstairs where she flicked on the living room light before running through the open door and into the garden.

Ben was sitting astride another man who was lying face down on the path. To Sandra's horror Ben was pulling his leather belt taut around his victim's neck making him thrash about frantically and grip the belt with both hands. However, the more he struggled, the more Ben clung to him with the skill and determination of a cow-boy on a bucking bronco.

From the light afforded through the open door, she could see Ben's face was ablaze with excitement, as if the act of attempting to kill had brought him to life. The other man remained pinned to the ground, emitting the most terrible rasps.

'Ben!' yelled Sandra. 'Stop! Get off him!'

Ben turned to look at her, giving his victim the opportunity to spin round and punch him in the throat. Ben's tongue shot from his mouth as his face reddened and he fell backwards, gagging.

The other man struggled to his feet, coughing then reached up, pulled back his hood and rubbed his muscular neck. It was then Sandra saw his dark hair but there was no disguising those long pale hands. She gasped, her whole body shaking, hardly daring to hope. Slowly, he turned to face her. She leapt towards him; her bare feet slipping on the moss covered paving stones.

'Carl, you've dyed your hair!' she exclaimed.

She hadn't seen her son in years, he had turned up unannounced in the middle of the night, her lover had all but killed him and all she could do was comment on the his hair colour? What was she thinking?

'Carl! My darling, are you okay?' she said hugging him and kissing his cold cheek.

He pushed her away forcefully. His thin, wiry body had become bulky and more muscular since she had last seen him, not like her Carl at all.

'What the fuck?' he asked looking at Ben.

'Oh love, I am so sorry. He thought someone was trying to break in.'

'Really? Intruders don't usually knock.'

She bustled around. Simultaneously, thrilled to see him but fearing for

178

his safety.

'What are you doing here? Didn't you get my message?'

'What message?' he asked as he coughed then spat onto the ground.

'I called you last night. Left a message on your landline.'

'I must've already left.'

He shrugged and ran the flat of his palm over his face. She flung her arms around him again causing him to wince.

'I'm sorry. Your neck must be sore,' she said brushing aside his hair to take a closer look.

Aghast at the sight of the red welts, she turned on Ben who was still doubled up on the grass.

'Look what you've done,' she screamed. 'You could've killed him. You could've killed my son.'

Ben groaned.

Carl laughed. It was a hollow sound. He pushed past Sandra and went into the cottage, still holding his neck. She followed him indoors unable to believe he was real, unable to believe he was really here. At last, she could see him, talk to him, touch him. Tentatively, she reached out and rested her palm on his forearm. He raised an eyebrow and she quickly removed her hand.

'Thank God you're safe. When the knock came, I didn't know what to think. I was worried it was the police coming to tell me something had happened to you.'

'Stop stressing. Thought you'd be pleased to see me.'

'I am, of course I am.'

She went to hug him but he backed away.

'My neck,' he said accusingly, holding his hand against his throat.

'Sorry, by the time I got downstairs …'

'... the bastard was trying to strangle me,' Carl interrupted looking at her disapprovingly. 'You should have warned me you had a Rottweiler.'

'But I didn't know you were coming, Carl.'

'Go and put something on for God's sake.'

She looked down to discover Ben's shirt had fallen open. Embarrassed, she immediately covered herself up. Carl looked at her and laughed.

'Oh, my God, Mum! I get it now. You're shagging him, aren't you? I know it's been a while but you didn't have to jump into bed with the first bloke who came along.'

'This is your son?' Ben asked incredulously as he staggered into the cottage.

'Yes, and you keep away from him. Don't touch him!' Sandra shouted, holding the folds of the shirt together with one hand, and thrusting the other in Ben's face.

'Well, how was I to know?'

'You only had to ask,' said Carl flatly pulling his Mother to one side. 'You wanna watch yourself. The bloke's a nutter. He tried to kill me. All I did was knock on the door.'

'Liar!' muttered Ben.

'Enough!' said Sandra.

'I thought he was our intruder,' persisted Ben.

'What?' asked Carl suddenly on edge.

'There is no intruder,' said Sandra. 'Ben just assumed it was someone trying to break-in. Anyway, it's all fine, Carl. You're here now and that's great. Why didn't you tell me you were coming? And why so late?'

'What does it matter, I haven't seen you for years?' asked Carl. 'Just go and put some bloody clothes on. I've told you once.'

Sandra gasped. What gave him the right to talk to her like that? She was about to say something then reminded herself to cut him some slack. Life had dealt him a duff hand. He was probably scared, just like she was. Why waste time arguing when all she wanted to do was love him?

Having shot Ben a glance to warn him off attacking Carl again, she ran upstairs. Quietly, she opened the wardrobe door, straining to hear what the two men were saying. She took off the shirt and picked out the first thing that came to hand, a wool dress. As she dragged it over her head, the zip caught in her hair. She went to cry out but stopped and silently pulled the dress down over her knees.

'Bit old for you, isn't she?' Carl asked Ben.

Hurt, she looked up to see her reflection in the mirror on the inside of the door. Eschewing Botox, her skin was more prune than plum and there was no denying the depressing line of liver spots on the left-hand side of her face. The only compliment she ever got these days was the stock back-hander: 'You're attractive, for your age.'

Feeling foolish, Carl's remark released the tears banked up since she saw him, standing there in her garden, her lover trying to throttle him. It was hardly surprising her emotions were in free-fall. What the hell was he doing, turning up out of the blue, in the middle of the night? With everything that had been going on, this was the last place he should be.

'Well, this is all very cosy, I must say,' Carl said, his voice shot through with sarcasm. 'Nice little love nest you've got here. Rent it by the hour, do you?'

'You little shit …'

Before Ben could finish, Sandra intervened and shouted down the stairwell.

'Carl! For God's sake, shut-up.'

Unable to contain her anger, she flew downstairs and into the living room. Ben, his head and shoulders lowered, looked like a bull ready to charge.

'Stop!' she shouted.

'But he called you a slag,' said Ben.

'Ah but you don't know my Mum like I do.'

'Carl. Not now,' she warned.

Only a few minutes earlier Ben had attempted to strangle her son, had she not stepped in there was no doubt in her mind he would've killed him. Her worst nightmare had almost become a reality, all because of a stranger, a murderer she had met on a train.

Suddenly, the room swam and she lost her balance.

'Grab her!' yelled Ben leaping up.

The next minute, Sandra felt his hands around her as he helped her to a chair.

'Get your Mum some water,' he ordered.

Carl did not move.

'I'm going to be sick,' cried Sandra, covering her mouth with her hand.

'Get a bucket! Anything!' demanded Ben.

Still Carl refused to move. Ben ran to the kitchen and returned moments later with the washing up bowl and a glass of water.

'Thanks,' she said taking a sip. 'I'll be fine.'

'You frightened the life out of me, Rosie.'

'Rosie?' scoffed Carl turning to look at them both. 'What's all that about? Her name's Sandra.'

Neither Sandra nor Ben spoke.

'Tut, tut. Have you been lying to your lover? Where's the integrity you like to ram down everyone's throat?'

'Don't speak to your Mother like that,' Ben said.

'Oh, drop the hard-man act.'

Sandra shook her head at Ben, silently imploring him not to react. Ben backed off.

'You've got him well-trained, Mum but then again you always were a control freak.'

'Shut-yer-mouth.'

'What you need to understand is that my Mum or should I say, 'Rosie', will always side with me. As a kid, she didn't so much mother me, as smother me.'

The criticism hurt her more than a physical blow. Something in his smug tone made her want to punch his contemptuous face but as she lurched forward, the room began to spin again. Luckily Ben was there to catch her.

'Come on, Rosie, sit down.'

Much to Sandra's surprise Carl bent down and hugged her but there was no warmth in his tight, hard embrace. She breathed him in wishing she could impart the love she had been unable able to give him for so long.

'Steady on, Mum, you'll make lover-boy here jealous,' he said, laughing and batting her away as if he was a celebrity and she just a crazed fan.

That was it. Sandra pulled away. It wasn't just his hair colour he had changed. She barely recognised this objectionable man as her son. What the hell had happened to him in the intervening years? Although loath to admit it, she struggled to find something to like about him.

'You really are sick,' said Ben.

Sandra's maternal instincts kicked in and she leapt to her son's defence.

'Leave him alone. He didn't mean anything.'

Bolstered by his Mother's support, Carl kept going.

'You heard her. In fact, I don't even know why you're here. Although I can make an educated guess which is more than you ever could.'

If Ben had picked up on the insult, he did not respond and for that Sandra was grateful. It had been one of the worst nights of her life; she just wanted it to end.

'I'm your Mum's friend,' said Ben simply. 'I'm here to look after her.'

'Well, I'm here now. Mum and I will be fine without you.'

'I'm not leaving unless yer Mum wants me to.'

Her son turned to look at her.

'Well?' he asked.

Chapter twenty-six

[Isle of Wight 2013]

'I'm very disappointed in you,' said Ben.

He was leaning over Sandra the second she woke, his face too close to hers.

'Sorry?' she asked somewhere between sleep and consciousness.

'You heard.'

His tone was harsh.

'I don't know what you're talking about.'

'Oh, I think you do. We agreed you weren't goin' call the police.'

'I haven't, I didn't, I ...' she faltered.

He held out the phone and jabbed at the display with his finger.

'Don't lie to me. You rang 'em last night at 10.14. There, look.'

'I didn't speak to them. Anyway, if I want to involve the police, I will. My son's here. His life could be in danger. I keep telling you, we need help, we can't do this on our own.'

'And I keep telling you, they're not going to help but you won't listen, will ya?'

Sandra tried to back away but he was on her, his face never less than three or four inches from hers.

'You disobeyed me, Rosie. I thought we were in this together. I thought you trusted me. But I suppose now yer son's 'ere you don't need me anymore. I might as well just piss off.'

'Ben...'

'Forget it,' he said, throwing the phone onto the bed and walking out of the room.

She picked up the handset, more determined than ever to ring the police. Something had to be done. The stakes were too high but before she spoke to the police, she needed to talk to Carl.

He kept her waiting until later that afternoon before he finally got up and appeared in the kitchen with his hair on end just how she remembered.

'You must've needed that sleep,' she ventured.

When he ignored her, she cut to the chase.

'So, Carl, what are you doing here? And why all the secrecy?'

'Where d'you keep the coffee?' he asked opening all the cupboards in quick succession.

'I've only got tea,' she said switching on the kettle.

He pulled out a chair and sat slumped over the table.

'So?' she prompted.

'So what?'

'Why are you here?'

She needed to know. His arrival had made a dangerous situation untenable.

'I've left the Programme, you know that. No police, no rules, no holds barred. I can do what I like, go where I want, see who I want. And I wanted to see you but I can go if you prefer. I don't want to interrupt anything,' he said sarcastically pushing back his chair.

There was something he wasn't telling her, she was sure of that.

'Don't be silly. I'm just worried because the situation ... it's not safe.'

'Give it a rest.'

Unfortunately, what should have been a loving conversation between her and her son turned into a one-sided interrogation.

'How's your girlfriend? Debs, isn't it?'

She made the tea and set a mug down in front of him.

'Is she okay? Pregnancy going well?'

'Fine,' he yawned, his tone low and patronising.

'So why didn't you let me know you were coming?'

He took a mouthful of tea then made a face.

'I don't take sugar anymore.'

Sandra ignored the comment.

'A spoonful of sugar is the least of your worries.'

'For God's sake. No-one saw me come here and even if they did they wouldn't have recognised me...' Carl pulled his hood up over his head, demonstrating how well it concealed his face making him look like just another street rat. '... and I got the night ferry and a cab here. Got him to drop me at the bottom of the lane. I was virtually the only one on the boat so you can stop worrying, can't you? But if I'd known I'd be greeted by a fucking nutter trying to kill me, I wouldn't have bothered.'

'How's your neck?' she asked noticing how the bruising had come out and looked far worse it did last night. 'Sorry, we thought you were an intruder.'

'Intruders don't knock.'

'True but it was late, you frightened the life out of us.'

'As warm welcomes go, it sucked.'

She smiled at him.

'Oh Carl. I have missed you.'

'Oh Mother,' he said mocking and mimicking her tone.

'So why did you come here?' asked Ben suddenly appearing noiselessly in the kitchen making Sandra start.

She hated the way he did that, crept up on her when she least expected it.

'Oh! It speaks!' exclaimed Carl. 'You have trained him well, Mum.'

'Stop it. For God's sake.'

Sandra tried to convince herself his attitude was all a front, just his way of coping. It had to be. He must have had to toughen up to cope with his life under the strict rules of the Programme. Stripped of his name, his home and his job, his past had been torn up and his future rewritten. She opened her arms but he just smirked at her.

'It's not me you want to hug, is it?' he said looking at Ben. 'It's him.'

'Why have you come here?' she asked exasperated.

Despite her instinct to make it all better, she couldn't; he was no longer a child. He was a grown man and, from what she could see, not a very nice one.

Ben looked at Carl. Sandra positioned herself between them.

'Heel!' sneered Carl. 'Good boy.'

Sandra, who was finding the dog analogy increasingly irritating, turned to Ben.

'Can you nip down the road and get some milk, we've run out?'

'Fetch!'

'Shut it,' snarled Ben under his breath as he walked towards the back door.

'Did you just tell me to 'Shut it'? God! I feel like I've walked into an episode of 'The Sweeney,' Carl laughed as Ben slammed out of the house.

Sandra pulled up a chair next to him. For the first time, she noticed how shattered he looked.

'Something's happened, hasn't it? I warned you not to leave the Programme.'

She silently admonished herself for saying: I told you so.

'Fancy a drink?' she asked joylessly getting up and taking a bottle of wine from the fridge and filling two glasses to the brim with wine. If he drank enough he might relax and open up to her.

'Bit early, isn't it?'

'Oh come on,' she said sitting down and handing him the glass. 'It's not every day my son pays me a visit. Cheers!'

She lifted her glass and nodded at him to do the same.

'Thanks for coming, Carl.'

'God Mum, you've got a problem. You always liked a drink but...' he broke off and pushed his glass away.

He shook his head as she downed her drink.

'Have a drink with me,' she ordered, draining her glass then instantly refilling it.

Carl refused and the pair sat in silence. The only sound was his heel tapping ceaselessly against the leg of his chair. She fixed her eyes on the door, desperate for Ben to come back. Fortunately, she didn't have to wait long. He arrived five minutes later carrying a plastic bottle of milk and a loaf of bread.

'Everything alright?' he demanded when he saw Sandra's glass.

He unscrewed the lid of the milk before slamming the bottle down on the table with such force the milk spurted up into Carl's face.

'Sorry about that, mate,' he said with sly sarcasm.

'What the …?'

Carl stood up, milk dripping down his front. 'You …'

Sandra grabbed a tea-towel and gave it to him. He dabbed at his tea-shirt before hurling the cloth on the floor.

'Let's all have a nice drink and calm down. Yes? No? Just me then,' she said taking a mouthful of wine, her hand going for the wine bottle.

Ben picked it up and placed it out of her reach.

'Hey! Give that back. If I want a drink, I'll have one.'

Carl gave her one of his disapproving looks. She didn't like being judged by her own son.

'Mum, I don't know what your problem is but you're doing my head in. I'm going back to bed; I'm knackered.'

'Whatever. We can talk later,' she said Sandra swigging back her drink.

'Later? You mean he's staying?' asked Ben incredulously.

'He's my son, of course he's staying!'

Sandra watched as Carl helped himself to a wizened-looking orange from the fruit-bowl. He peeled it, removing the skin slowly in one long spiral that he dropped onto the table. Then he ate the orange, segment by segment, turning occasionally to spit the pips into the sink. His eyes danced mischievously as if daring his mother to reprimand him but the wine had mellowed Sandra. After a few glasses, the world seemed a better place.

'So how come you're here and yer girlfriend ain't?' Ben asked.

'Not now; he's said he's tired.'

'For fuck sake, Rose! Tell 'im.'

'Tell me what?'

Sandra looked at Ben.

'Mum? What is it?'

'Rosie, stop pussy-footing around him. You can't sit here playing happy-fucking-families.'

'Shut-up!' she cried covering her face with her hands. 'Just shut-up.' Carl ran the tip of his tongue over his upper lip.

'What's he going on about?' he demanded, his tone no longer complacent but fearful.

'Nothing, nothing for you to worry about,' she replied airily.

She took a step towards the door. Carl pulled her back.

'I'm not fucking six-years-old anymore. Tell me what's going on.'

'Everything's fine,' she replied.

'Fine? It's because of him you're in this mess, fucking tell him.'

Sandra was sweating even though the cottage was cold. Everyone was in danger and there was nothing she could do about it. Suddenly, her legs gave way as the floor moved from under her. She grabbed the back of a chair.

'Jesus, Mum, you're drunk.'

'You little shit. Your Mum's had a lot to deal with. She's got a stalker. He's been terrifying the life out of her. And he's been in the house.'

'What here?'

Ben nodded.

'Yeah, and he's been to her work.'

Carl looked at his Mother.

'What the fuck? Why didn't you tell me? I would never have come.'

Clearly, his selfishness knew no bounds.

'I didn't dream you would turn up in the middle of the night, unannounced. Besides, I didn't want to worry you and ...' she paused and looked at his dark hair, dyed an unconvincing shade of black suddenly remembering her conversation with her boss. 'Did you... have you ever been to my work?'

'No, of course not. Why would I?'

'Just... oh nothing, I just thought...'

'Our little visitor has got a knife,' interrupted Ben.

'How do you know? Have you seen him?'

'Yer Mum's carving knife's gone. No, we ain't seen him.'

'Have you told the police?' Carl asked clearly on edge, agitated.

'Yes, but they can't help because he hasn't actually done anything,' said Sandra slurring her words.

'Any idea who it might be?'

'No but he's posing as you. That's what he said when he went to the hospital,' said Ben. 'But apparently he's a good-looking bloke and you're an ugly fucker.'

Sandra leapt up and slapped his face. Ben did not flinch. It was as if his cheek was made of steel.

'I reckon it's your mates, the Elliotts,' said Ben.

Carl went white and his body shook uncontrollably.

'The Elliotts. How d'you know about them?' he whispered.

Ben glanced at Sandra.

'You told him? What did you do that for?'

'Don't have a go at yer Mum. It's my fault. I forced her to tell me. If I was going to protect her I needed to know everything.'

Sandra regretted hitting him. It had been a terrible mistake; she could see that now.

'I'm sorry.'

'Don't worry about it.'

'I'd like some time with Carl. Can you give us a minute?'

He nodded.

'Call me if you need me,' he said, his hand on the banister.

Carl drummed his fingers on the table. Every time she thought he had stopped, he would start again. Then he suddenly reached into his back pocket, pulled out a white crumpled envelope and handed it to her.

'What's this?' she asked recoiling.

'Just open it.'

He didn't sound like Carl; his voice was too thin and reedy. As she took the envelope it was as if his fear had transferred to her. Her hand was shaking.

The envelope was addressed to Carl, at his new home in Primrose Hill. The handwriting was unfamiliar, big and loopy with a pronounced back-slant.

Tentatively, she reached inside and carefully slid out a card. At first glance, the picture seemed innocent enough, a drawing of a stork flying across a blue cloudless sky, a white fluffy bundle in its beak. She read the message quickly, it was equally unremarkable, picked out in simple blue lettering across the top:

Congratulations on the birth of your baby.

Confused, she looked to Carl for an explanation.

'Sorry, I don't understand.'

'For fuck's sake! Read the bloody thing!' he shouted.

She opened the card and looked inside. It was blank.

'Sorry, I ...'

'Look! Here!' he said stabbing at the greeting with his forefinger.

There, crudely inserted between the words 'your' and 'baby' and written in the same hand, with the same ballpoint pen was one of the most powerful words in the English language. Just four letters but the last adjective anyone would want to use to describe a baby.
'Dead.'

'Congratulations on the birth of your dead baby.'

Her hands flew to her face, as the card fell to the floor. Carl picked it up, stuffed it back in the envelope and into his pocket.

'What do I do, Mum?' he asked, his callow mask slipping to reveal the terrified young man beneath.

'I don't know. This is awful. Is that it or has there been anything else?' she asked, her voice breaking.

'That's enough, isn't it? Or would you prefer they sent a wreath too?'

'Carl, I ...'

He interrupted her.

'There's no postmark. It was hand-delivered. Whoever it was came to my house. It's got to be the Elliotts.'

'Has Debs seen it?' she asked anxiously.

He shook his head.

'But, she needs to know she's in danger. You have to tell her, Carl.'

He was tapping his foot on the floor.

'For God's sake, Carl. I can't believe you've left her alone. She's carrying your child.'

'Never mind about her. It's me they're after.'

'And your baby by the sound of it.'

His attitude was unbelievable. In the past, she had always made excuses for him. Blaming the fact he came from a broken home and had her for a mother and a cold fish for a father. But the days of letting him get away with his callous behaviour were over. There were too many other people involved.

'Where's Debs?' she demanded. 'Not in the house alone, is she? Somewhere safe, yeah?'

He hung his head, his face concealed behind his long fringe.

Suddenly Ben reappeared making Sandra jump. She had not heard him come back down the stairs. For such a big man he had an unnerving ability to move noiselessly about the cottage.

'Where the fuck is she?' Ben demanded, looking as if he wanted to crush the life out of Carl.

Chapter twenty-seven

[Isle of Wight 2013]

'Are you mad, Carl?' asked Sandra jumping up, her heart beating too fast. 'Debs can't come here. It's not safe. The Elliotts are onto us. God knows how long they've been watching me.'

'How was I supposed to know? You never said.'

Slumped on the chair, his hair over his eyes, it was difficult to read his expression. His tone was a clearer indicator of his mood, petulant and resentful.

'They'll be watching you now,' said Ben. 'They know you're 'ere. Yer can bet yer life on it. Go now, while you still can.'

He shook his head.

'I can't.'

'You don't wanna mess with 'em. They would've known the minute you got 'ere. Bet they've been onto you since you left the Programme.'

Sandra suspected Ben's motives for wanting rid of Carl were not entirely concerned with his welfare. She took hold of her son's hand.

'Look, I'm sorry but you can't stay here and neither can Debs. It's not safe.'

By way of reply, he tapped his feet on the floor, the uneven beat adding to the tension.

'As soon as that card came I knew they were onto me. I had to get out. This was the first place I thought of. Somewhere remote, somewhere no-one knew me.'

Sandra placed her hand on his thigh. She hoped it came across as supportive but really she just wanted to try and stop his leg from shaking. It was driving her mad.

'You're not listening to me. This isn't just about you. You have got to look after Debs, she's your main priority, her and your baby.'

'Yeah, yer Mum's right.'

Carl thumped the table with his fist making Sandra jump.

'But I've got nowhere else to go,' he whined. 'We can do this together, look after each other, like we used to, eh? Let's tell the police, they'll help us. Please Mum.'

The word 'Mum' embedded itself in her heart, like a pearl in an oyster, softening her soul. She could see Ben was watching her closely, all the while tearing and chewing at his cuticles.

Keeping Carl concealed at the cottage was not the answer. The problem was she had no idea what the solution might be.

'Listen,' she said forcing him to look her in the eye. 'Debs can't come here. Do you understand?'

'It's too late. She's on her way.'

'What? You've got to stop her.'

Events were unfolding too quickly and nothing she said or did could prevent them hurtling to a conclusion no-one wanted.

'Phone her and tell 'er not to come,' ordered Ben. 'She must 'ave mates or family she can stay with?'

Carl shook his head.

'She's only got me.'

'God help her,' muttered Ben,

Carl shot him a look as he tap-tapped his feet to a new, even more erratic rhythm.

'How about I put you both up in a hotel for a few days?' suggested Sandra. 'Just until you sort yourselves out?'

'Are you kidding? We'd be sitting ducks. They must've...

TAP

...been keeping...

TAP

... tabs on...

TAP

... me for...

TAP

... a while and...
TAP.

'For fuck's sake, stop that!' yelled Sandra. 'For once in your life, accept you're wrong and do the right thing.'

TAP. TAP. TAP.

Her head began to throb. She pressed her fingertips against her temples. It was impossible to think clearly when a man with a knife was running amok in her head.

'Why the hell did you have to leave the Programme and get some poor girl pregnant? What were you thinking? But that's just it, isn't it? You weren't thinking. You just did what you wanted to do and to hell with everyone else. You haven't given me or your girlfriend a second thought, let alone your unborn child.'

'Finished?' Carl asked.

TAP. TAP. TAP.

She rushed at him over the kitchen table. He reared backwards.

'Oh my God. You're fucking crazy,' he sniggered. 'Calm down, Mother, you've got to be careful at your age; you'll give yourself a heart attack.'

She wanted to slap him.

'Have you told yer girlfriend anything about your past?' asked Ben.

'No, of course not. I'm not a fool.'

'Oh, I think that's exactly what you are,' said Ben. 'Leaving the Programme, getting some girl up the duff, turning up 'ere uninvited, you're a bloody idiot.'

'This is none of your business,' replied Carl.

'It is his business, very much so,' she said her voice spiralling out of control. 'You see, he's here, looking after me, protecting me. You could learn a lot from him, Carl. Oh, yes, remind me, what does Debs think your name is? Steve? Sean? No, hang on. It's 'Sam', isn't it? She thinks you're called Sam. The mother of your child doesn't even know your real name let alone what you're caught up in. Start as you mean to go on, Carl? Or should I say Sam?'

'Shut up, you thick bitch.'

She could hear the insult long after he had spoken it. It wormed its way into the corners of her mind where it infected even the happiest memories. Too shocked to respond, Ben spoke for her.

'Oi! Apologise. Now.'

It was asking too much of the word 'sorry'. It was not enough to heal the hurt.

'What did you just call me?' she asked incredulously not imagining he would dare to repeat the insult.

'Thick bitch.'

He spoke the words as if they had no meaning.

'Let me at him,' said Ben.

'Don't touch me.'

'You called me a thick bitch?' she asked the anger taking hold, burning like a flame inside her.

He nodded as if he had paid her a compliment.

This was not her son talking. He sounded more like her ex-husband.

'I think you're the 'thick' one,' she told him. 'Now you shut-up and listen to me. Debs is not coming here. No way. Either you tell her or I will tell her everything.'

'Please Mum, don't.'

This time the word 'Mum' did not have the desired effect. Instead of wrapping itself around her heart like an embrace, making her yield to his wishes like it once did, it stuck to her insides like a layer of fat clogging her vital organs.

'Okay, I can't do this anymore. I'm going to do what I should have done when all this started, I'm going to call the police.'

'No,' shouted Ben. 'I keep telling yer, they won't help yer.'

'They will now Carl's here.'

Even Sandra was surprised at how controlled she sounded.

'I told you I'd sort this and I will,' said Ben.

'What...

TAP

...are...

TAP
...you...

TAP
...saying?'

Ben smirked and drew his finger across his throat.

'No!' screamed Sandra. 'You can't, not again.'

'Oh my God. You mean he's killed before? You've shacked up with a fucking murderer?'

'That's right. Even more reason not to bring your precious girlfriend 'ere.'

Carl laughed, an unnerving rattle as he stretched his lips into a long thin smile.

'Oh that's just where you're wrong. Our very own resident killer? I've lucked out. Looks like I couldn't have picked a safer place.'

A confused expression fogged Ben's features.

'Am I going too fast for you?' asked Carl sarcastically. 'Let me explain. You are going to protect me and Debs. You are going to be our bodyguard. And if you have to, you're going to take a bullet for us.'

Sandra gasped. This was not her life. All this talk of cutting throats and taking bullets was alien to her. Ben began to shout.

'No way. You can't stay 'ere. And neither can your girlfriend.'

He used his rough and ready accent like a weapon before pushing the heel of his hand into Carl's chest.

'You don't get it, do you?' Carl said calmly removing Ben's hand. 'You're the hired gun. It's your job to look after the three of us, four when the baby's born.'

'I don't take my orders from you,' Ben spat before charging out of the house.

Sandra's heart was beating double-fast. What if he didn't come back? She couldn't cope without him. She looked at Carl; he was no use. She needed Ben.

'Now look what's happened. Well done, Carl.'

He shrugged.

This was not the homecoming she had pictured for her son. Where there should have been love, there was loathing and instead of happiness only fear. In the intervening years it appeared Carl had become less of a boy but not more of a man.

Her cold attitude rocked her to the core. How could she love her son but not like him? It made no sense. Such feelings couldn't be natural, could they? The guilt weighed heavily on her, making her head spin and chest ache.

She sat down and tried to rearrange her thoughts into some sort of maternal order. It wasn't easy. Whether she liked it or not, her boy was low and cunning. She wouldn't put anything past him.

'Debs will be here soon,' Carl announced as if he was in charge. 'Don't you dare say anything to her.'

She stared at him in disbelief.

'Oh don't worry. I'm not going to tell her anything. You are.'

'No!' he protested, running his fingers through his long, floppy fringe and pulling it back to reveal his twisted features.

She held his gaze for longer than was comfortable eventually forcing him to look away.

'Phone her and tell her the truth.'

'For God's sake, Mum. Why are you being like this?'

Over the years, she had discovered that sometimes saying nothing gave her all the power where her son was concerned. Without her words to twist, he had nothing to use against her.

He tried all his usual tricks to try and goad her into retaliating: sneering, smirking, finally jabbing his finger in her face then, when that didn't work, shouldering past her. But this wasn't some tin-pot row about him not doing his homework; this was serious, she needed to remain steadfast.

She watched as he slid his phone from his pocket, scrolled down and clicked. She had won. He was going to do what she wanted.

'If she leaves me, it'll be your fault. Don't blame me if you never see your grandchild.'

Emotional blackmail. She wasn't falling for it.

'Text her and tell her to go home or I will tell her everything.'

'Why would you do that? You are such a bitch. This is my chance. Fresh fucking start. Clean slate. All that shit. Please, Mum.'

His mood was all over the place, swinging between audacious insults to pathetic pleading. He was close to tears as his fingers hovered over the keys.

'Your relationship is a sham. You've chosen to live on the edge but you can't expect her to do the same. You might be able to justify involving her in all this, but I can't. I will not stand by and watch you screw up not only your life but hers and my grandchild's.'

That was her best shot.

'You don't know her. Debs will do anything for me. She loves me.'

The misuse of the word 'love' got to her, shredding her nerves as easily as a fork through slow roasted pork.

'She loves Sam, not Carl. She doesn't even know who Carl is.'

'Don't ruin this for me.'

'Oh you don't need my help, you're doing a very good job yourself,' she looked at him, searching his face for clues as to what he might be thinking.

Nothing. Sandra never had been very good at reading him and was just desperate to provoke a reaction to make him see sense.

'Do you love her?'

He refused to meet her gaze and put his phone back in his pocket.

'I thought not. For God's sake, you don't care about her at all, do you? You're just using her.'

'Yada, yada, yada! You're not going to say anything to her; you wouldn't dare. We both know you'll welcome her with open arms when she walks through that door and Lover-Boy is going to make sure no one harms a hair on her head. You can't just throw her and your grand-child to the wolves.'

He was standing beside her, his long bony finger inches from her face.

She took a step back but he pursued her and drove her into the wall, the impact sending shards of chalk crumbling to the floor.

'Carl, stop it.'

'Carl, stop it,' he parroted. 'You don't get to tell me what to do anymore. All your 'do the right thing' crap. Look where that got me. Thanks to you I turned into the Invisible-fucking-Man. I've lost years of my life, thanks to you, hidden away in a shit house, in a shit place in a shit job.'

'You did the right thing. You'd seen a murder; you had to speak out. Thanks to you, that poor woman who lost her son got some justice.'

The same old speech, even she was tired of hearing it.

'Oh, shut-up.'

He wasn't getting it.

'I don't think you understand, I've been under siege in this house.'

Her voice sounded coarse and strained.

'It's been terrifying. I can't put you and Debs through that. Thank God Ben was here otherwise I would've had to have coped all on my own.'

'And we all know whose fault that is.'

'Not mine.'

'Keep telling yourself that, Mum. But from where I'm standing you ruined my fucking life. Not content with forcing me to go to the police and give evidence, you cut off my fucking allowance, didn't you?'

'You've got a nerve. Your new job paid well enough. Anyway, I couldn't afford to keep putting money into your account, not once I gave up my job in London.'

'It was your way of trying to punish me.'

'Don't be silly. We both had to make sacrifices.'

She gestured to the simple interior with its shabby, down at heel furnishings.

'But living here was your choice. You didn't have to get out of London. I did. You could've stayed in your big house with your fancy job and snobby friends.'

'I couldn't, not after everything that had gone on. Besides with you gone, I had nothing to keep me there. I'm sorry things worked out they way they did for you.'

'So am I,' said Carl walking away and plonking himself on the sofa.

She sat down tentatively beside him.

'At first, I had no idea who was stalking me. It took me a while to make the connection between you leaving the Programme and the Elliotts coming here to find you. I guess I didn't want it to be them. The thought was too terrifying.'

'It might not be them.'

'It must be. It's too much of a coincidence otherwise. But, I don't understand. You must have known they would find you once you went back to London? With their connections, they would've known the second you got on the Tube.'

'If it is them, I'm sure they're just trying to frighten me. Get me off their patch,' he said sounding like a cocky teenager.

Who did he think he was kidding?

'Get you off their patch? What d'you mean?' she asked suspiciously. 'Your evidence got one of their family put away for life, surely they want rid of you, full stop?'

He looked at her but said nothing, lifting the toe of his shoe as if preparing to break into another tapping session. Her nerves stood to attention, waiting.

'No, they just want me out of London.'

'Bullshit,' said Ben suddenly appearing behind him.

Again, she wondered how long Ben had been in the house, concealed, listening to her conversation. He should wear bells, like a Morris Dancer. At least that way, she could hear him coming.

'Don't kid yerself, they want you dead, mate. It only takes one bent copper to tell 'em you left the Programme and they'd be straight onto yer. Don't take a genius to work out you'd head back to London, and sooner or later turn up at yer Mum's.'

'He's right. Look at that disgusting card they sent. They're animals. You know that.'

Ben sidled up to Carl, his voice a low growl.

'I've done a bit of thinking and I reckon I've sussed what's goin' on. You're just using Debs to protect yerself. You know there's no way even the Elliotts would take a pop at a pregnant woman. I'm right, aren't I?'

Sandra gasped. It was true; she could tell by Carl's expression. Before she could say anything, his phone buzzed. He clicked on the display.

'Text from Deb's. She's in a cab heading to Portsmouth. Be here in about four hours.'

'A taxi all the way from London? Blimey, that's goin' cost her,' commented Ben.

'It's small change to her.'

'Ah, I geddit, so she's loaded,' said Ben.

'Well, no-one's queuing up to offer me a job. I've got a degree but even I can't ...'

'You're unbelievable. There's no way I am going to be party to this,' said Sandra.

'Tell her not to get on that ferry.'

She caught hold of his arm, pulled him to his feet and marched him over to the door.

'You can't do this. If anything happens to Debs or the baby, it'll be your fault,' he said. 'You can't just abandon me and your grandchild.'

She faltered. He was right. What was she thinking? Had she really spent a lifetime caring for her son only to turn her back on him when he needed her the most? There was no way she could send him out there to his death. She had to look after him and his girlfriend. They could stay. Just for a while.

'Okay you can both stop here, just for a few days, until you sort yourselves out,' she looked at Ben, imploring him to help.

Much to her relief and surprise, he was quick to nod in agreement

'If that's what your Mum wants, I'll protect yer, on one condition. You do what I say. That means you stop blaming yer Mum for everything. It ain't her fault yer life's shit. Say yer sorry.'

Carl nodded, his black fringe flicking in and out of his eyes.

'Sorry. Can I go now? I need some space. I'll be in my room if you want me.'

He had only been here five minutes and had already commandeered the spare room.

Immediately, she ran to the sink and threw up. It was just bile, her stomach was raw and empty. She turned on the tap and splashed cold water on her face as she blinked back the tears.

Had her life unravelled to such an extent, she didn't know where she began or ended anymore? Worse was to come, she was sure of that. Everyone was in position, just like the pieces in her ex-husband's chess set, ready and waiting to be knocked off the board.

Chapter twenty-eight

[Isle of Wight 2013]

The Elliotts must know Carl was here and Debs on her way. They had probably sent the card deliberately to frighten him and flush him out and were outside right now, lying in wait.

Sitting in her room, Ben dozing on the bed, she mulled over the problems, pulling them apart until they became such a mess as to be unsolvable.

Why had she agreed to let Carl and his girlfriend stay? She had no choice. She couldn't just let them take their chances with the Elliotts, could she? Yet, a pregnant woman in the midst of this mayhem was madness. Debs would be here soon. Once she arrived Carl would have to step up and look after her. She was his responsibility, not hers.

Then again, why bother coming here at all? The cottage wasn't safe; she knew that. If Carl hurried, he could get to Portsmouth before Debs and the pair of them could travel back to London together.

She crossed the landing to tell him, tapping urgently on the door then waiting a few moments before pushing it open. She could just make out a shape under the duvet.

'Carl, are you awake?'

When he didn't answer, she took a closer look. The bed was empty.

'Carl! Where are you?'

He must have got up to use the toilet. She went across to the bathroom and listened at the door. Silence. Panicking, she skidded downstairs, her feet missing the last step. The living room and kitchen were both empty.

Where the hell was he?

'Come on, come on, for God's sake,' she cursed as her fingers worked frantically to free the new locks on the back door.

Drawing back the last bolt, she pulled on the handle but the door would not budge.

'The key! Where's the bloody key? Ben! Where's the back door key. Ben!' she yelled, opening drawers and cupboards and pulling out the contents onto the floor. 'Carl's gone! Ben!'

She ran upstairs. A sudden noise made her pause outside the bathroom. Tentatively, she pushed the door. It swung open. Her hand reached for the cord. The strip light flickered into life illuminating the small, sterile space. Someone had pulled the shower curtain taut along the length of the bath. Her heart thudding and her hand shaking, she gripped the curtain and yanked it back to discover Carl with his eyes closed and the water up around his neck.

She caught her breath. There was no doubt in her mind. He was dead.

'Carl! No! God no!'

She fell forwards and reached out to pull him out. He opened his eyes and looked at her.

'What the hell?'

'I was worried about you. I checked your room and when you weren't there I just thought ...'

He yawned, making no attempt to take the towel she was holding out to him. 'Well, I can't get out with you standing there, can I?'

He waved her away as she left, embarrassed at being made a fool of.

When she went back to her room, Ben was snoring. How could he sleep through all that? It was hardly reassuring. What if Carl really had gone missing? What if Elliott had turned up? She grabbed his shoulder and shook him awake.

'What?' he asked opening his eyes.

'Didn't you hear? I've been going crazy. I thought Carl had been taken.'

'Taken Carl? Nah, no-one would want him. Ssch, Rosie. Go to sleep.'

With that he closed his eyes again. It was pointless trying to talk to him. Sure enough, within seconds his breathing changed and she could tell he was asleep. It annoyed her. Really annoyed her. She went to punch his arm then realised how tired she was. The stress of Carl's arrival had taken its toll. She lay down next to him and closed her eyes. But as she drifted off to sleep, she was greeted by the now familiar disembodied voice, lodged like a bullet in her brain, the one that liked to blame and shame her.

'Look what you've done, bitch. Happy now? You've surpassed yourself this time. Your son, his girlfriend, your grandchild, even your boyfriend, their lives hanging in the balance because of you.

How does that make you feel? Proud?

I can't help you in your quest to 'do the right thing'. As you know only too well, I am only concerned with the wrong thing. A concept your son is all too familiar with. You have been apart for some time, soon you will be together for eternity.

Welcome to hell. I hope you'll be very unhappy here. Please let me know if there's anything I can do to make your stay even more unbearable. I wish you a miserable time.'

Thankfully, Sandra was ejected from her nightmare the moment the knock came. Carl must have been waiting downstairs because the door was answered almost immediately.

'You're late. What happened?'

'Oh Sam, I have missed you,' said a well-spoken female voice. 'I told you we should have travelled down together. I have had the worst journey ever.'

She over-emphasised the word 'ever' making her sound slightly American and she called him 'Sam', the girl didn't even know his name let alone what she was getting messed up in.

'It's okay, Debs, you're here now. Come on in, Babes.'

'Babes'? Since when was Carl given to terms of endearment?

Sandra got out of bed and ran across the landing to the top of the stairs where she stood quietly and listened.

'The cab fare cost a fortune. We got stuck in traffic. Oh my God, it was awful. The whole of south London was gridlocked. It took over twenty minutes to cross Battersea Bridge. Then, we'd just got out of London when the baby started pressing on my bladder making me want to pee! At one point I thought I was going to have to wee in my handbag!'

'Never mind, you're here now.'

He already sounded bored.

'By the time we got to Portsmouth, we'd missed our ferry and had to wait ages for the next one. I fell sleep. The driver had to wake me up because for some reason we weren't allowed to stay in the cab on the crossing. Then, when we finally got to the island, it took ages to get here. Why does your Mum want to live in the middle of nowhere?'

'Ask her yourself. She can't wait to meet you.'

Sandra shrunk back, hoping he wouldn't dart upstairs to fetch her. Thankfully, Debs sounded more considerate.

'Oh don't disturb her, please. She's probably in bed now, isn't she? She's not well; let her rest. How is she at the moment? Still imagining all sorts?'

'Y'know how it is, some days are better than others. She doesn't know what she's saying half the time so if she comes out with anything weird, humour her and go along with it.'

Sandra bridled. So he was still peddling the line she was unstable. What the hell was he playing at?

'Anyway, she asked me to let her know the minute you arrived. I'll get her and she can make us something to eat.'

'No she can't,' thought Sandra, furious with Carl for even suggesting such a thing.

Again, Debs was having none of it.

'Don't disturb your poor Mum. It's way too early. I'm not hungry, I had something on the boat.'

'It's fine. She has problems sleeping; it's the medication. She'll be glad of something to do.'

'Okay but hang on, I haven't had a kiss yet.'

'Ow! Careful! We mustn't harm the baby,' he said, sounding just like his father.

'Sam, don't be so silly! A little hug won't hurt her.'

Sandra couldn't take any more and walked as calmly as she could down the stairs.

'Hello there, you must be Deborah,' she said warmly.

With her lustrous hair and perfect complexion, the girl was beautiful. The photograph Carl had sent did not do her justice.

'Call her, Debs, everyone else does,' said Carl dismissively.

She kissed Sandra's cheek and grasped her hand, the diamonds glinting on her fingers and the Tiffany bracelet jangling expensively from her wrist.

'Hello, how lovely to meet you, Sandra. Sorry to turn up without an invite. Blame Sam. It was his idea!' she smiled, looking up lovingly at him.

'Pleased to meet you, Debs. Yes, Car… Sam … Sam…can be very spontaneous.'

He shot his mother a look as Debs bobbed down and unzipped her little case on wheels.

'Oh! Here, I've brought you a gift, just some bubbly and chocolates.'

She produced a bottle and a box of Fortnum and Mason fondant creams and handed them to Sandra.

'Sorry, not very inspiring, but if you're anything like me, you'll love them. The raspberry ones are to die for.'

'Oh thank-you, that's very kind of you,' she said taking the presents while examining the exquisite packaging. 'Wow, Dom Perignon, how lovely. And these chocolates, my favourites …I used to buy them all the time when I lived in London. How did you know?'

She looked at Carl in the vain hope he had been considerate enough to tell her.

'Just a lucky guess!' exclaimed Debs. 'Then again, you can't go wrong with chocs and champagne, can you? I would've got you roses too but I didn't think they would survive the journey.'

'I love roses,' she said touching the floral pendant at her throat.

'That's pretty.'

Debs stepped forward to take a closer look.

'Yes, it's lovely, isn't it? It was a gift from… my son,' Sandra replied unable to bring herself to call him 'Sam'.

Carl pretended not to hear as he disappeared upstairs with Debs' case. When he came back down he was decidedly upbeat.

'How about I make us all some tea? I can do some scrambled eggs too if you like?'

It was the first time her son had ever offered to make her a cup of tea, let alone something to eat. She assumed the sudden character change was for his girlfriend's benefit and not hers.

She seemed pleasant enough and with her perfect features and beautiful figure, it was obvious why Carl liked her but she wondered how he coped with the incessant chattering. Her obvious wealth probably helped.

'Come and sit down, Debs,' she said suddenly feeling sorry for the poor girl with her long thin legs looking like they might snap under the weight of her swollen belly.

'So why didn't you two travel down together? It's a long way to come on your own,' asked Sandra determined to find out the truth.

She took Debs gently by the arm and guided her towards the sofa. Carl's face appeared around the door, glaring at his mother.

'I told you, Mum I was down this way catching up with a mate. I could have crashed at his for the night but I thought you'd rather I came straight here.'

He sounded so plausible.

'Excuse me, where's your loo?' Debs asked.

'Upstairs, straight ahead.'

'Thanks.'

Carl waited until he was certain she was out of earshot before rounding on his Mother.

'Shut the fuck up.'

'Don't speak to me like that. I'm keeping a very big secret for you. I don't like lying to her. It's not right.'

'Bit late for integrity. You've already told her my name is Sam.'

'Your lie, not mine. I just want to keep you both safe but God knows how.'

The last thing this killer cocktail needed was a pregnant woman in the mix. She tugged her hands through her hair.

'You've gone grey,' he commented, seemingly oblivious to his part in her premature ageing.

Sandra ignored the remark. She had more important things to worry about.

'So how much does Debs know?'

'How much do I know about what?' asked Debs, as she came down the stairs.

'Looking after a baby,' Carl replied without missing a beat.

Sandra was horrified the way he could easily make a lie sound like the truth.

'Mum was just wondering how you were going to cope, weren't you Mum?'

She refused to be drawn in as she heard him bring the lie to life.

'Obviously, when it comes to kids, she's been there, done it, got the T-shirt, haven't you Mum? Anything you need to know, she's your girl.'

He spun round, a clown-like grin on his face and pointed both index fingers at Sandra. It was intolerable to watch him being so false and jovial. If she could see through the act, why the hell couldn't Debs?

'Oh, you don't want me interfering; I am sure you would rather ask your own mother for advice,' she said trying to avoid the issue.

Debs looked away and gripped Carl's hand. He made a show of putting a protective arm around her shoulders.

'Debs' Mother is dead. You know that. I told you. I put it in the letter, remember?'

Sandra was upset with herself. With everything that had been going on she had forgotten. But there was no excuse.

'Sorry about that, Debs. I told you Mum gets confused. It's not her fault,' Carl said enjoying having the upper hand.

'I am so sorry, Debs. I didn't mean … sorry,' Sandra faltered.

'It's okay, please don't worry. Really, it was a long time ago.'

'I am sorry, Sam did tell me. I just forgot. Oh, look can I get you a drink? I've got wine, beer…?'

'For God's sake, Mum, she's pregnant and you shouldn't be drinking; you're on tablets,' Carl said clearly relishing the moment.

'But I'm not taking tablets.'

He shot Debs a look as if to say, 'I told you she'd lost the plot.'

Then he turned to Sandra.

'Whatever, look, why don't you just go and make some tea, eh?'

'Yes, of course. Milk and sugar, Debs?' she asked desperate to make amends.

Tea, why was it always about the bloody tea? No matter how grave the moment, the mundane always intruded, demeaning the situation.

'Milk, one sugar. But please don't go to any trouble.'

'Make that two teas and we'll have both have an omelette, cheese for me, ham for Debs,' shouted Carl, then seeing his girlfriend's shocked expression added. 'Thanks, Mum.'

By the time Sandra had fed them both, it was almost morning. She had no choice but to put them in the spare room even though it was damp. It was hardly worth going back to bed but she was exhausted. She slid in beside Ben who was still asleep. Unlike her, he could afford to switch-off, being in the enviable position of not being emotionally involved. Carl was not his son and Debs was not carrying his grandchild.

Chapter twenty-nine

[Isle of Wight 2013]

It was gone ten when Sandra got up and went downstairs. She glanced out of the kitchen window where she could see her neighbour's back garden clearly. It was surprisingly messy, in stark contrast to the front with its regimented rows of flowers in patriotic bands of colour, red, white and blue, a hangover from the Jubilee. Stephen visited his house so rarely these days, he probably had more pressing things to do than gardening. The last time she had seen him was when he brought round Carl's letter. An odd man, the sort who kept himself to himself but managed to winkle information out of other people.

'Morning,' said Ben startling her as he opened the fridge.

Sandra turned.

'Where did you come from? You were dead to the world the last time I looked.'

'You woke me up.'

'Sorry.'

She poured boiling water into mugs and dropped a tea-bag into each.

'Carl's girlfriend didn't get here 'til the early hours. Then we chatted. I haven't had much sleep.'

'Is she nice?' Ben asked.

Sandra nodded.

'You should've woken me,' he yawned.

She spooned the bags out of the cups and into the bin before adding milk to the tea.

'You okay?' he asked putting his arms around her.

She relaxed into his embrace.

'Not really. What a horrendous situation. How are we going to look after the pair of them?

'Well, we can't them keep holed up here forever. They're goin' to have to sort themselves out.'

'But you said you'd protect them. What happens when the baby's born?'

'Baby? How long are they staying, for fuck's sake? We agreed a couple of days.'

'Ben, she's pregnant. She's going to need some help. Carl's no use. He's just like his father. I don't know what to do for the best. Any ideas?'

He didn't reply but then he didn't respond well to questioning. No doubt a hangover from all the years spent repeating 'No comment' when being interrogated by the police.

She took her drink up to the bedroom where she peered anxiously through the gap in the curtain. The lane was empty save for the birds that had gathered on the telephone wires and the field opposite was full of corn.

Temporarily reassured they were not in immediate danger she went back to bed. Last night had really taken it out of her. She wanted to cry with tiredness. Much to her frustration, there was no chance of a nap; Carl and Debs were awake and chatting in the next room. She didn't want to listen but the cottage was so small it was impossible not to hear every word

'If you loved me, Sam you'd bring me tea in bed,' said Debs.

'I'll text Mum, she can do it.'

You've got some nerve, thought Sandra.

'Text your Mum? Don't be so lazy. You make the tea.'

He must have relented because a few moments later, Sandra heard the door open and Carl thud downstairs.

She wished Debs would tell him where to stick his milk and two sugars. Then she remembered Ben was still in the kitchen, a potentially explosive situation. She thought about joining them to try and keep the peace but if Carl was going to be staying a while, he and Ben would have to learn to get along.

Within moments, overwhelming fatigue, worked better than any sleeping draft. She fought hard to stay awake. That way she couldn't hear the voice, the one that had wormed its way inside her head and never missed an opportunity to berate and torment her. She knew the voice only too well. It was hers.

She couldn't bear to listen to it and tried to get up but someone was piling lead-weighted blankets on top of her, cover after cover, each one heavier than the last. Finally, she felt herself being tethered to the bed as straps were belted across her chest, pelvis and ankles. The more she struggled, the tighter the bonds became.

'Lie still. You know the rules,' instructed the voice. 'I want you to think about your son. Is he Carl or Sam? Do you know? Do you know who your son really is?

You did your best with him but you have to remember his father is a very unpleasant man and that will come through in his offspring.'

She struggled, pushing against the restraints.

'Lie still. Your son is about to become a father himself. Let's think about that for a moment.'

The notion of Carl bringing up a child made her blood run cold. Although she was reluctant to admit it, she did not trust her own son and was just glad for the baby's sake that Debs seemed such a decent, if gullible, girl.

'What values will he teach his offspring? What genes will he pass on? What qualities will he impart?'

Teachings? Values? Qualities? Carl lacked the lot.

She fought against the restraints, pulling and tugging to free herself. When she snapped open her eyes there were no blankets, no straps, just her duvet. Relieved to be free, she leapt up and went into the bathroom. Someone had left the light on and she immediately caught sight of herself in the mirror. It was hard to believe the haunted eyes

219

and ragged features belonged to her. Backing out of the room, she could just make out Ben and Carl talking downstairs. Their voices were low and guarded.

'Nah, nah, nah Carl, you might be able to fool yer Mum but not me.'

'If I were you I...'

'If I were you I wouldn't fuck with me,' Ben warned.

Sandra held her breath.

'You've been a naughty boy, haven't you Carl?'

'Shut-up. Debs might hear.'

'Oh, sorry, I forgot she thinks your name's Sam,' he said letting out a throaty laugh. 'Can't 'ave her knowing the truth, can we?'

'I don't know what you're talking about.'

'Yer punchin' above yer weight, Carl.'

'Fuck off!'

He sounded more desperate than defiant.

'Yer goin' need more than a few naughty words when the Elliotts get their 'ands on you, Carl.'

'Stop calling me Carl.'

'What d'ya want me to call yer? I can think of a few names.'

'You're supposed to be protecting me not ....'

'Nah, Carl. You don't get it, do yer? I'm here to look after yer Mum. And I've promised her I'd keep an eye on you. But even you must see I can't be in two places at once. You understand what I'm saying, don't ya?'

'If you had to choose, Mum would want you to save me.'

'Carl, you ain't listening. You ain't nuffin' to me. You ain't worth a carrot. I don't give a fuck what happens to you.'

Sandra was furious with Ben for being so contemptuous of her son and angry with her son for being so contemptuous of her. Her first instinct was to intervene but thought she learn more by staying put.

'Yer Mum told me all about you, Carl.'

'She did what?'

'Apparently, you grassed up an Elliott? Tut, tut. Silly boy.'

'I did the right thing.'

'You reckon? Elliott got life and so did you. Witness Fucking Protection? That ain't no life because it ain't your life - just some shit made up by a copper.'

'I'm out of all that now.'

Sandra could hear the fear in his voice.

'More fool you. Anyway, where were we? Ah yeah. Yer Mum told me what happened that afternoon. Apparently, you was walking along minding yer own business when you only go and witness a murder. Fancy that.'

Ben's voice was a hazardous mix of sarcasm and suspicion. Sandra's heart was thumping against the walls of her chest. What the hell was he implying?

'I don't know what you're talking about.'

'Oh I think you do, Carl. The thing is, it don't add up. None of it.'

Sandra was willing her son to say something, anything that would quash Ben's line of thinking but he stayed silent.

'So, you see some poor sod, with his throat cut, bleeding to death and you don't do nuffin? You don't phone an ambulance? You don't shout for help? You just clear off and run back home to Mummy?'

'The killer had a knife. What was I supposed to do?'

'You left a dying man, Carl. That's not nice.'

'I panicked. The killer knew I'd seen him. I could've been next.'

'Nah, nah Carl. That was never goin' happen, was it? You was always safe. And we both know why, don't we?'

There was a heart-stopping silence as Sandra waited and waited and waited for her son to answer.

'You never called for help because you wanted him dead. You as good as killed him.'

She shook uncontrollably and thought she might be sick.

'That's a very serious accusation. You should watch what you say. The prints on the knife were Elliotts. His DNA was everywhere.'

'Cos it was. You're a clever boy, Carl. You weren't goin' have blood on your hands.'

'I'm not listening to this.'

Sandra sunk down, her body knotting into a ball as she willed Carl to defend himself.

'You didn't call no-one cos you arranged the whole thing and the last thing you wanted was the Old Bill sniffing about.'

'No.'

'Oh Carl, come on. I ain't yer Mum. I don't think the sun shines outta your arse. We both know you as good as killed that bloke.'

'Be careful what you say.'

Ben laughed. Then immediately his tone changed.

'Who the hell d'you think you're talking to?'

There was a long silence.

'You're forgetting, I've been inside with scum like you. I know how your little mind works. Like mine, only slower.'

'So what am I thinking?'

'You're thinking you're about to shit yerself. I'm right, aren't I, Carl?'

Carl made an odd sound, like a rabbit dying in a trap.

The tops of Sandra's arms hurt from where she had been pinching them. An urgent pain gripped her stomach, then her insides loosened. She fought the urge to rush to the toilet and instead stayed in the hope she might learn the truth.

'What yer Mum told me didn't make no sense. So I made a few calls. Asked a few questions.'

She needed to be with Carl and went to get up but her legs buckled under her as if her bones were nothing but marrow.

'D'you know I killed a man? Ten years I got for that. Inside, I mixed with all sorts, men who've done terrible things; stuff you can't even imagine, Carl. And you get talking. People tell yer things, things you don't wanna hear. But once they've said it, it's too late, it's in yer head.'

'What's all this got to do with me?'

'When someone blabs you don't know if what they're saying is true or not. So you wait, you wait until you hear another little whisper, then, another and another. Until one day, it ain't a whisper no more, it's a fuckin' great ROAR!'

'So now you can't ignore it. You're sitting up, takin' notice. Cos now you know yer onto something. Then a funny thing happens, Carl. Well, I think it's funny cos I've got a very sick sense of humour, Carl.'

'What?' yelled Carl. 'What happens for fuck's sake?'

'What happens? I'll tell ya what happens. It's the middle of the night and there's a knock at the door. I open it and who should be standing there but the bloke everyone's talking about. You.'

'No.'

'Yes, Carl. Everyone knows it was you what arranged it. And if it hadn't been for that jogger who saw yer there, you'd have got away

223

with it. But he went and told the police so then you had to make sure you stayed in the clear. So you landed Elliott right in it. And let's face it, the police ain't gonna believe an Elliott over a nice posh boy like you. They'd been trying to fit him up for years and there he was covered in blood, his prints on the knife. The police must have thought they'd won the fuckin' Lottery.'

'How do you know? How could you possibly know?'

Sandra froze. Had Carl really just admitted to murder?

'How do I know what? That you killed that no-mark? You didn't, you paid Lee Elliott to do it. When you turned up in the park that day to check up on Lee, he didn't have a clue who you were cos you'd always stayed in the background, The-Invisible-Fucking-Man, giving the orders, paying money for someone else to do your dirty work. But I made a few enquiries and worked out it was you all along.'

Sandra tried to tell herself she had misheard.

'Who told you?' Carl demanded. 'Who told you I was involved?'

'You.'

'What?

'You just told me, Carl. Two minutes ago, I didn't know nuffin'. Only what I'd seen on the news, what yer Mum told me and a few little whispers.'

'But you said....'

'I didn't say nuffin'. You did.'

'I'll deny it all. The police won't believe you over me.'

'Calm down. Don't get excited. I ain't goin' tell no-one.'

'Really? You'd do that for me? Thanks.'

His relief was as palpable as it was pathetic.

'I ain't goin' tell no-one. You are.'

'I can't. I'll go to prison.'

Sandra felt as if her body had been turned inside out and all the soft parts, long protected by skin and bone, had suddenly become exposed. Her mind shot back to when Carl was younger, presenting her with a dark montage - memories of his childhood.

Did killing a dog, having no friends, bullying and lying make him a killer? Probably, possibly.

There had been other things too. Signs she had chosen to ignore. He had been just three-years-old when next-door's tabby wandered into the garden and rubbed its body against his bare legs. Running his hand repeatedly along its back, the cat had shown its appreciation by purring. Carl had looked perplexed, bending down and pressing his ear against its side as if trying to work out where the noise was coming from.

The memory had always ended there but now Sandra could clearly picture the cat walking away from Carl and him reaching out, grabbing its tail, pulling it hard and using it to drag the animal, yowling across the grass.

She had shouted at him to let it go but he had ignored her, running in the opposite direction and laughing, still pulling the cat, like a sledge behind him. She had raced across the grass and caught up with him, slapping his hand away. The terrified animal shot off, his tail dragging behind him. Weeks later she learned from her neighbour the poor creature had suffered nerve damage and had had to be put down.

Only she and Carl knew about his part in its demise.

What was she thinking? An unfortunate childhood prank had no bearing on a murder. This had to be a misunderstanding. Carl was tired and exhausted. What was Ben thinking, interrogating him, twisting his words and tricking him? Powered by anger and indignation, she ran downstairs and flew at Ben, her arms outstretched, her nails talons, weapons to gouge eyes, claw flesh and tear hair.

'Lying bastard!' she cried.

He caught hold of her wrist.

'Get off!' she screamed, hitting his face hard with her one hand as she managed to twist free.

'Stop it, Rosie. Calm down.'

'Just get out. Go!'

'You heard her, leave, before I call the police,' said Carl getting out his phone.

'You wouldn't fuckin' dare. The last thing you want is the Old Bill turning up.'

Carl sheepishly slid the mobile back into his pocket.

The red fog of anger lifted and Sandra could see how hurt Ben seemed and how quick Carl had been to back down. Had she made a mistake? Could Ben possibly be right about Carl? There was no denying her son had changed out of all recognition. Perhaps he did know more about the murder than he had originally let on but surely that was impossible. Neither the Prosecution or Defence had cast any doubt on Carl's version of events. Why would they? Elliott was guilty as charged. Everyone knew that. There was no arguing with the DNA evidence and there was never any question her son had been involved.

Until now. Until Ben had interfered. How dare he accuse her son of murder when he was no better himself?

'I heard you, bullying a confession out of him.'

She unlocked the front door and held it open.

'No, Rosie it wasn't like that,' he insisted standing his ground, refusing to leave. 'He's admitted it.'

'No. You kept on and on until he told you what you wanted to hear.'

Ben turned to Carl.

'Tell her.'

Carl stood with his arms folded, a smile spreading like a seeping wound across his face.

'She knows the truth, don't you, Mum?'

She knew one man's truth, was another man's lie. That was the trouble with honesty; it didn't exist, not really.

'Rosie, I know he's yer son and all that but you can't trust him.'

'And I'm damn sure I can't trust you. You're a killer. I must've been mad letting you into my life.'

She spat out the words like they were slime to smear on Ben.

'Rosie, he's as guilty as fuck.'

His words made her so angry she could have burst into flames. How dare he cast aspersions on her boy? She moved her face close to his, her voice barely audible.

'Carl's my son. I love him but I hate you for what you just did to him.'

'That's a shame because I love you.'

The three words that a few days ago would have lifted her heart, fell flat.

'Don't say that, Ben.'

'Why not? I love you, Rosie.'

Totally numb, her head was a jumble of fact and fiction. She didn't know who or what to believe. She suspected the truth was trapped like a fly somewhere in the web of lies. Too much had already been said. It was time to listen to her son. Silently, she nodded at Ben, motioning him to leave.

'Rose, you're kidding, I can't leave you.'

'I'm here now, I'll look after her,' sneered Carl.

Ben looked at Sandra. She turned away.

'Okay, have it your own way. I'll leave you to it, but I'll be back soon.'

Chapter thirty

[Isle of Wight 2013]

'What were you thinking getting together with him? I bet he only had to say he loved you and you fell for it.'

Sandra glared at Carl, too angry to speak.

'What?' he asked sounding like a petulant teenager.

She watched her son closely, this man she no longer knew.

'For fuck's sake,' he said throwing himself down onto the sofa. 'What you looking at me like that for? You don't believe him, do you?'

Again, she did not reply, giving him space to open up, hoping the less she said, the more he would divulge.

'You do, don't you? You believe a murderer over your own son?'

She stood in front of the inglenook, looking straight ahead, hardening herself against his cheap emotional strikes.

'They were your words, Carl, not his. I was upstairs; I heard what you said. Everything.'

'Fuck you.'

She lunged forwards.

'Get off me.'

'Carl, I could ...'

'Shut the fuck up!'

'No, I won't. I've stayed quiet for too long. It's time I had my say. You are a ...'

He leapt up. She thought he was going to hit her but he settled for shouldering past and running upstairs. She flew after him and caught him on the landing. He spun round, his face in hers, taught with anger.

'Carl, I …'

'Shut-up,' he hissed. 'Debs will hear you. She doesn't know anything about …'

With that the door to the spare bedroom opened and Debs appeared, barefoot and still in her pyjamas, looking quizzically from mother to son.

'Why are you shouting?'

Sandra stared at Carl hoping he might, just for once, do the right thing but there was nothing in his defiant expression to suggest he had any intention of answering her honestly.

'Will someone please tell me what's happening?' said Debs her hands protectively guarding her swollen belly.

At that moment, there was a sudden noise from above. Sandra looked up to see someone leap out of the loft hatch, landing awkwardly on Carl and knocking him to the ground.

Sandra screamed.

There, squatting like a toad and grinning at her just like he had that day in court, was Lee Elliotts brother, Gaz.

'Hello, again,' he said to Sandra, his eyes devouring Debs.

Sandra pushed her back into the bedroom and pulled the door shut.

'Lock it,' she told her. 'And don't come out until I tell you.'

Her heart was beating so fast she thought she might collapse. She turned to see Elliott scampering like the rat he was, across the floor towards the knife. It was her knife; he must have dropped it when he jumped.

It was within Sandra's reach. Like wild animals, their eyes met briefly before she grabbed the handle and turned the blade on him.

It felt wrong. She had only ever used the knife as a kitchen utensil, never a weapon. Her nerve faltered but she reminded herself she had used it to bone and carve pork, more than adequate preparation to deal with a pig like Gaz Elliott.

'Sam!' screamed Debs, her terrified face suddenly appearing round the door.

Sandra spun round, giving Elliott the opportunity to grab both her and the knife.

With the point of the blade in the small of her back, he marched her across the landing, pausing beside Carl who was still lying on the floor, his eyes closed. She tried to tell herself he was just badly winded but by the look of him, he was seriously injured.

To her horror, Elliott pushed her up against the wall, the knife still in her back before letting go of her. She turned her head to see him calmly unzip his fly. Using his penis as a wand, he urinated in the shape of a 'C' over Carl's torso. When he had finished he did up his trousers, took hold of Sandra and shoved her towards the wardrobe.

'Get in,' he ordered, pulling open the door.

With all the attention on her, she saw the chance for Debs to escape.

'Run, Debs. Run!'

Sandra glanced over her shoulder to see Debs kneeling beside Carl.

'Please, wake up, my darling, please.'

'Leave him, Debs. Run!'

'Shut the fuck up!' shouted Elliott elbowing Sandra into the cupboard and locking the door. Immediately, she turned and put her eye to the crack in the door. Elliott was striding towards Carl and Debs, knife in hand.

'Go you two!' she called.

'Get up you piece of shit,' said Elliott, booting Carl in the chest.

'Stop,' Debs said.

Sandra frantically threw herself against the door.

Then Elliott pointed the knife at Debs' distended belly as he spoke to Carl.

'Open your eyes, you coward. I've got your girlfriend here. She looks like she's about to drop any minute. Did you get my card, by the way?'

At the mention of the disgusting *'Congratulations on the birth of your dead baby'* card Sandra shouted and rained her fists against the door.

'Dad was right, he told me if I waited long enough, you'd run back to Mummy.'

He left Sandra in no doubt as to who her unwelcome guest had been as he shouted over to her, 'Cosy little attic you got up there, love. In case you was wondering, I had my own private entrance – your neighbour's back door. Oh you might wanna let him know, he's got a dodgy lock. Dead handy him never being here, I could come and go as I pleased. Did you know you shared the loft with him? Oh and I owe you for the toast and Marmite, here you go.'

With that he reached into his pocket, took out a handful of coins and tossed them onto the floor in front of the wardrobe before delivering another blow to Carl's kidneys.

'Wake up, mate! You're missing your family reunion! Look! I've got you, your Mum, your girlfriend and yer kid. Four for the price of one!'

'Not my baby,' Debs cried.

'Did you hear something?' he asked sarcastically as he cocked his head to one side. 'Ah, yeah it's your girlfriend. Listen, they might be her last words.'

He let out a laugh.

'Do what you want to me but leave her alone,' cried Sandra from the wardrobe.

'Thanks for the offer, love but you're a bit old for me. This one's more my type.'

He leered at Debs while still pointing the knife at her stomach.

'I've always wondered what it was like doing it with someone who's up the duff.'

'No! You sick bastard,' yelled Sandra, shouldering the door.

Crafted out of oak, screwed to the wall, the lock solid brass, the wardrobe was too well made to yield to her weight.

'Sorry, love I know you want me but you'll have to wait; this little lovely is gagging for it.'

With that, Sandra saw Carl open his eyes. At last. Thank God. He would protect Debs.

'Stop it!' Sandra shouted in an attempt to distract Elliott long enough to give Carl time to do what he needed.

It worked but not in the way she had hoped.

Carl leapt up and grabbed Debs from behind, pulling her to her feet. Sandra assumed he was trying to protect her but then she realised, he was just trying to protect himself, holding her in front of his body like a human shield. Debs' eyes popped from her head like two hard-boiled eggs as she looked down at the bulge concealing her unborn baby.

Elliott made a half-hearted move towards Carl but backed off. There was no way he could get at him without harming Debs. It seemed Ben had been right: the thug was not prepared to attack a pregnant woman.

What the hell had she done telling Ben to leave? She needed him more than ever.

Debs' jagged cry sliced through the house. Carl clamped his hand over her mouth but not before she emitted a second, terrifying sound. It reminded Sandra of the terrible noise cattle made holed up in a truck, on board the ferry, on route to the mainland to be slaughtered. They had no way of knowing what fate had in store but judging by the noise they made, they understood only too well.

'Here, take her, she's all yours,' Carl shouted flinging his girlfriend at Elliott as if she were nothing more than a shop dummy. As she fell to the floor, Carl rattled down the stairs with Elliott just seconds behind him.

'Debs! Are you okay?' called Sandra.

'Fine,' she said scrambling to her feet as quickly as her top-heavy body would allow and making her way over to the wardrobe where after much fumbling with the key, she eventually unlocked the door.

The two women fell into each other's arms. When Sandra felt Debs' swollen tummy pressing against hers, it was as if they were both giving the baby a much-needed hug.

Sandra heard shouting. Going over to the landing window and pulling aside the curtain, she could see Elliott standing in the road. He had his back to her and was peering through the hedge into the field opposite, whooping, cheering and punching the air.

'What is it?' asked Debs, desperately trying to see what was going on.

'Elliott is going crazy but I don't know why.'

She stood on tiptoe to get a better view. Once she could see clearly, she wished she was blind.

There, at the edge of the field, parked behind the hedge, was a tractor and impaled on its hay-baling spike was Carl. He hung there, limp and lifeless, an empty costume of skin.

Sandra opened her mouth but no sound came as she pawed at the window like a crazed animal.

'Carl!'

'Who's Carl?' asked Debs, her voice splintered with uncertainty.

'My son.'

'His name's Sam.'

Sam? Carl? It didn't matter anymore. He was dead.

Sandra couldn't breathe. She was gasping for air. Suffocating, she pushed Debs out of the way and ran helter-skelter down the stairs.

But Elliott was at the front door, knife in hand, barring her way. Sandra tried to dodge past him but he grabbed her hair, twisting the strands between the fingers of one hand as he jabbed the knife into her side.

'The bastard could shift when he wanted,' he joked dragging her backwards like a crab up the stairs, deliberately letting her head bang on every step. 'I kept telling him to slow down but he wasn't listening and jumped straight through the hedge into the spike.'

Sandra made a noise; half gurgle, half choke. When they reached the landing, Elliott pushed her roughly down onto the floor next to Debs.

'Murderer!' Sandra cried.

'Not this time,' he said brandishing the blade. 'I waited years to get that bastard then he goes and does the job for me.'

'You killed him. It was your fault,' Sandra screamed. 'He was running away from you.'

'Blame the farmer. He left the spike sticking out. Accident just waiting to happen.'

'Sam's dead,' cried Debs.

'Sam? The piece of shit hanging by his balls is Carl and trust me, no-one's goin' miss him.'

The two women stared incredulously at him.

'You don't know, do you?' he sneered, enjoying having the upper hand.

Then he laughed even though nothing remotely funny had happened.

'You don't know this but Carl, Sam whatever he called himself was a loan shark. He could turn very nasty if people didn't pay up. He'd do anything to get what he was owed, even forced girls onto the streets to get the money.'

Sandra shook her head.

'You're lying.'

Debs had collapsed on the floor, her arms over her head. Sandra couldn't tell if she was even listening.

'He made a fortune. Mind you, he had a bit of dosh to begin with. That's how he got started.'

Sandra's insides contracted; that 'bit of dosh' must have been the thousands of pounds she had given him when he went to university. She had hated to think of him scraping by like all the other students. She had the money, and at the time, it had seemed the right thing, to make his life easier.

'Carl didn't like late-payers. He hurt them. Well, he paid Lee to. It was a nice little earner for my brother, as it goes. All he had to do was turn up, do the business and clear off. No questions asked.'

Sandra felt the vomit rise to the back of her throat.

'Lee usually worked alone and never knew who gave the orders. He'd just get a text with a picture of who he had to sort and where and when to find 'em. He'd do the business, then collect his money from a drop-off.'

Sandra didn't want to hear what he had to say. She just wanted him to shut-up.

'But, that day was different. That day your son turned up for a nosey around. He should've kept on walking and kept his mouth shut but when that bloke jogged past, Carl panicked. He couldn't be in the frame and grassed up my brother. He grassed up an Elliott. Silly fucker.'

'My son told the truth.'

'And look where it got him, skewered like a fucking kebab.'

Elliott smiled.

'Still, now he's gone, you and me can have some fun,' he said stroking Debs' cheek.

If Debs felt his touch she did not react.

'Get your hands off her,' shouted Sandra.

'Calm down. I ain't goin' hurt her. You ain't bad-looking, for an old girl,' he said looking Sandra up and down. 'And you like younger blokes, don't you? I saw yer at it with Lover Boy. Bet you didn't know you had an audience, did yer? Amazing how much you can spot through a little crack in the ceiling. I watched you in the bath. I was going to come down and wash yer back but I couldn't let you know I was there, could I? Still, I enjoyed myself all on my own, know what I mean?'

He made an obscene gesture with his hand and laughed exposing his little pointy yellow teeth.

Sandra shrunk back and pinned her knees together. Debs stared blankly ahead. Where was Ben? Hurry up, please hurry up.

'What was I saying?' Elliott continued. 'Ah yes, big mouth Carl told the police he saw Lee cut the bloke and that was that. All they cared about was nailing one of us. Lee got sent down for life and Mummy's boy got off scot-free. Well, not quite,' he said gesturing towards the field. 'Now, that's what I call justice.'

He laughed as Sandra lay shaking next to Debs.

'Our Mum lost her boy. Only fair you lose yours.'

Sandra tried to close her mind to what he was saying and huddled closer to Debs.

'Don't move,' he instructed, pointing the tip of the blade first at one woman, then at the other.

Debs began to sob uncontrollably.

'Shut the fuck up!' he yelled. 'What you crying for?'

Footsteps! Sandra heard someone run into the cottage and up the stairs. Please God let it be Ben.

Elliott pulled her up and pressed the blade hard against her throat. It felt different. This time, it felt like he really meant it.

'Rosie!' shouted Ben as he appeared on the landing. 'Put her down, you fucking bastard.'

Sandra's heart thumped in joy and dread.

'Ah mate. I've been watching you for so long, I feel I know you,' laughed Elliott.

'Let go of her,' Ben repeated steadily.

'Sorry, can't do that. When I do a job, I like to finish it.'

He tightened his grip, pushing the knife against her flesh.

'Rose!' Ben cried, training his eyes on her hand and nodding.

She knew exactly what he meant. In one swift movement, she thrust her hand up hard and fast, just like he had shown her, breaking Elliott's grip.

Ben lunged forward, knocking Sandra onto the floor and out of the way. The two men struggled. One second Elliott had the knife, the next Ben had wrestled it from him. Then, it was if it had taken on a life of its own, lashing out, stabbing and slashing. Suddenly, there was blood. Lots of blood.

'No!' cried Sandra.

Debs was screaming, hard and fast.

Ben's white T-shirt had turned a violent shade of red as he doubled over, clutching his stomach.

'That looks nasty. Here use these,' Elliott could hardly speak for laughing and thrusting his hand into his pocket pulled out a pair of knickers, Sandra's black lace pants, the ones that had recently gone missing.

He sniffed them, smiling as if transported to paradise before stuffing them inside the slash in Ben's stomach. With Elliott distracted, Ben lurched forwards, grabbed the knife and plunged it into Elliott's chest.

Both women screamed and scrambled across the floor until they hit the wall, where they sat, recoiling from the sight of Elliott's face set in an eternal smirk.

Never mind him. Ben could die. Sandra ripped off her top and balled it up, using it to pack the wound.

'Press hard,' she instructed, placing his hand against the fabric.

'Sorry, Rosie,' said Ben struggling for breath. 'I saw Carl.'

It was too late for her son. She needed to focus on the baby.

'Are you okay, Debs?'

She nodded, her hands covering her belly.

Ben opened his mouth, when he spoke his words were barely audible.

'Police, ambulance...on... their way.'

'Don't try to talk, Ben.'

'Told you I'd get him for yer, Rosie.'

She nodded. Elliott was dead but so was Carl. Yet again, two mothers had lost their sons. One had been stabbed to death but her boy had been killed the only way possible, with a stake through his heart.

Chapter thirty-one

[Primrose Hill, London 2014]

Sandra, her grand-son, Josh cradled in her arms, flung open the French windows onto Deb's garden. The baby screwed up his eyes against the sun. It was set to be a blisteringly hot day, the sort London did so well with the intense heat of the city warming the coldest hearts, persuading people to bare theirs arms, legs and even their souls.

'Morning, Sandra,' said Debs appearing in the kitchen in her dressing gown. 'Thanks for getting Josh up. Sorry, did he wake you?'

'No, I couldn't sleep.'

'I bet. You must be excited. It is today, isn't it?' asked Debs with a wink.

Sandra changed the subject.

'It's a beautiful morning, fancy breakfast in the garden? I'm so lucky to be here with you and Josh.'

'I'm the lucky one. I'd be lost without you. I'm not cut out to be a single mum and Josh adores having you here. Look at him. He's growing so fast. He's going to be tall, like his...'

When Debs hesitated, Sandra finished her sentence.

'Like his Dad. It's okay, you are allowed to talk about Carl.'

Debs did not reply. Instead she chewed her lip and busied herself securing a bib around the baby's neck.

In their different ways, both women were still suffering, trying to come to terms with all that had happened. Their pain was shared but unfortunately not halved.

'Shouldn't you be getting ready?' asked Debs eyeing the clock. 'You are still going, aren't you?'

Of course she was. She had waited a long time for this day.

The clock had started ticking the minute the police arrested Ben on suspicion of Elliott's murder, holding him in custody while the case was referred to the Crown Prosecution Service. Fortunately, having seen he had acted in self-defence and had been protecting Debs and Sandra, they dropped the charges.

Ben being Ben, it wasn't that simple and he was soon behind bars for receiving stolen goods. The bolts and locks fitted on Sandra's cottage had been part of a much bigger consignment purloined by one of Ben's mates. She smiled to herself at the irony a thief securing her house with contraband to keep out another criminal.

She went upstairs to get ready and thought back to the last time she had seen Ben. Wormwood Scrubs was not the most romantic of venues but he had been as upbeat as ever. Prison suited him. It really was his second home. He took great pride in telling her about his latest scams and his new mates but most important of all were his plans for the future. He couldn't wait to set up home with Sandra, anywhere provided it was within staggering distance of a pub. She insisted they were somewhere close to Josh and Debs. Hampstead, Camden or Belsize Park would fit the bill. As always, the session had ended too soon. She hated leaving him, especially when he winked at her, in that way of his.

'See ya soon, Rosie.'

Now that day had finally arrived. She couldn't wait to be with him again and applied her make-up as carefully as a teenager getting ready for a first date. She had treated herself to new underwear and when she put it on, it transformed her, making her feel young and desirable again. Her clothes, carefully picked out the night before, completed the transformation.

As she brushed her hair, her phone rang. She considered not answering it but changed her mind when she checked the display and saw who it was.

'Rob! Sorry I can't talk. Ben's coming out today.'

'I told you he was in denial.'

'You wish,' she giggled.

'Ah well, a boy can dream. Anyway, I remembered today's the day he stops pleasuring Her Majesty and just wanted to wish you luck.'

'Ah thanks. Listen, I've gotta go, meeting him at Hammersmith tube in an hour…couldn't face all that prison gates stuff.'

'Give him my love. And anytime he wants to experience my bedside manner, I'll be at the hospital waiting for him. I'm a manager now y'know and …'

She cut Rob off in his prime, checked her reflection and ran downstairs where Debs was cleaning Josh's mouth. She looked up at Sandra.

'Wow! You look fab.'

Sandra smiled in nervous anticipation.

'Do I? Not too much make-up? Nothing sexy about the whiff of mutton.'

'Oh please! You're not old. Now, promise me one thing? You won't let the past spoil the present.'

Sandra furrowed her brow.

'Don't be silly.'

'You don't have to pretend, Sandra. I hear you crying, talking to yourself. You still have nightmares about what happened, don't you? If you're blaming yourself, please don't. Carl was a grown man. He made his own decisions.'

Sandra nodded. The voice in her head was still there. Thankfully it berated her less frequently these days. Debs inviting her to live with her and the baby had been a life-saver. The girl was so easy-going and brilliant with Josh. He had lucked-out having her for a mother.

Debs held out her little finger for the baby to grasp.

'Bet you can't wait to see Ben. I hope you two can make a go of it, even if it means losing my live-in babysitter.'

Sandra wanted to be with Ben but didn't want to tempt fate.

'Oh, it's early days and …'

Debs didn't let her finish.

'He loves you. He killed for you.'

'Don't say that. I had no love for Gaz Elliott but …'

Debs reached out and took hold of Sandra's hand.

'It wasn't your fault.'

Josh squealed and they both turned to look at him. What a welcome distraction, with his gleeful smile and animated limbs, shooting out in all directions. But Debs joy at her little boy was short-lived.

'What if my son is…?'

'…like mine?' said Sandra.

'I didn't mean that.'

'Yes, you did and understandably so. But, Carl isn't here. You are. And you're the best mother Josh could wish for.'

Sandra hugged Debs.

'I'm sorry. I'm being silly. Hey, look at the time; you need to go.'

Sandra then checked her pocket to ensure she had her Oyster card, the one Ben had left at the cottage the first day they met before smoothing her cream skirt.

'Love that top. Suits you. Is it new?' asked Debs.

'This? No, I've had it years.'

It was the one she had worn that fateful day. The day she met a man on a train. The day she met a murderer on a train.

Now, she was wearing it to meet Ben off the train.

Chapter thirty-two

[Hammersmith, London 2014]

Ben waited for the right moment to speak out, to voice his thoughts but he knew no-one was interested in what he had to say, they made that obvious when they gagged him. His wrists and ankles were sore from where they had pulled the rope taught and his eyes were taking a while to adjust to the light having the blindfold ripped off.

He was lying, trussed up like a hog roast, his cheek grazing the concrete floor. There were no windows, just an inspection lamp, slung over a hook in the breeze-block wall.

The bastards had been lying in wait for him around the corner from the prison. He should've been on his guard but he'd been thinking about Rose. That was the trouble with a one-track mind. It only thought about one fucking thing at a time.

He knew he had it coming. He just hadn't bargained on it being so soon. He moved his hands discreetly, trying to work the rope free. Rosie would be at the tube by now, waiting for him. Fuck these bastards.

The air was filled with nicotine, thick and heavy. Three men stared at him. One lit a cigarette and inhaled deeply before taking a step forward and exhaling a rush of smoke in Ben's face.

The oldest man was sitting behind a makeshift table, grinning. Ben knew that expression and understood what it meant. No one spoke for a long time. Then the old man moved his lips slowly, deliberately.

'You want it over?' he asked as his cracked voice broke into a laugh.

In a room that already stank of death, it seemed the old bastard had found something amusing. He leant forward, his face, papery and puckered like he was about to say something but he just sniggered. Ben was sweating, really sweating. The old git was leaning back in his chair now, his eyes never leaving Ben's. The younger man took a final drag on his cigarette before dropping it on the floor and grinding it under the heel of his shoe. It was only a fag butt. To watch him, you'd think it was a scorpion he was annihilating.

'You killed my boy,' whispered the old man calmly.

Ben opened his mouth but the words had dried to dust in his throat. He glanced at the door where two other men stood guard. Two men he hadn't known were there. Two men who looked just like Gaz Elliott, only younger. Ben closed his eyes and thought of Rosie.

THE END

Thanks for reading this book. If you enjoyed it, a short review on Amazon would be appreciated.

Please keep in touch, I'd love to know what you think of the work, stop by www.joan-ellis.com and follow me on twitter @joansusanellis

Disclaimer: All persons are fictitious.

By the same author:

Humour / Contemporary women's fiction

I am Ella. Buy me.

*'I am a ginger tom. I am a boy racer. I am a housewife.
I am a pain in the arse.'*

Ella David is Bridget Jones meets Peggy from *Mad Men*.

Working in Soho's mad, bad Adland in the sexist 80s, she is a rare beast, a woman in a man's world, dodging her sleazy boss, Peter, on her way to the top. This funny, fast-paced tale is set against a backdrop of Thatcher's Britain when money trumps morals and lust is a must. Ella knows love is more powerful but can two unlikely friendships help her go from a girl in the firing line to a woman calling the shots?

Based on Joan's experiences as a copywriter in top London advertising agencies.

'This book is like real life; funny, sad and wise and true.'

Paul Burke, author.

☆ ☆ ☆ ☆ ☆

'Crackling dialogue dances off the page.'
'Pure entertainment.'

Book Addict UK

☆ ☆ ☆ ☆

'Fans of Mad Men will be enthralled.'

Natasha Presky

'I am Ella. Buy me.' is one of the sharpest and wittiest books I have read. Ella is a brilliant lead character.'

Bookaholic Confessions

☆ ☆ ☆ ☆ ☆

'I absolutely LOVED Ella David. She made me laugh endlessly. There was a smart wit about her. Ella was the sort of woman that I'd love to sit across from in an office. I'd be endlessly entertained! The characters were superbly developed.'

Becca's Books

'The writing style was humorous, serious and heart-breaking. With feelings and a good moral compass Ella could be a role model for women.'

The Bookshelf

'It's fast-paced and very believable especially if you are old enough to have lived in the 80s when sexism and a lack of morals in the work place were tolerated.'

Girls Love To Read

'One of the things I liked most was the reminder it gave that, however much we may still be struggling to achieve equality in the workplace, there has been a lot of progress since the yuppie days of Thatcher's Britain.'

Book Addict UK

Coming soon: Psychological thriller

Guilt

'You died on August 8th 1965, a month before your fourth birthday. You were probably dead long before Mum downed her third gin with Porky Rawlings.'

Seven-year-old Susan is alone with her younger brother when he dies of an overdose. The guilt informs the rest of her life. When it threatens to destroy not only her but also her family, she must return to her past to discover the truth.

Coming soon: Autobiography

The Things You Missed While You Were Away

'Being paired with a chair at the local National Childbirth Trust anti-natal classes did nothing for my ego. Unlike the other mums who were with their husbands, the only arms supporting me through the breathing exercises were wooden ones.'

My daughter's childhood in the 90s was very different to my upbringing in the 60s. As neither of us knew what it was like to have our Dads at home, the book is written as a letter to my Father highlighting the moments he never got to share. It is for anyone who has been a child, if only to prove when we lose someone special, love comes from unexpected places to fill the space in our heart.

Made in the USA
Charleston, SC
16 June 2016